INSEVERABLE

A Carolina Beach Novel

Cecy Robson

"[Cecy] Robson's O'Brien family has the hottest brothers ever! . . . It's impossible not to keep your fingers crossed for an HEA, but the author knows exactly what she's doing as readers hold their breath during this roller-coaster ride of passion!"—**RT Book Reviews**

"Make room on your list of book boyfriends for Curran O'Brien! This bad-boy cop is fiercely protective of the feisty Tess, and the sexual tension between these two is off the charts!"—*USA Today* **bestselling author Lauren Layne**

"Robson has once again captured my attention with these wonderful characters [in Once Pure]." —**Everyday eBook**

"[The Weird Girls] is a fantastic new paranormal series, and I highly recommend Cecy Robson for those looking for steam and sass"—**USA Today, HEA**

"Once again, a new Cecy Robson book wrecked my plans for a productive weekend. Let Me made me laugh, cry, and squirm in my seat (in a good way)--sometimes all at once." —**Teri Anne Stanley**, Author of *Accidentally in Love with the Biker* and *Drunk on You*

"I love her characters, her topics, the emotion and the romance. She always manages to snag me in with her stories..." —**Rainy Day Ramblings**

"It is with eager anticipation and excitement that I pick up every read by [Cecy] Robson...She truly is a talented writer that never ceases to amaze me with her words." —**My Guilty Obsession**

"Ms. Robson's books don't come with easy endings. It's why I love her work." —**Under the Covers Book Blog**

"Cecy Robson does a great job with character development and making you care about her characters and the obstacles they face... Cecy has a way of bringing a big dose of reality into all her stories and it is pleasure to read her books."
-- JB's Book Obsession Blog

"Damn it Cecy you made me cry!!! Of course you also made me laugh, smile and swoon too. I loved their story."
— Caffeinated Book Reviewer

"WOW!! Just WOW!!! I have to say that Cecy Robson has completely blown me away with Let Me." —**Devilishly Delicious Book Reviews**

"One of the things I love about Cecy Robson is that her books are always true to life. She makes sure her characters are flawed as we all are in some way and she always gets it right. She's not afraid to tackle the difficult issues and she does her homework. She is truly flawless and close to perfection as an author." —**OMG Reads**

"Overall, A Cursed Bloodline is the proof that Cecy Robson and her Weird Girls series deserve its place on the prize list of the best paranormal romance series. I recommend this title to every Weird Girls series lovers. Of course, to anyone out there who are looking for something new, hot, intriguing and refreshing to read, Cecy Robson will fulfill your desires!"
—Proserpine Craving Books

BY CECY ROBSON

The Shattered Past Series

Once Perfect

Once Loved

Once Pure

The O'Brien Family Novels

Once Kissed

Let Me

Crave Me (coming soon)

Feel Me (coming soon)

The Carolina Beach Novels

Inseverable

Eternal (coming soon)

Infinite (coming soon)

The Weird Girls

A Curse Awakened (novella)

The Weird Girls (novella)

Sealed with a Curse

A Cursed Embrace

Of Flame and Promise

A Cursed Moon (novella)

Cursed by Destiny

A Cursed Bloodline

A Curse Unbroken

Of Flame and Light (coming soon)

DEDICATION

To all those with wounded hearts. May you find the strength
and love to once again be whole.

ACKNOWLEDGMENTS

I am blessed to have many wonderful people to thank. Some who have been with me forever, and others who have recently jumped aboard the crazy train that is my life.

To my agent, Nicole Resciniti, who continues to help me all because she believes in me. Thank you, Nic, for waving that wand and helping me make my dreams come true.

For Jamie, my strength and the one who makes whole. Thank you for all the hugs, all the "it's going to be okay" talks, and all the times you've lured me out from beneath the bed with the promise of Buffalo wings. That whole growing old thing? Yeah, couldn't picture a better man to spend a lifetime with. Love you, babe.

To my babies who have shown me what real love is. Mommy loves you more than this writer could ever put to words.

To my girls, Amanda Flower and Kate SeRine. Thanks for laughing, screaming, and crying along with me.

To my publicist, Lisa Felipe. I bet you didn't know what you signed up for, huh? Thank you for your patience, for "blowing my launches up", and for your tireless work. I'm so proud to have you on my team.

To my copy editor Gaele Hince who cries and cheers for my characters! Thank you for your kindness and hard work.

Most of all, to the members of are armed services, past and present, you'll never know the extent of my gratitude, or respect.

For ways to help our wounded heroes and their families, please visit https://www.woundedwarriorproject.org

Prologue

Callahan

Three days.

That's all I have left until this shit ends.

Three days shouldn't feel like forever, not compared to the eight years I've bled to the Army. Thing is, good men have been killed in less time. In as quick as a blink, a squeeze of a trigger, or a small breath right before a grenade blows is all the time it takes to shove someone right out of life and well into death.

That's what makes three days as long as it is. Three days is plenty of time to die.

My eyes tear when the wind picks up and shoots grime through the small hole of my lookout point. This blown out piece of cinderblock is only big enough to allow me a view of the street below, but not so small I don't get smacked in the face with more filth. The tarp flaps above me as I spit out another layer of the dirt-sand mix spackling my teeth. Christ Almighty, I need a swig of the water resting near my elbow. But my thirst, like everything else has to wait.

I have a job to do.

I adjust my hips against the cracked cement of my bed, bathroom, and home all rolled into one, thankful that the agonizing ache stretching over the lower half of my body has settled into a now familiar numbness.

Out of all the points I'd scouted, and all the accumulated years spent in this position, I should be used to it. And in a strange way, it should almost be home. Yet nothing ever has been home.

But in three days, maybe something finally will be . . .

I shove my thoughts away and breathe as my fellow Rangers stalk along the street. It's then I see them, a mother and daughter walking straight toward my team. Less than one city block separates them from the men counting on me to keep them alive.

The hell? How did they get past the other sniper unreported? Rogers is new on watch. But the quick paces these two are taking should have clued him in that something's up. I train my scope on their faces; their expressions are blank, unreadable. 'Cept that's not what keeps my attention.

The little girl can't be more than five. So why the fuck isn't her mother holding her hand? I lift my radio and bark a warning, dropping it beside me as I lock my scope dead center on the woman's head.

The radio crackles and Modreski chimes in, yelling at his team to hold their positions. He asks me what my plan is, knowing if something's caused the short-hairs on my neck to rise, he and the boys damn well need to listen. But I don't hear him, with a breath and a squeeze of the trigger, I leave a kid without a mother.

Just beneath the sleeve of her *abayah*—the dress completely covering her body—I see it, a detonator that would trigger the explosives likely strapped to her chest. A few Rangers I know—Simons and Boreman, rush forward. I start to mutter a curse, pissed at her for making me shoot her in front of her kid. But the curse lodges in my throat when I see the kid isn't looking at her mother lying next to her dead.

She's watching my advancing team as she lifts the detonator clasped tight in her hand.

Chapter One

Trinity

"Trin! You coming?" Hale calls.

Even over the steady hum of the ocean, his deep voice cuts through the small opening of our lifeguard station.

"I need five more seconds," I yell back, my thick southern accent drawing out each of my words.

"That's what you said nine minutes ago," he complains.

"But I didn't mean it last time," I holler back.

I grin because even though I can't see or hear him, I know he's chuckling, no matter how much he's trying to hold it in. I hurry and finish writing the schedule on the white board and cap the dry erase marker, before tossing it in the small cup holder to join the rest.

No sooner do I reach for my beach bag and throw the sandy thing over my shoulder than the office phone rings.

Most people would run away, ignoring it, after all by now it's seven thirty and way after closing. But I've always been one of those goody-goody responsible types—you know the ones the teachers assign as classroom monitor and who always turned in her library books a day early? What can I say, I'm all about a good time.

I lift the receiver before it finishes ringing. "Magenta Groves Beach Resort, lifeguard station seven, this is Trinity speaking. How may I help you?"

"Trin. Screw the whiteboard and get in the damn car!" Hale yells through the receiver. I whip around as his voice echoes behind me, as well as through the phone. He hops up the steps as he disconnects, laughing like that was the best prank ever.

"Why did you do that?" I ask.

"Because I knew you'd stop to answer the phone, even though the rest of us have been waiting on you."

I pretend to scowl, but don't quite manage. Me and scowling don't go hand and hand. Life's too short to wrap your mind around everything that's wrong with it. So I grin, because that's something I can do and do well.

"You think you're so smart. Don't you?" I ask, placing the phone back on the charger.

"You forgot good-looking," he says. "But I'll let it slide on account of I'm modest, too."

I laugh, but don't argue—at least about the good-looking part. We've only been back at Kiawah for a week, but already Hale's wavy blond hair has bleached significantly and his skin tone deepened to a light bronze. His steps are slow and purposeful as he crosses the small space separating us and stops in front of me.

"Let's go, Trin," he says, hauling me along. "You've done enough for the day."

I readjust my bag over my shoulder, and follow him out of the office, the usual bounce to my walk kicking in despite my heavy bag.

"Here. I'll take that," Hale offers, reaching for my bag.

I step just out of reach, knowing he has his own stuff to carry. "I've got it, big guy," I tell him.

"You sure?" he slams the door behind us. I stare out to the beach where a young couple is chasing after their little toddler as Hale fumbles with the lock.

"I'm sure," I reply, my attention staying on the young family. "Hey, Hale, you know how I always mind my own business."

"Nope," he says, leading me forward.

"Well, this time I can't," I continue, ignoring his comment. "For your own good, I have to tell you that this maybe your last chance to do something about Becca. The summer hasn't quite started, but it won't be long before it's gone."

"Yeah. I know," he mumbles.

"And?" I ask, turning back to him.

He tugs on my long ponytail. Unlike Becca, my best friend in the world, I'm neither tall, blonde nor leggy. My hair is as black as midnight in winter, and I'm just barely five feet three. And where her eyes are light and striking mine are a dull brown. But I do have something my bae doesn't have. Freckles. Y'all feel free to envy me at any time.

"Well?" I press. "You going to do something about that girl or aren't you?"

He shoves his key into the pocket of his long red lifeguard shorts and glides the sunglasses perched on top of his head back onto his face. "I guess we'll just have to wait and see," he tells me.

His smirk widens into that grin of his—the one capable of sizzling panties like coals over a fire. I shake my head. "Boy, between that smile of yours and that face it's a wonder Becca's not running to you rather than away."

He flings his arm around my shoulders as our feet dig through the sand. "Now, sugar, I'm sure I don't know what you mean," he says, keeping his grin in a way that tells me he's lying.

"Come on. You can have anyone you want. And if it's Becca, you need to act fast before those girls slapping each other just to lie their beach blankets near your post lead you astray and down a long dark path of sin, sex, and STDs."

"Is that so?" he asks.

"I'm just watching out for you," I say, stepping with him onto the gray weathered steps leading to the lot. "It's the kind of friend I am. You know, the kind who likes to pretend you're still a virgin and not the man whore you've become."

He laughs hard enough to shake us both as we reach the edge of the pier. Ahead of us in the sandy lot, Sean, Mason, and Becca look up from where they've been waiting for us.

Mason's dark skin glistens with sweat, likely from having dragged all the heavy equipment we weren't using back into the shed. But he's got the muscle and the stocky build for it. Poor Sean has the endurance to swim a few miles and back, but his long-limbed body is better suited for reaching things the rest of us can't, and his personality is best for those who don't mind the occasional dip in the gutter and can appreciate his not-always brilliant remarks.

But of course it's Becca Hale hones in on.

I can't blame him. Becca is leaning against the Jeep, poised like Miss America and as alluring as Miss Universe.

"What the fuck's taking y'all so long?" she yells.

But that mouth of hers makes her all Becca, so does that smile that pulls Hale closer.

"You know how she gets," Hale hollers, hooking his thumb my way. "Had to get the floors waxed, the office dusted, and mend that sea gull's broken wing before setting it free."

"You did all that shit?" Sean asks, moving forward. "Man, and here I was thinking you were just working on the schedule."

Mason who tends to be the most serious among us just shakes his head and laughs, because that's what we all do around Sean.

Becca backs away toward the driver's side, keeping her grin as she points to our boys. "Alex Pettyfer, Nathan Owens, Channing Tatum, y'all got the back," she tells them. She grabs my bag and tosses it onto the floor of the passenger side. "You, get to ride with me, cutie."

I almost ask to switch with Alex Pettyfer, aka Hale. But I've known Becca long enough to know something's up. So I hop in the front, barely snapping my seatbelt in place before she shifts in gear and tears out of the lot.

We catch the road leading out of the resort. Mason tugs on my hair just like Hale had, just to say "hi". Like most men I meet, he thinks I'm cute. As in a kid sister or a BFF cute. Not cute as in, "hey how about you let me rip off your thong with my teeth?" You know what I mean? The kind of "cute" that really matters.

I've pretty much resolved myself to BFF status, even though I wish I could be more.

Hale, whether because of what I said, or because he realizes time is running out for him to make a move, leans in between the seats, his attention fixed on Becca. Unlike me, that's not sand filling out the cups in her swimsuit.

"Hey, Becks, how about we catch dinner Tuesday after work? Maybe even a movie?"

Becca's wild hair—highlighted in alternating shades of blond and blonder—slaps around her gorgeous features as she grins. "I don't know. The boss may not like me dating a co-worker." She looks at me then. "Isn't that right, Boss?"

I crack up. All my lifeguards can do whatever they want during their time off. But these four in particular? These four that have been my friends since before any of us learned to read, swim, or cuss. I know they're a good bunch. I know they have my back. For all we joke, the minute their toes dig into that smooth white sand, it's on.

I perch my legs up and over the dash and cross my arms behind my head. "As your fearless leader, I hereby let that be your call, ma'am."

Okay. Maybe I'm not so fearless. And "leader" is a pretty loose title considering all I do is run a few drills each day and make sure everyone has a shift.

"I'll think about it," is all Becca tells him.

Hale is a good guy. Good enough to slink back and give her space. Like all my male besties, he's had a crush on Becca since he hit puberty and his male parts saluted her in celebration. Capable of stirring erections with a single glance was Becca's super power. Mine is the ability to make people snort drinks through their noses at my jokes. I adjust my head beneath my hand after another glance at my beautiful friend. We all have our gifts, and if mine includes making others smile, I can't complain.

Her grin widens as she takes the road that leads to Your Mother's Coconuts, better known to the locals as "Your Mother's". Once off the resort we're no longer lifeguards expected to abide by the rules. We're just fresh college grads ready to run amuck, do some skinny-dipping, and partake in all the fun our young selves demand.

In less than a minute, Becca is screeching to a halt at the far end of the half-filled lot. It is a quarter to eight on a Friday and our work week is done. With a hoot and a few hollers, our buddies jump out the back, rousing the other lifeguards who beat us here to do the same.

"Where the hell have y'all been?" the new girl calls out. "I'm thirsty."

Sean holds his hands out. "Then what're you newbies waiting for? Order up the first round."

"Us?" she asks, looking at her friend. "*We* have to pay?"

"Damn straight, yeah," Sean says like it's obvious. "Everyone knows virgins always buy the first round. Ain't that right, boys?"

The rest of my team, even those loitering on the outside deck, start chanting "virgins, virgins, virgins," pumping their fists in the air.

"Aw, hell," her friend says. "Come on. Let's go get our cherries popped."

They walk in, but we don't follow. Becca's made no move to slip out so I know she means to talk. I smile softly. "What's up?"

She looks to the ocean, where the waves sweep in to bathe the sand with all its salty heaven. But I doubt she really sees it, even though like me, Kiawah is a part of her. She crinkles her nose and then takes my hand. "Last summer," she says.

"Yeah, last one," I answer quietly, knowing how she feels because I'm feeling it, too. I squeeze her hand, my tone mirroring all the emotions fluttering inside me. "Time to grow up, right?"

"I wish we didn't have to," she mumbles, keeping her stare on the sea as if trying to gather some strength from it. "You still serious about applying to the Peace Corps?"

I was hoping we didn't have to have this conversation any time soon, but I've kept things from her long enough. "I applied over winter break, Becks."

Her mouth slowly falls open. "I told you to wait—to not do something drastic just because of what those douche heads did to you."

The "douche heads" she's referring to are Hunter, my ex-boyfriend, and Blakeney, my ex-friend. They once held my heart, until I caught them in bed and they ripped it from my chest.

Her words chip away at me. Not because I'm not over Hunter, or Blakeney. I am. I'm just not over their betrayal. I could never hurt anyone I claimed to love or called a friend. But they didn't feel the same.

I try to smile, knowing Becca needs my reassurance. But I can't quite manage this time. "You know I've always talked about going and serving. Ever since I was little."

"So you're telling me, if he'd stayed faithful and been a real man instead of a little bitch—if you'd agreed to marry him like he kept talking about—that you still would have signed up to join the Corps? Come on, Trin. Finding him fucking Blakeney was like a pen being slapped in your hand, forcing you to sign on that dotted line."

"No, it wasn't," I insist.

I don't want tonight to be about the bad things of the past. Not with the five of us together after too many months apart. But here we are, focusing on things I've tried hard to forget. "Becks, as much as I thought I loved Hunter, and as much as I believed that he wanted to marry me, I realize now we never would have worked out. I'm going into the Peace Corps, exactly like I've always planned. But knowing who he is— who he *really* is—he wouldn't have waited for me, and he sure as anything wouldn't have joined up just to be with me."

Even through her sunglasses, I can tell Becca's eyes are narrowing. "He's still a douche head, and so is she."

"I won't argue with you about that," I tell her. My head falls against the seat rest. Do you want to know something about Becca? She's sweeter than maple syrup and about as kind as people get. Until you hurt someone she loves. I'm among the lucky few she loves. But it's because she loves me, that she reacts the way she does.

She pushes her sunglasses up to her head, pegging me with enough disappointment to make me ache. "When do you leave?" she asks.

"September. But I won't know my placement for another few weeks." I answer so softly, I'm not sure if she hears, but her tensing posture assures me she does. "Daddy used his connections at the UN and arranged it so I'd have time to take my boards and have one last summer here with all of you."

"So from Princeton to the Peace Corps. From rich kid, to just another volunteer risking her life."She sighs in that way she does when she's trying not to cry. "Nice," she says, not that she means it.

My attention falls to our hands and to how hard she's holding me. "It's the right thing to do, Becks," I tell her.

"Helping people *is* the right thing to do. Signing up for twenty-five months with no way out, that's above and beyond." She shakes her head. "Hunter and Blakeney are assholes for what they did to you."

They are. But she needs to know that's not why I applied. "Becks, it's time to grow up and move forward, and to do the things we've always planned."

"What if I don't want to?" Her voice splinters and tears glisten her eyes. "What if none of us do? I don't want life to go on without the five of us together—you, me, Sean, Mason, and Hale—especially you, Trin."

Like me, she wishes she could stop time, and that somehow things could be different. But somethings can't be helped, and this is one of them.

Her parents and mine had offered to send us backpacking across Europe, but we chose to come back here. Back home to spend one last summer doing what we loved, and to pretend to be forever young, forever free of life's demands, forever friends. As I look to my pseudo sister, I swallow hard and hope that the latter stays true.

Tears trickle down her cheeks, causing my eyes to sting. But Becks doesn't need me crying with her. Right now, she needs my strength, and maybe a little of my humor.

"*Trin, Becks!*" Sean hollers from the deck. "What the hell?

We've got shots waiting and horny women who can't wait to have a piece of me."

"Sorry!" I yell, hopping out of the jeep. "Becca dared me to spell my name across her belly with my tongue and I couldn't refuse."

Instead of taking it for the joke it is, Sean freezes. "No, shit," he says.

Becca doubles over, practically falling out of the driver's side seat. I hurry around to steady her and lead her forward. Sean continues to stare at us, his eyes clouded with whatever dirty thoughts are swimming through his mind as we stumble into Your Mother's.

My laughter fades as I look to where the rustic blue double doors open up to the rear deck. But I'm not staring at Hale as he points to his raised shot glass filled to the rim, or at Mason who's smiling politely at the women admiring his muscles. And my, I barely notice Sean shooting past us.

I'm too busy gaping at the smoking hot bartender with the Army Ranger tat inked to an arm as thick as my thigh.

Holy Baby Jesus in a manger sleeping on a bed of hay.

"Hmm," Becca says in a purr. She leans in close to whisper in my ear. "Who do we have here?"

Brown strands of wavy hair spill around his strong features and startling light eyes, and a thin beard lines a jaw I could probably pound horseshoes on. If I knew anything about horseshoes. Or horses. Or, pardon me, what was my name again?

Not to be rude, or inappropriate—I do have morals, after all—but that tight blue shirt stretching across his broad chest is one pec flex shy of ripping in half. Or me ripping it in half when I straddle him.

"You want to straddle him?" Becca asks, a delighted gleam fixing on her face.

I look at her, realizing I spoke out loud. "No?"

She busts out laughing. This time, she's the one dragging me forward. "Come on, Trin. Time to have fun."

We stroll toward the hot guy. Or as I call him, 'my future baby daddy' because for the first time in too long I'm looking—we're talking full-out gawking—at a man. He has my attention and whether he means to or not he's not letting go.

I smile his way, not because of what he looks like, but because I can't seem to help myself. I think maybe Becca smiles at him, too. But "sex in a tight T-shirt" isn't impressed by her charm, and he sure isn't captivated by mine. He scowls—as in *scowls*—which of course earns him a wink from me.

Hey, sticks and stones, or whatever, I'm going to get this guy to smile. Even if it's clear he doesn't want to smile at me.

Chapter Two

Callahan

I mutter something that's supposed to be a curse when Jed nudges me.

"What's up, Callahan?" he asks.

"Is this the way it's going to be?" I reply, motioning to the group of lifeguards and locals chatting it up and arguing about which song's next on the old jukebox.

Jed laughs. "Partner," he tells me. "It's only end of May. The season hasn't even started. Things are going to heat up fast come the second week in June."

"Christ," I mumble.

When I pictured Kiawah, I pictured a real island. Something secluded and quiet, tucked away from the rest of existence. And when I first took over my uncle's place it was. But that was March. Back then, feeling like I was—hell, like *I am*—the sun rising and setting along the South Carolina shore was the only proof I had that the world continued to spin even though I no longer felt like I was part of it. Now, with temperatures rising and the increase in traffic along the back roads, Kiawah is anything but quiet, especially the moment this bunch walked in.

The young woman, with the long dark hair is especially loud. And perky. Lord, I hate perky. I know her type, pretending no war is going on while kids younger than her have their limbs blown clean off. She smiled when she walked in with her friend. What in the hell did she have to be so happy about?

I glance up in time to catch her rip a dollar out of an old man's hand and wave it in front of him. The guy reaches for it, grinning as he tries to snatch it back. "Uh, uh, uh, Mr. Perrington," she practically sings. "Fair is fair. One Cupid Shuffle in exchange for one Electric Slide."

"You tell 'em, Trin," the lady next to him says.

The brunette shimmies, that's right, *shimmies* all the way to the jukebox even though the song is long over and nothing's playing. She slides the dollar in, hits a few buttons, and the music starts. But that's not enough, she motions everyone forward. And when I mean everyone, I mean every last person here.

Like a herd of sheep they follow. I wouldn't follow her anywhere except to the door, and only then to lock it behind her.

The base of this crap song is heavy enough to rumble my shit kickers. It takes all I have not to mutter another swear. But seeing how even Jed has jumped into the horde of people hopping back and forth instead of mixing that prissy drink on the ticket, I curse anyway.

I make the drink and head to the rear storage room, taking longer than I need to rearrange the kegs closer to the door and haul back a case of Corona.

With my attention ahead and away from the dance floor, I return to the bar, lowering the case to the floor in front of the fridge. I don't think I'm done shoving half of the beers in when I hear, "Excuse me. Excuse me, sir?"

I close my eyes and sigh, knowing who it is even before I straighten. I recognize her voice. This homecoming queen or whatever pep squad she leads is loud for a little thing.

I lean back on my heels and cross my arms, not bothering to smile. "Yeah?"

She grins, her large brown eyes blinking with something what, Lord help me, resembles excitement. "I don't think we've met. My name's Trinity, Trinity Summers."

Of course it is.

She waits, still smiling, I suppose for me to shake her hand or something. When I don't, her smile fades a little and she glances over her shoulder to where her friend, the tall blonde is sitting. Her friend taps on her ear and quickly turns away.

I don't know if it's some secret girl code she's doing with the blonde until she yells, "I said I don't think we've met. My name is Trinity. TRI-NI-TY SU-MMERS. You know, like the season?"

Right now, I can do little more than blink, wondering if there's some kind of hidden camera trained on my face and what the hell she snorted before she walked in here. No one is this high-strung sober. No one.

She leans into the bar, keeping her smile. "And you are?"

Someone not named after a porn star, that's for damn sure.

It wasn't too long ago that the same "please die" look I'm pegging her with would have sent dangerous men running. Instead this woman here giggles. *Giggles.*

"Well, if you're not going to tell me your name, I'll have to give you one." She twirls her dark hair, so thick it looks like a wet towel slapped on her head. She sits up and beams even more, if that's even humanly possible. "I know. How about Spanky?"

How about you skip along the beach with a band of puppies and leave me the fuck alone?

"No," I respond.

"You sure?" She frowns, like she's confused. "You look like a Spanky."

If I were a pit bull, my lips would be peeling back from my gums. "My name is Callahan Sawyer."

She clasps her hand over her mouth, her eyes wide. "My stars, he speaks." She drops her hands and offers an exaggerated wink. "Or should I say Callahan speaks?"

I'm annoyed on multiple levels, don't get me wrong. But the fact that Tinkerbell here has tricked me into telling her my name pisses me off more than it should. "Do you want a drink or not?" I manage, grinding my teeth.

"Sure," she says, oblivious to my growing desire to strangle her. "Pour me a taste of your finest."

I pour her a shot of Tequila and step back. She looks down at the shot, then back at me.

"What? No lime. No salt?" she asks. She leans forward, resting her arms across the bar in a voice that sounds husky, but I determine is grossly sarcastic. "I thought this was a classy establishment, sir."

I bang the bottle of salt in front of her and pass her a lime punctured with one of those tiny swords, careful not to actually touch her. She licks the salt she added to her hand, slams back the shot, and attempts to suck on the lime.

I expected the usual, for her to actually *swallow* the damn thing. But no. Not this woman. Instead she spits the booze out, spraying me in the face with enough force to slap the lime against my mouth.

The mangled piece of fruit falls back on the bar as I swipe at my skin. This time, I do blink. A lot. Booze to the eyes will do that to a man. As I watch, a deep shade of red creeps up her neck and into her face.

"I'm so sorry. So, so very sorry!" she says. She whips back around to look at her friend who now has her face buried in her hands. "Um. If you give me a second I think I have some tissues in my bag."

She spit tequila at me—and a Goddamn lime!—and she thinks I'm going to let her wipe me down with *tissues*. As the sting eases from my eyes, I take a moment to question her sanity, and my ability to snap her neck without anyone noticing.

She covers her mouth. "Oh, my God. You look like you want to kill me."

And she's right. But then she starts laughing, because clearly this woman isn't loud enough. Her face reddens further. Maybe she's embarrassed and maybe she does feel bad. But something in the way that she blushes . . .

"I'm really sorry, Callahan," she says. "That's never happened before. I think it went down the wrong way."

"It's fine," I say, tearing my eyes off her. I reach for a

clean rag beneath the bar to wipe my face only to have her lift it from my hand.

"Here, allow me," she says, dabbing my nose.

She passes the towel along my skin, using care that I'm not used to. I step away from her reach, wondering why the hell she touched me, and why the hell I let her.

"Look, Trixie—"

"It's Trinity," she answers quietly, her bright smile returning like I invited her to Disney to meet Mickey Mouse or whatever the fuck. This woman can't possibly be real. No one is this . . . *her*.

"I really am sorry," she says yet again. Her eyes, despite their dark color, sparkle beneath a veil of thick lashes, and the way she looks at me, it's like she's known me forever.

But she doesn't know me. No, not at all. I slap the rag on the bar and wipe it clean in angry circles.

"So . . ." she says, resting her chin on her hand as she leans against the bar. "If it's not too much trouble, would you mind pouring me another shot?"

I'm ready to tell her that I do mind—that something's wrong with her, and that maybe she should skip back to her friends and far away from me. But those words lodge in my throat when I catch sight of her face, and notice something beyond that smile she's pegging me with.

Before I can figure out what exactly that is, I pour her another shot, focusing on my task and once more wrenching my eyes off her.

Chapter Three

Trinity

I wave to my new best friend on our way out and throw in a big grin since that's how I roll. "Thanks, Callahan. It's been real!" I call to him. He pauses in the middle of shoving a chair beneath a table just to narrow his eyes. But I'll admit, it's my, "See you next week" comment that causes his upper lip to curl.

That man is all sorts of crazy about me.

I hop down Your Mother's worn wooden steps and join the rest of my crew gathered at the bottom. "Trin!" they yell when I reach them.

Since I'm the last one to exit the premises save for Jed and that Yummy Callahan, my presence is everyone's cue to disperse. The designated drivers do their best to shove their drunk passengers into their cars, most of them swearing and cranky since they're the ones scheduled to work in the morning and not the ones who got to slam back shots.

Mason, and a young co-ed visiting for the week are talking softly by the Brewsters' Jaguar. He bends and kisses her slowly—very unlike the way Sean had made out with her friend on the dance floor right before closing. Goodness, Sean and his lady friend were like a pair of horny dolphins during mating season, except not as graceful and certainly not as chipper.

The Brewsters simply shrug and use it as an excuse to take a walk along the beach. The Brewsters have always been cool like that. So have Jimmy and Millie Rossen who are getting pretty friendly all over the hood of Mr. Rossen's latest muscle car. Hopefully, the cops won't catch them naked with Mrs. Rossen bent over the hood like last Christmas. And Easter. And yeah, Arbor Day, too. Lovely couple, the Rossens.

Hale hurries to my side, but I suspect it's because Becca's next to me. "Can I crash at your place, too, Trin?"

He asks me, but is looking at my very sloppy yet gorgeous friend. "Of course," I say.

"Cool," he answers, although yup, still giving Becks the eyes.

As per our usual Friday night festivities that come with every start of the season, we leave Becca's jeep at Your Mother's and head toward my place which is only a mile up the road. With Momma, Daddy, and Landon gone, I don't mind the company. And they don't mind their presence whether they're home or not.

My folks are awesome. They always have been. For as long as I remember, our house was burstin' at the seams with my friends and Landon's. When I went away to college, that's the first time I noticed my parents begin to age. No more kids running in and out of the house to keep them young.

It made me sad. But I suppose it made them sadder.

So now instead of trekking through malaria-infested jungles, with Landon and I in tow to immunize children or rock sick babies to sleep, Momma and Daddy spend their retirement travelling the world in style. Well, if anyone deserves a happily ever after, my folks sure do.

Becca swings her arm around me, a friendly gesture, and also one that will keep her walking straight up the incline. "Love you, Trin," she half slurs, half yawns.

I push up on my toes to kiss her cheek. "Love you, too, Becks."

Out of the five of us who started, I'm the most sober. And because Mr. Perrington, who is one Viagra-inspired-ejaculation away from an early grave, decided to go beer for beer with some of my boys—Mr. Perrington won by the way—we picked up another three lifeguards too drunk to drive home. They stagger behind us, excited that they're not the ones on-call tomorrow.

"Where's Sean?" I ask.

"Throwing up in the bushes," Hale replies, smirking.

"And where's that girl he was with?" I ask.

Hale laughs. "Her friends shoved her in their car when she tried to pull down his shorts."

"Good call," I say. I glance behind me. "Sean, you okay?"

He jogs up to me, his long limbs and condition causing him to stumble into a rather graceless swagger. "I'm good, Trin. Must've been that last beer."

"Or the three shots you did off Mrs. Brewster's belly," I offer.

Sean nods thoughtfully. "That, too. You know, for a woman who's well over sixty, she's surprisingly fit."

"Hmm-mmm" the group of us concurs.

Becca leans in closer to whisper in my ear. "What happened between you and that hot bartender? You spent a lot of time talking with him."

She's right, although I'm the one who did all the talking. He mostly did his best to ignore me. My multiple and animated attempts to draw his smile, only drew more scowls, and a few annoyed grunts. And yet I can't stop my grin as I think of him. "He wants me, bad. I know he does."

"Yeah?" Becca asks.

"Nope, not even a little bit," I answer, laughing.

My smile diminishes as I think about Callahan's stance: arms crossed, stare hard, and mouth clenched shut. Men can be dangerous. And scary. But those kind of men carry a certain look in their eyes. My Daddy had once compared this look to a door opening and revealing the darkness of the soul.

Callahan doesn't have that darkness Daddy speaks of, despite the intense leveling stare. He has something more akin to the kind of grief I'd seen too many times—the type that numbs you and makes you forget what it's like to feel.

The trips helping those in need that my parents took us on were intense, involving countries crippled by war, disaster, or poverty. Some of the people there had that same expression Callahan wears: anger, sadness, and disappointment mixed with despair. Emotions so devastating they hollow out the soul, leaving only a vacant shell behind.

Like those people from those countries, Callahan has experienced his share of torment. If that Special Forces tat hadn't given him away, the lines hardening his features, and those eyes—*man,* those heartbreaking blue eyes—spilled the truth. He's broken . . . and probably all kinds of lonely.

"So you're giving up on him, Trin?" Becca asks, yawning yet again.

I adjust my arm around her waist. "You saying I should?"

She thinks about it. "Yes, and no. I mean, he's like the first guy you've actually taken an interest in since . . ." She clears her throat. "It's just nice to see you notice someone you don't have to save from drowning," she adds quickly.

"I don't know. I wouldn't mind a little mouth to mouth action there," I admit. My comment causes Becca to clutch me tighter and squeal with a little too much enthusiasm. I try to loosen her hold so she doesn't choke me and only mildly succeed. "*Becks,*" I croak.

"Oh. Sorry, sugar."

She repositions her arms around me, but thankfully her hold is tamer than what it was, allowing me to move and breathe as I increase our speed up the small hill. Just a few more yards until we reach our property, and a few more after that before we fall into a soft bed.

I breathe in the salty sea air fluttering my hair as I stop in front of the electronic keypad. The house, while a good distance away from the beach, is still only a short walk from the shore. My parents purchased the property when they were first married, but didn't build the house until Landon was a few months from starting school. They liked the view and the close proximity to the beach, they just preferred not to be smack dab in the face of a hurricane should one hit.

I punch the keypad, causing the gate to open with a mild

creak and allowing my drunk cohorts through. "Open sez a me," I say a little too late.

Sean who's crashed here before jogs ahead, likely to call dibs on a bed. Hale and Becca have stayed over more times than I can count, but they remain by my side. The rest of our party walk slowly behind us, the solar powered lights casting their glow against the weeping willows, palmettos, and dogwoods, allowing them to take in the property.

"You live here?" the girl who made out with Mason asks. I hadn't noticed that she'd tagged along.

"I do," I answer. I offer a smile over my shoulder, making sure to catch Mason's stare. He tilts his head, his way of telling me he'll keep an eye on her. While I like to think most people are genuinely good, I still have to be cautious of who I allow in my home.

My attention returns ahead to take in the light brick color Momma and I wanted, and Daddy and Landon did not. It's a great shade, bordering on tan with traces of peach, and even in the darkness, it seems to welcome us home.

I hurry up the steps and unlock the door. For a brief moment, I wonder if I should have invited Callahan with us. It's a stupid thought—he would have said no—not to mention I'd just met the guy. But maybe I should have. Like I said he seems so lonely and . . . well, doesn't everyone deserve a smile?

"Trin?" Hale says.

"Uh, sorry, what?"

He cocks his head. "I asked where you wanted us?"

"You can have my room. Becks and I will take my parents' room."

"Okay," he says, looking back at Becca. "Hey, Becks. Want to hang out on the terrace for a little bit? Maybe kick back some water instead of more beer?"

"No, shug. All I'm thinking about is warm sheets and a long sleep," she answers, yawning.

Disappointment swirls along his features as he watches her trail inside with the others. I punch him the arm affectionately. "It's a marathon," I whisper. "Not a race."

He shoots me a sideway glance, and oh yeah, there's that panty melting grin again reminding me he's not giving up hope yet.

"Trin?" Mason calls from the kitchen. "Can we heat up the frozen pizzas in there? I'll swing by tomorrow with a few more to pay you back."

I shove Hale away when he pulls me into a headlock and tousles my hair. "Sure," I answer, Mason. "But consider yourself in charge, 'kay? I'm tired and going to crash."

"No problem, Trin," he says.

By his serious tone, and that stiff nod he offers, I know he means it. I hurry up the steps behind Becca. "Spare toothbrushes still in the linen closet?" she asks when reach the top.

"Yeah. Be a pal and see who else needs them, okay?"

"All right," she says, hurrying off.

I grab some clothes for us out of my room and my toothbrush from my bathroom before crossing into the other wing and slipping into my parents' suite. I've already showered and have my hair up in a turban before Becca returns and slips into the bathroom with me.

My hair falls against my shoulder blades with a smack as I tug off the towel. I reach for a wide tooth comb and pass it through the length as I think back to Callahan. He didn't notice me like I wanted him to. In fact, some might call my first impression disastrous.

As friendly as I can be, I'll admit I was more than a little intimidated by him. The fact that he's gorgeous may have had something to do with it, and so might the little tidbit that those hands could bust a skull open with a single squeeze. That doesn't mean that I won't try again. He's not exactly enthralled by my charm, mind you, but right around closing, I did catch him looking at me. His stare didn't linger . . . yet it was there, totally taking me by surprise.

What surprised me more was he didn't seem to notice Becca.

I glance at her as she shoves the shorts down her tiny waist and long legs, her large breasts bouncing as she shimmies her hips. Y'all, *everyone* notices Becca!

Except maybe Callahan.

It affirms my suspicions that he's seen, or maybe done, more than his conscience could live with. And it breaks my heart. But his sadness draws me, making me determined to get to know him, and hopefully lift his spirits.

In a way, I'm actually freaked out that I'm attracted to Callahan. It's something I haven't felt or wanted in like, forever. And again, while I don't know him, I can't suppress my grin every time I think about him.

Those hands—how they passed along the bar in smooth motions—makes me wonder if he's a gentle lover or one who takes full control. Not that it matters now or maybe ever. Men, especially who look like him, always think "little sis" not "little minx" when they see me coming. It's not that I think I'm ugly, but no way will I win him over with my looks—not with the supermodel types scattered all over Kiawah. So tonight I'd used what I had, my personality, even though it accidently ended up all over his face with a touch of lime.

I meant to make him laugh when I spoke to him, or at the very least smile. He did neither. Given I'm stubborn, I see his rebuff more like a challenge. And given my insane need to save the world, and leave it a little brighter, I also see him as something more.

"What you smiling about, shug?" Becca asks as she fumbles through the linen closet for a towel.

"Callahan," I answer truthfully because it's Becks, and I can.

"Fair enough." She turns on the water and blasts it until steam starts to cloud the glass doors. "How do you think he'd be in bed?"

I laugh because it's so like Becks to go there with me. Southern ladies are like that, all proper and polite in public, but not so much in private. "I'm thinking rough and hard," I admit, remembering the ease with which he carried that keg in from the back room. "What about you?"

"Oh, girl, my guess is that man will ride you like a bronco

straight from the gate until a rodeo clown runs in to save you." She strips out of her bathing suit, revealing a body that's totally unfair and hops in the shower. "Did you get me something to wear?"

"Yes," I answer. "But I think you're better off in one of my daddy's T-shirts."

She runs the soap over her melons as I drop away my towel and stare at my strawberries. "For the love of all," I say, when they appear to be laughing at us.

"Don't complain," she insists when she catches me eyeing my so-called rack. "You've got plenty. I have too much. It's a wonder I haven't bumped into a grade schooler and killed him."

"Or blinded one during winter," I agree, pulling my nightshirt over my head.

She cracks up, slipping out of the shower as I head into my parents' room.

I toss her one of Daddy's old T-shirts when she joins me. She's pulls on a pair of the panties I'd brought from my room because not only is she big on top, but tiny on the bottom. Sometimes the scales of sexy totally tilt in someone else's favor, regardless of the rest of us jumping on the other side.

Becca shifts into bed after me, we roll to face each other just as we've done a thousand times over the years. "Can I ask you something without you thinking I'm feeling sorry for myself?" I ask.

She brushes a strand of my wet hair from my face. "You know you can ask me anything."

I know I can, but it doesn't make what I have to ask any easier. "Do you think I could get someone like Callahan interested in me? I know he's different from other guys I've dated, but . . . do you think I might stand a chance?"

She analyzes me closely, her eyes searching my face as her hand slips away from my hair. "Trin, you're smart, you're beautiful; you can have any man you want."

I shake my head, but not at the sting her words cause. "We both know that's not true," I remind her softly.

A flicker of anger finds its way into her face, and voice.

"You're better off without him, *and* her."

I know she's right, but it's not just Hunter I'm talking about. After years of too many men calling me their best friend, it's hard to consider myself the man-killer Becca is trying to make me out to be. Hunter was the first cute guy I liked, who thought I was cute back. The only guy to ever pledge his love for me, only to ultimately betray me. It's not exactly a stellar record on my end.

"I don't want to think about them," I admit truthfully, wanting to leave the past where it belongs. "Let's get back to Callahan, okay?"

"All right," she says, softening her tone and her expression.

My short nails skim along the mattress. "Be honest with me," I tell her. "Can someone like him maybe like someone like me?"

She watches me carefully. "As more than a fuck?" she asks.

Considering I asked for the truth, I'm no longer sure I want to hear it. "Yeah."

"I don't know," she says, taking a moment to mull through her thoughts. "A man like that is hard from life, and probably more, Trin."

"I figured as much," I confess. "That doesn't mean he doesn't deserve some good and maybe a little happiness in his life."

"Maybe," she says. "But can I ask you something? Why him?" She holds up her hand when I shoot her a look. "I get that he's hot, Trin. Hell, the man is sex, dipped in honey, with a cherry on top of his penis for the lickin'. But he's no boy—not like the ones we know who are just now barely men. He's different, steely, and from what I can tell, someone who's innocence was lost a long time ago."

There's a whole lot of truth in what Becca says. The young men who generally pique my interest are like Hunter: more Abercrombie and Fitch, and usually on the smaller, leaner side. Callahan is jeans, work boots, and I have to crane my neck to meet his face.

"For someone who was all excited, that I was all excited, you don't sound very excited anymore," I remind her.

"That's before I knew you wanted more than something to ride."

Yeah. I think she's right about that.

She purses her lips. "If you're looking for something more, Trin, I'm not sure this guy is a good place to start."

I adjust my head against the pillow, more to give me a moment than something I really need to do. "So is that a no?" I ask.

"It's a *be careful*," she answers me truthfully. "You're a good girl—an angel always willing to sweep in and save people. But, Trin, some people don't want to be saved."

Chapter Four

Callahan

I throw open the back door, grumbling from exhaustion and step onto the deck in my bare feet. As I lean in to stretch against the rail, a breeze sweeps in through the break in the trees. For a moment I still, expecting the grime to once more coat my face with its filth, and the smell of sweat and death to fill my nose.

Instead, only salty air strokes my beard in a gentle caress. I release a breath, remaining tense and unable to shake the memories that haunt my dreams every night. The squats, the presses, and the pull-ups I do during my grueling daily workouts only temporarily distract me. I need to run along the beach until my thighs burn, my muscles ache, and my brain forgets—everything. Feelings are bullshit. It's numbness I seek. That, and to escape from everything and everyone.

I take off in a sprint, desperate to free myself of all thoughts, and eager for exhaustion. Only through exhaustion do I ever manage a few hours of decent sleep. It's not easy, pushing my body the way that I do. But it beats those meds the army docs kept trying to get me to take—drugs that lock you into the nightmares with no way out.

Another breeze sweeps in, cooling my sweat-soaked brow as I reach the shore and turn left. It's early, real early, the sun's rays just starting to build in intensity. But already a few locals are out.

An old couple dip their spotted feet into the water, waving to me as I near. I tilt my chin, but not much more. I can't give much more, and hell, I don't want to.

The next group I pass is a cluster of old women speed walking, heads up, arms pumping, their focus tense and straight ahead. They don't say shit, and neither do I.

A wave crashes along the beach, strong enough to cover my ankles and drench my shins. I ignore the cold sting it causes and push on. I'm only vaguely aware of the water's withdrawal, losing sight of where I am, and who's around me. And I'm glad.

Maybe I'm lost. But that doesn't mean I want to be found.

"Spanky! Is that you?"

Jesus. H. Christ. No . . . just . . . no.

I know who's there even before my stare cuts left. The brunette, the little one from the other night abandons the buoy ropes she's untangling and waves, a big grin lighting up her small face.

I jerk my chin ahead and away from her, spitting every swear word I know through my teeth. My fists clench tight as that now familiar, annoying—hell, did I mention annoying?—voice appears way too close in behind me.

"It is you!" she drawls.

I try to run faster, but I already ran a mile, and worked out close to two hours. So when the small graceful steps grow louder, and Cheerleader Skipper bounces to my side, it's all I can do not to fall to the sand and beg God to take me.

"Wow, you're fast. I almost didn't think I'd catch you."

She only sounds mildly out of breath which means she keeps talking.

Fuck. Me.

"I love running on the beach. Don't you, Spanky? It's like exhilarating and fun all at the same time—"

"Do *not* call me Spanky."

"Iron Man?"

"No!"

"Batman?"

I turn enough just to glare at her. "*Batman*?"

She shrugs and continues to run like she's prancing through a field of daisies, pointy toes and all. "You know," she says. "Because you're all broody and your voice is really deep—like Batman." She beams up at me. "Take it as a compliment. Batman's all sorts of hot."

"There's something wrong with you," I tell her truthfully.

I continue to run. And so does she. For a tiny thing she's freakishly athletic. She's also fairly quiet which is more than shocking.

As I start to get winded, I notice her face is only mildly flushed. I make the mistake of sweeping my gaze along her form. She's wearing a black sports bra, and shorts that are more like panties than pants. Her hair is pulled back in ponytail revealing a round face and bright brown eyes.

A small spray of freckles pepper her nose and cheeks, and although it's still only May, her skin has begun to tan. The girl is a stick and would probably shatter if she tripped. Yet despite her puny frame, there's definition to her arms, legs, and flat stomach.

My gaze lingers longer than it should because she notices and yeah, *giggles*.

"If you'd like, I can flex for you," she offers.

I release a heavy breath. This woman can't possibly be this, this, *grrr*.

"So where you from?" she asks, ignoring the way I continue to shoot daggers.

When I don't answer, she keeps talking like I did, and then some. "I'm from South Carolina, born and raised right here on the island. My folks—well, you can call them modern day hippies—used to take me and my brother—his name is Landon—all over the world every summer break up until I was in eighth grade."

"To Europe," I guess, even though I more than intended to keep my mouth shut.

She laughs. "Sometimes. Mostly Asia and Africa. We went to England and Italy a few times, but primarily hung out in soup kitchens in the cities, and churches in the rural countryside, tending to those in need of care."

I frown, confused as to why anyone would drop what had to be several grand to visit Europe only to hang out in soup kitchens and I'm guessing are homeless shelters. But of course, I don't ask. And of course, that doesn't stop her from answering.

"They were volunteers, kind of like missionaries without religious intent. More because they could, and wanted to help."

I'm listening, even though I don't want to. That doesn't mean I bother to respond.

"Ever been to Asia?" she asks.

I don't answer.

"Africa?"

Again, I don't say a word.

Her voice quiets. "Been to Iraq?"

My head whips her way. And even though I don't doubt my face shows she's hit a nerve, she doesn't flinch. She motions to the ink on my left arm with a tilt of her small chin.

That arm carries the sniper rifle beneath the Death Before Dishonor banner. My right arm is all Ranger. A soldier's outline covering the entire upper arm that took four hours to ink in.

"I appreciate you serving, more than you know," she says carefully. "But it must have been hard, protecting your country like you did."

I almost scoff at her words, but then I don't, holding in my anger, for my sake and hers. Hard is running along a sandy beach after you've worked out for the past two hours. Hard is surviving Special Forces training. Hard *isn't* killing a man you never quite get to look in the face—or watching your friends bleed out in your arms—or lifting your buddy's severed limb from a dirty pile of rubble—hoping like anything they can somehow stitch that shit back on.

Iraq wasn't hard. Not in the least. Iraq was pure hell.

I want to rage then, and tell her as much—tell her how she doesn't know shit. But I don't. She's a pain in the ass, that's for damn sure. And while I'm far from kind, I won't be cruel. Not to her.

For all I don't want or need her company, she doesn't deserve the fury that threatens to choke out the last bit of me that remains.

So instead of raging and going all beast, I continue to run. And so does she, diligently beside me like we have all the time in world. I grit my teeth and push past the stress of another mile, wondering if she's a punishment for my sins. I'm convinced that she might be when I reach the three-mile mark.

Of course I don't tell her this. Instead I angle around without speaking. Surprisingly, she does too.

My pace slows to a steady jog. Rainbow, or whatever the hell her name is—wait, Trinity, that's it—keeps up. Her breathing is more pronounced, and her skin more flushed, but she continues to move her slender legs in time with mine.

In the silence, and based on the conversation, my mind should return where I don't want it to. Back to Iraq. Back to my team. Back to that time when only three days remained. Instead it latches onto what she said about her parents volunteering all over the world, and her working in a soup kitchen.

No wonder she's screwed up. Who the hell does that?

I focus on the horizon ahead, doing my best to ignore her. But for some asinine reason my mind starts trying to figure her out. Why is she here, with *me*? Isn't it damn obvious I want be left alone?

I open my mouth—ready to tell her she's wasting her time, and warming up to the wrong man, when the blonde—her friend from the other night—hops down the lifeguard tower and calls to her.

"Trin—"

Her smile fades when she sees me with her, and catches the scowl tensing the muscles along my jaw.

Trinity simply grins. "Coming!" she yells. She pats my arm. "Catch you same time tomorrow."

As if it's the most natural thing in the world, she runs off, while I almost stumble—trying to understand what just happened. *Catch you tomorrow? What the fuck?*

Against my better judgment I glance over my shoulder. Her friend seems wary and she should be. Trinity is, well, *not*. She ignores my scowl and continues to grin. "Nice butt by the way," she calls.

I jerk my attention in the direction of my house, thinking I might need a restraining order to keep her away. She's relentless, nosey, and unbelievably irritating.

I mutter another curse. So then why the hell am I smiling?

Chapter Five

Trinity

I rest my rescue can on my chair and adjust the umbrella so
it's actually providing shade where I want it. It's only seven
thirty in the morning, but that notorious Carolina sun heating
my arms is making it clear we're in for a hot one.

As I toy with the large bulky umbrella, I sneak a peek
down the beach, trying not to look desperate, and failing
miserably. The spot where Callahan usually materializes like
a hot, sexy, brooding mirage is empty of his presence.

Come to think of it, the only signs of life I see are the
speed walking ladies no sane human being would be foolish
enough to cross. I won't lie. I'm disappointed. So much so
that the little balloon of hope I usually carry deflates with an
almost audible whiz.

I finish positioning the umbrella and look once more.
Humph. It's getting late. If Callahan doesn't come soon I
won't be able to run with him. I try not to laugh. And
wouldn't that just ruin his day?

"Trin!" Sean calls to me.

"Yeah?" I answer.

"I can't find the damn surfboard we use for rescues."

I give his comment some thought. "You mean the spine
board?"

"Yeah. The surfboard we use for rescues," he repeats, like I'm the one saying it wrong.

I drop my whistle beside my can, climbing down the lifeguard chair as I speak. "The pediatric one or the adult?"

His long arms swing against his sides as he walks. "The pediatric one—that's the little one, right?"

"Right," I answer. "Hmm. Did you look in the back room behind the desk?"

"Looked everywhere." He pulls off his shirt and tosses it up to the chair since he and I are sharing watch duty today.

I think about it. "There's an old one in the shed. It's dirty and will need to be washed, but so long as it's not cracked we can use it until we find the other one."

He makes a face. "And what if it's cracked?"

I tighten my ponytail. "Then we'll have to call the local EMTs and see if they have a spare. Can't be without something we might need. Have Mason and Hale check on their side—and call Becca, too, at her post. With all the training exercises we've been doing, it probably got moved."

He reaches for his radio and calls it in as my hot and studly running partner appears down the beach. I can't see his face. Not yet. But I know it's him by his large frame and the way he runs. If those squared shoulders and clenched fists don't scream, "I was in the military and I'll whoop your ass" I don't know what does.

I'm not looking at Sean, but I know he's looking at me. "You gonna run again before opening?" he asks.

I take a moment to stretch my legs, trying to look casual, and once more failing miserably. "Yup. But don't you worry none. I'll be back in time."

"Oh, I know. I wasn't worried about that none." He waits, then says, "Trin, you sure about this guy? I mean, he barely talks to you. I don't think he said two words to you last Friday night."

I rise from a deep crouch and grin. "But he's no longer snarling, and only rolled his eyes at me once yesterday." I waggle my finger at him as Callahan nears. "That, my friend, is progress."

"Aw, hell. If you say so. But you're, you know, fuckable. Maybe you should try for someone who's fuckable in return."

I pause in the middle of stretching my arms. "Sean, you know how we've talked about those deep thoughts of yours you should probably keep to yourself?" I ask.

"Yeah?"

"That was one of them," I point out.

I stroll away from Sean, unable to stop my smile. Maybe another girl would be put off by his comment. But I know him well enough to recognize his heart is in the right place. My, how long have we been friends now? Twenty years? Doesn't seem like that long, but considering we went to the same preschool together it sounds about right.

My feet kick back little scoops of sand as I walk to the water's edge in time to meet the man who can't live without me. Okay. Not really. But in his own grouchy, grumbling kind of way he—

I was going to say he seems to enjoy my company. Perhaps, "enjoy" is too strong a word. More to the truth, he no longer attempts to flee at the sight of me.

"Morning, Callahan," I say brightly, picking up my pace so we run side by side.

He doesn't say anything back. But—score!—he doesn't scowl either. See? Progress. Now that's what I'm talking about. We plow ahead, falling into a smooth and easy rhythm.

He keeps his focus down the beach, and I let him. But once my legs warm up I convince myself something's missing. Oh, I know! Mood music. And what's better than a little Flo Rida as we run along the Carolina coast?

I start with *I Cry*, humming to the beat as best I can before I move on to *Low*. But hey, I love that song so it's not long before I'm singing the words out loud, alternating between deep and high voices with each beat of our steps—just to keep it interesting.

"*She hit the floor. She hit the floor. Next thing you know, Shawty got low, low, low, low, low, low, low.*"

He briefly closes his eyes. "Do you have to do that?"

By now I'm sort of shimmying as I run and sing (no easy

task, mind you) so I'm not sure which part he's talking about. Shame he's not impressed by my moves and coordination.

"You mean shimmy?" I clarify.

He doesn't answer, swallowing as if in pain.

I try again. "Surely you don't mean my singing?"

He makes an irritated gesture down my body. "It's the whole package."

I pretend to think about it. "Maybe it's just the song. If you want, you can pick the next one. I take requests."

He opens his mouth only to shut it. I back off and take in how those messy waves trail just above his blue eyes, before my gaze falls to his beard. The beard looks . . . thinner as if freshly trimmed.

I reach up, mostly because I can't help myself, and attempt to stroke it lightly. Thing is, we are running, so the stroke turns into more of a slap and I sort of ram my middle finger up his nose.

"Oh, gosh—sorry!" I say as we both stumble to a stop.

I shake my hand out and run into the water to rinse my finger even though I don't think there's anything on it. For a hot beach bum, Callahan is surprisingly well-kept. I glance over my shoulder as my fingers splash along the waves to find his narrow eyes locked on my . . . butt?

I grin and throw in a wiggle. "Like what you see?"

His head jerks to the side, and his jaw tightens. When he turns back to face me, that now familiar scowl is set firmly in place. "Did you just slap me?"

I skip back to his side, ignoring the heat behind his accusation. "Of course not. Why would I slap you?"

He regards me like I'm the stupid one. "You seriously need medication," he tells me.

Okay, now he thinks I'm crazy. But that doesn't stop me from smiling.

"Why are you smiling?" he asks, his tone clipped.

I step in a little closer, my grin softening. "I guess because in the last seven days we've run together, and in the two days I've seen you at Your Mother's, this is the most you've ever talked to me."

Sean was right. Friday night when my team and I returned to our favorite dive bar, Callahan barely acknowledged my presence. And the days we've run, he's mostly said "Christ" when he's seen me and "Jesus" when I've said something that annoyed him.

Such a nice religious boy that Callahan.

But every so often, I'd catch his eyes on me when he didn't think I was looking, and the barest hint of a grin tugging at his lips when we ran. Those tiny flickers gave me hope that maybe I'm starting to reach him, and that smile I'm gunning for isn't far beyond my reach.

At the bar, I'd grinned at his scowls, but had given him space. But today, maybe I need a little more. I inch up to him. "I didn't mean to slap you, and I'm sorry if that's what you think. I'd never disrespect you like that."

"Then why were you touching me?" he bites out.

His choice of words cause me to tilt my head and make me wonder who if anyone is allowed to touch him. "I wasn't trying to hurt you," I explain, keeping my voice quiet. "I was trying to stroke your beard."

His expression is stony and one I can't quite figure out. I'm not sure if he believes me so I show him I mean what I say.

I lift my hand, ignoring the way his narrowing eyes watch me closely as my fingertips gently graze his jaw. I keep my motions light, barely making contact, and trying real hard not to let my fingers sweep upward and smooth the wavy strands of hair dangling along his brow.

The short, prickly hairs of his beard tickle my fingers and widen my smile. "There," I whisper. "That's all I wanted to do."

His expression remains unreadable, and his mouth closed as my hand drifts away from his face to fall at my side. I motion down the beach. "Want to keep going?" I ask. "It's still early yet."

Instead of answering, he backs away and starts down the beach. In a few quick strides, I reach him, but only because he's not moving very fast. This time, I keep the Flo Rida tunes in my head. It's only when we reach the end of Magenta Groves Beach and turn around that he finally speaks.

His tone is tight, not quite angry, but not very friendly either. "Why did you touch me?" he asks.

It's almost the same thing he asked me before. Almost. But there's more to it this time for sure. "You trimmed your beard," I respond.

"That doesn't answer my question."

I take a deep breath and let it out slowly, then do it again, trying to gather the courage to answer him honestly. "I wanted to see what it felt like," I admit.

"What it *felt like*?"

I can't figure out if he's angry or genuinely surprised soI respond the only way I know how—by cracking a joke, because that's one thing I can pull off."If I had a beard, and I trimmed it, I'd let you touch it. In fact, I might even thank you for it."

"You want me to thank you," he says slowly.

"Only if you liked it," I answer, laughing, because I know he just *loves* the way I laugh.

He doesn't respond, forcing me to throw out the big guns. "Are you a virgin?"

He does a double-take. "What?"

"Are you a virgin?" I repeat.

"Why the hell would you ask me that?"

I try to keep my expression quizzical instead of full out laughing at my own ridiculousness. "I'm not trying to judge you—really I'm not. I'm just trying to figure you out. Now, it's nothing to be ashamed of. But if you were it would explain your shyness."

"You think I'm shy?" he asks in that slow way he does when he can't believe the things shooting out of my mouth.

"Among other things." The ocean breeze picks up, and the waves crash, forcing me to speak up to be sure he can hear me. "You can tell me if you are. I promise not to tell anyone, cross my heart."

It's not that I believe there's a snowball's chance in Hades that this boy hasn't single- handedly popped enough cherries to make a pie, it's more like I want him to keep talking. No, I *need* to keep him talking. Me and Callahan . . . I don't know. I think we're actually getting to know each other. And I really like who I'm getting to know.

"No. I'm not a virgin," he admits, something that may or not be a smile lifting the corners of his mouth. "What about you?"

I almost can't believe he went there, mostly because I can't believe he's speaking all on his own. I smile to myself thinking I should've checked on his hound status long before this.

Instead of answering, yes or no, I say, "If I tell you I am, would you believe me?"

"No."

"No? You callin' me a slut?" I ask in my thickest southern accent.

And good day in the morning, that's when I see it, his very first grin—even though he's fighting with all that he has to beat it down.

"Maybe," he finally manages.

"*Maybe* you're calling me a slut?"

That smile he's trying to destroy turns into a laugh—we're talking full-out guffaw. And right then and there I can't tell who's more stunned, me or him.

His expression darkens, as if embarrassed or angry he allowed that long-denied laugh to release. So instead of pushing him too far I give him space. A lot of it. Maybe too much.

I spot my lifeguard stand just ahead, saddened that our very first and real conversation is quickly coming to an end.

"I meant you could be a virgin, but I doubt it."

His words are so low they barely register over the sound of waves splashing along the shore. But I hear them well enough.

"Why?" I ask.

I slow to a stop just in front of my designated perch. Already the first of the beach goers are pulling into the lot. In the distance, a man grunts and curses, likely trying to lift something heavier than sin followed by the delighted squeals of a few children, and their momma's urgent voice telling them not to run.

Callahan stops a few feet away from me, and although he knows I'm still behind him, he keeps his back to me. I kick the sand at my feet, but my attention remains on him, waiting for him to tell me more before this moment between us is gone for good.

Right about where I'm standing has become our unofficial drop off / pick-up point. It's where I say hello, and usually wave goodbye—followed by an inappropriate comment on my part of course.

As I continue to watch him, I decide he probably intended to make a quick escape. He easily could have, knowing my duties would keep me from chasing after him. Instead he waits with his hands on those baby-makin' hips of his as if wrestling with what to say.

This time I don't move. I'm not playing games, not really. I'm mostly just being my goofy self. But if we're going to be friends, real ones I mean, I can't always be the one running after him. So I wait, certain he won't walk back to me.

But then he does.

His steps are slow and purposeful, halting about an arm's length in front of me. When he says nothing, and I know our time is quickly running out, I decide that maybe I'm the one who needs to speak.

"What did you mean by what you said?" I ask him.

He works his jaw, appearing just a little shy as those baby blues fix on my face. "I just figured at least a few guys have tried to get with you."

"Maybe. Maybe not. But you're assuming I said yes," I tell him. "At least a few times, by the sounds of it." It's what I say, but this time, I'm the one who's suddenly shy.

"I'm not judging you if you did."

His thick brows draw in tight. To anyone passing by, he may appear angry. But I catch the trickles of concern in his tone. He thinks he may have insulted me.

"You could have said no," he adds. "And you probably did

for a long time. But pretty girls like you don't usually stay virgins for long."

My lips part and I feel myself straighten. "You think I'm pretty?"

His eyes widen as if he can't believe what he just said—or what I just said—or *something*.

"Trin!"

His stare locks on mine.

"Trin!"

I stand there waiting.

"Trin!"

And still he says nothing.

"*Trinity!*"

I whip my head around. "*What?*"

Sean stops short. I didn't mean to yell. But every girl needs a moment with a cute guy. Can't he see I'm having mine?

"Found the surfboard we use for rescues," he says.

I throw my hands out. "That's *awesome*—" I realize I'm still yelling and try to calm. "Sorry. That's good. Good. Uh. Thank . . . you."

He nods, backing away with his hands out. "PMS. I get it. I'll try to find you some chocolate."

I turn my head to say something—anything—to Callahan. But he's gone, long gone. With a sigh, I watch his brawny form disappear down the beach.

Chapter Six

Callahan

Jed wasn't messing when he said the start of the season would kick in come June. Bobbie Lee, the owner, hired three cocktail waitresses and another two bartenders to mix in the outside bar. The combined forces should have been enough, but they weren't. Not with the tourists coming in in droves, and the die-hard regulars who never miss a Friday night.

I fill a tray with shots of rum and hand the waitress a bucket of ice stuffed with Coronas. Cindy, Sally—something like that—gives me a wink and a not-so subtle thrust from her chest.

"Thanks, Callahan," she says, adding yet another wink in case I missed the first.

I ignore her and keep pouring, working fast. The only good thing about the crowd is that my shift is flying. I'm beat, and beat up. Haven't slept much this week despite all my grueling work-outs and my even longer runs.

A familiar laugh catches my attention out on the deck. Trinity. Of course she's laughing. That woman probably hasn't known a bad day in her life by the sounds of it. She glances up and catches my stare. Her smile vanishes when she sees me and she looks away, back to those friends she always skips in with.

I can't really blame her considering I'd spent the entire week ditching her. Instead of running at seven like I had been, I run at five (I'm up anyway)or wait till sundown on nights I don't work. I say it's because I don't want or need the company she offers. I tell myself she annoys me. And I do my best to convince myself that being alone is the right thing for a man like me. Don't need friends. Lost too many as is.

It's what I tell myself constantly. But after last night, I know it's all bullshit.

Magenta Grove Beach Resort officially closes at seven. What I mean by "officially" is that the lifeguards are no longer on duty and it's a swim at your own risk deal. I thought I was safe waiting for that moon to rise. But when I reached her post, she was there. My eyes cut to where she and a couple of lifeguards were piling out of that small shack they use as an office.

Near as I could figure, they were finishing up a meeting. Her laughter trailed as I neared so I knew she saw me. This time she didn't wave. Didn't smile. Didn't have anything to say. In a way, I expected her to say or do *something*. What I didn't expect was that look of hurt I caught as I passed by.

Shit. That hurt barreled over me like a rolling tree.

I told her she was pretty. And I meant it. She damn well is. What I didn't mean was for it to come out of my mouth. Same way I didn't mean for that laugh to escape. Lord, I can't remember the last time I laughed. Or smiled. Except with Trinity.

I shake my head. *What the hell's wrong with you, soldier?*

I fill another tray. Margarita on the rocks here, a shot of Jaeger there, and more Budweiser bottles than that skinny waitress seems capable of carrying. She hefts it onto her shoulder, barely spilling a drop and heads over to the table filled with frat boys who can't seem to shut the fuck up.

Jed keeps his eyes on them and our new waitress, knowing they're probably seconds from starting shit. But while I know I should watch them too, my attention returns to Trinity.

I wasn't sure what she expected to achieve running alongside me. For being a big ballbuster, it's clear she's plenty smart. And it doesn't take a smart woman to figure out I want to be left alone. But she wouldn't leave me until I made her.

The thought pisses me off. I had no right dumping her like she was nothing. As annoying as I find her, she's not a bad person.

I fill another pitcher, pour more shots, trying to keep my head on work where it belongs. I don't want to feel *anything*. Maybe that's why Trinity pisses me off more than she should, around her I feel . . . everything. The way she—aw, hell—I don't know. There's just something about her . . .

A redhead slinks into the barstool in front of me and waves a few bills. I glance up, so she knows I see her. "What'll it be?" I ask.

She grins and leans forward so her rack presses against the bar and elevates it slightly. "Three blow jobs." Her eyes travel downward and she laughs. "Or whatcha think, maybe four, cowboy?"

I make three shots, take the bills, and then walk to the opposite register when she and her friends make a show of swallowing them down. The frat boys holler, of course, egging them on. I roll my eyes only to find Trinity standing right in front of me with two empty pitchers clutched in her hands.

She offers me a weak smile. "Hey," she says.

I nod, but that's all I offer. She's not drunk or rude, not like some of the assholes that have stumbled in tonight. But that doesn't mean I'll be any friendlier. For all I think it was a dick move to ignore her like I did, what's done is done, and I shouldn't encourage her.

"What are you having?" I ask.

She blinks back at me, like she wants to talk and not just order. But then she swallows hard, speaking quietly. "Just Bud, please."

I reach for the pitchers and move down the bar to the taps. One of the frat boys, the biggest in the group, abandons the redhead when someone else catches his eye. He stalks forward like he's hot shit. My grip on the handles tightens as I watch him plop down next to Trinity.

"Dude. You're spilling your beer," a guy in a bright yellow shirt points out.

I switch the pitchers, keeping my eyes trained on Trinity. Frat Boy leans on the bar, making a show of checking her out. I half expect Trinity to talk to him. Hell, she talks to everyone. 'Cept even though he seems to be talking to her, she keeps her attention ahead.

He asks her something. Whatever it is has her shaking her head, either in disbelief or rejection. He leans closer, pressing his mouth close to her ear.

Trinity whips around, smacking him across the face as she wrenches away from him, her bright eyes firing with anger. I can't be sure if his mouth actually made contact with her, or if he said something that offended her. At this point, I don't really care. I'm already to them, set to pummel the shit out of this asshole no matter what he did to her.

I slam the one pitcher I'd managed to fill directly in front of him. He's so close to her, Trinity had to slip off the stool just to put some space between them.

"The hell?" Frat Boy yells when the beer sloshes and soaks his shirt.

I don't ask what his problem is. I don't tell him he's had enough. What I do is lean forward and shove my face in his. "Get the *fuck* away from her."

I'm vaguely aware of the advancing crowd. Frat Boy's friends are edging forward, and so are Trinity's.

"Break his jaw, Clayton," one of the other frat boys yells.

"Shut up, asshole," Trinity's friend fires back.

Yelling and taunts ensue. Every local there has had enough of these pricks. I don't pay them no mind. Every speck of me is focused on Clayton, or whatever the hell his name is. He's big. Probably plays ball. And based on that shit eatin' grin cutting a line into his face, he probably thinks he can take me.

Problem is, he's messing with the wrong soldier.

"It's okay, Callahan," Trinity insists, her hand gripping my arm.

"No, it's not," I rumble.

"Trin!"

Trinity's friend, the blonde, tries to haul her back. Good, get her out of the way. It's just me and him now. But here the crowd is too dense and this guy plays for keeps, he drags Trinity back before her friend gets her far and squeezes her ass, all the while looking at me.

I barely catch the punch Trinity nails him with because I'm already flying over the bar and grabbing him by the throat, hauling him away from her. With a turn of my hips, I slam him to the floor.

Something hard cracks against the base of my skull. I shake off the pain and nail the frat boy who hit me with the beer bottle across the jaw. It's then all hell breaks loose. Everyone's fighting, and I mean everyone.

Fists are flying as me and Clayton go blow for blow. I'm punching him with all my weight, steering him toward the front doors.

The crowd moves with me, beating the piss out of those limp dicks. I keep swinging, keep connecting, and forcing Clayton outside and into the lot. My last punch connects with his head; he stumbles back and lands on his ass beside a sedan.

I turn around, knowing he's not getting up, and scan the lot for Trinity. Her blonde friend is being hauled off the redhead who was hitting on me by another lifeguard. The lifeguard's lip is split, and his shirt's ripped, but he's laughing his ass off as he pulls Trin's friend against him.

"Calm down, tiger," he tells her.

Mr. Perrington—the old man who takes his little blue pill with a shot of Captain Morgan—is waving his cane at another frat boy. I'm guessing the frat boy's not intimidated by crazy Grandpa, but the lifeguards flanking the old timer are a different story.

I push my way around them, wondering where the hell Trin is and what trouble she's gotten herself into. I start yelling for her, but her name gets stuck in my throat when I see—oh, *hell* no—her *anchored* to some guy's back, her little fist punching him for all she's worth. I barrel toward her, ducking out of the way of another flinging fist.

This guy gunning for me is so wasted, he can barely keep his feet. I snatch him by the collar and fling him onto the beach. He rolls onto his stomach, lifting his sand-covered face, his eyes widening when he sees me stalking forward. I don't think I take more than four steps before he takes off. But I don't care about him.

As quick as I can, I'm back to Trin, ripping her off the guy who's seconds from throwing her off and hurting her. She fights me, not realizing I'm the one who has her. She's wriggling so badly, I barely manage to kick the guy across the knees when he lunges at us.

He crashes to the ground. But like his friends, he's had enough. He stumbles to his feet and backs away. Slowly at first, and then faster when he sees a few more locals closing in.

By this point, Trin is spitting mad, screaming and flinging her limbs like the lunatic she is. Me, I'm laughing. Hard. So hard, I can't catch enough air to tell her it's me. Apparently, she doesn't find this situation funny, nor does she like to be laughed at. She lifts her elbow and pegs me hard in the gut.

I fall back onto the sand-pebbled lot, taking her with me. She pushes off my chest with her hands, her face red and furious until she realizes I'm the one lying under her.

"Callahan?" she asks.

"Fuck," I respond.

She scrambles to her feet and offers me a hand. Cute. But I'll be damned if I let this little thing haul me off my ass. I rise slowly, broken pieces of shell falling off my back as I stand.

I fix my scowl on her as the crowd thins. "What in the *hell* were you thinking taking on a man twice your size—shit, taking on any man at all?"

Everyone seems to be rushing to the edge of the lot that hugs the main road. But Trin and me only have eyes for each other—well, y'all know what I mean.

She frowns. "He was going to hurt you."

"*What?*"

She hooks a thumb behind her. "He picked up one of those

outside stools and was going to hit you with it. I had to save you."

"You had to save me," I repeat slowly.

She rams her fists on her hips and juts out her chin, all insulted-like. "Well, yeah. You're welcome by the way."

I don't remind her that I was the one saving her ass. Or that I had to do it twice. I don't even point out that she nailed me in the solar plexus as a reward. Instead, I let her have her moment.

"Thanks," I mutter.

She grins. The gleam in that smile and in those eyes taking her from pretty, straight into beautiful . . . even though I don't want it to. Damn, with all that dark hair, her toned body, and spray of freckles set in all the right places along her sweet face, why the hell is she wasting her time on me? This girl must be beating men off with a club.

In a way, I can't blame that frat boy for seeking her company. He was an asshole, and for sure out of her league. But as a man, even one as fucked up as me, I can see why he'd want her.

Even while I think these thoughts, and even though it pisses me off that I do, I maintain my scowl. But there she is, grinning up at me like we're having a friendly conversation. She steps forward and before I know it she's stroking my beard again.

"You're welcome, Batman."

I close my eyes and choke down a swear. Now here's a woman who knows how to ruin a moment.

Chapter Seven

Trinity

I don't work the next day following the brawl. It's good in way because I get to sleep in. But it's bad because I'm not on the beach waiting to see if Callahan will magically show up as I'm prepping for watch. Either way, I don't sleep in as much as I probably need to, my mind busy wondering where we stand.

Will he show up looking to talk to me? Or at the very least run when he used to so I can join him? I don't want him avoiding me like he's been doing, but I won't pound on his front door either. My stalker tendencies do have their limits, after all.

I rise and stretch, giving up on sleep. After a few failed attempts at a yoga work out, I turn on the TV and flip through the channels.

My phone buzzes just when I find a classic *Buffy the Vampire Slayer* episode on TV—Oh! And it's that creepy one where everyone loses their voice, too.

I pick up the phone as I settle back into bed only to jerk up when I read Becca's text.

Call me. Call me NOW.

She picks up on the first ring. "What happened?" I ask her. "Is someone hurt?"

"Nope," she answers.

"Becks! What's wrong?"

She clears her throat like people do when they have something important to say. "Guess who ran by when we were setting up?"

"Who?" I ask, rushing to the edge of my bed.

"Hawkeye!"

"Who?"

"Hawkeye!" She pauses. "Isn't that what you call him?"

Poor girl never could keep her superheroes straight. But I'm too busy grinning to correct her. "Callahan ran by during set up?"

"Girl, not only did he run by, but he looked over by your chair, the office, *and* toward the parking lot."

"That doesn't mean anything, does it?"

In all actuality, I know it does, seeing how Callahan keeps his focus ahead so he doesn't have to engage anyone. But I need Becca to confirm my suspicions—tell me I'm not crazy—or imagining things—insist that there is hope—and convince me Callahan can't live without me. It's what best friends do, after all.

"Of course it does! Trin, he was looking for you. He never looked your way all those times you joined him on his run. At least not around us." She makes a funny noise so I know she's moving something. "Did he say anything to you after the fight broke up?"

"Only that he had to help clean up."

"And nothing happened?" she asks. "Nothing?"

I flop back down on the bed. "You know if it did I'd be telling everyone who'd listen."

"True—Hold on. Sean, could you take this for me . . . Thanks, hon. Trin? You still there?"

"I am."

"So what are you thinking?" she asks.

I adjust the phone against me. "I don't know. I'm hoping it's a good sign. Last night, things sort of changed between us. Callahan didn't have to come charging when that idiot shoved his tongue in my ear. I could handle myself—and you, and

Hale, and everyone were already moving in. But not only did he swoop in and get involved, he was majorly pissed."

"You're not kidding. When I looked up to check on you, he was clear across the other end of the bar. I don't think I had the chance to blink and he was suddenly there, ready to pound that shithead to dust for getting too close to you."

Becks was right. Callahan had been watching out for me, something I hadn't been expecting. And that rage he met that guy with? That there was a wolf set to pounce on his prey.

"Did you know he fought his way through the crowd to find you?" she says, pulling me out of the memory of him leaping over the bar.

"What? *No.*"

She laughs. "Hale was trying to rip me off that slutty girl—you know the one wearing those awful orange shorts?—and when he finally did I saw Ninja Turtle go all Transformer looking for you."

As her best friend, I semi-interpret this to mean Callahan got mad and raced to find me. "And you didn't tell me this *why*?" I press.

She waits. "I sort of forgot seeing how Hale was giving me the eyes. I think my catfight with that tramp got him all hot or something—"

"Becks!"

"Hey. I'm sorry. Hale was . . . well, you know how cute he is—anyway that's why I'm telling you now!"

I scrunch my eyes closed. "So you think I may have a shot?"

"You may not have lassoed him, but you sure did snag his attention." She sighs. "Just be careful. If I didn't think he was dangerous before, that all changed when he grabbed that monster of a man by the throat like he was nothing. Trin, he knows how to fight. . ." Her voice trails. "And judging by how he handled that asshole, he knows how to do a lot more than knock someone on his ass."

I'm not stupid. And I'm not as naïve as people think. But there's something about Callahan that tells me there's a lot more to him than brute strength.

My voice softens. "Callahan wouldn't hurt me," I tell her. "I'm sure of it. But even if I'm dead wrong, you know I'd never allow anyone to mistreat me."

"Trin, I hear what you're saying, and I am listening," Becca says quietly. "But there are ways a man can hurt you that have nothing to do with his hands."

Sunday comes. Two days after the brawl at Your Mother's. My hair is brushed to a sheen and I'm wearing my best—well, dark blue bikini top and jean shorts that is. I show up an hour earlier than usual to set up, even though I'm off today, too.

I finish prepping, adjust the schedule per requests, clean up the office, and then spend the next twenty minutes twiddling my thumbs. There're only so many things you can do with that whistle.

Mason does a double-take when he sees me and finds everything done, the muscles along his stocky build bulging from his early morning workout. Unlike Sean, he tends to be more staid. Well, except around me.

"You working today, Trin?" he asks.

"Darlin'," I reply. "I'm what you might call a responsible team captain. Even when I'm not working, I'm working. My heart and soul are part of this crew and this here beach. If you bleed, I bleed. If you weep, I weep. If you need a snack, I eat one right there with you."

He looks at me over his sunglasses. "You're waiting for Callahan, aren't you?"

Wow. It's like he has super powers or something.

"Is it that obvious?" I ask.

"It is," he says, nodding thoughtfully. He straightens. "But it looks like you don't have to wait much longer, here he comes." My head whips to the side. "Made you look."

I'm smacking his arm silly when he motions down the beach. "Oh, wait, Trin. He is here. He's coming now."

"Yeah, right. Fool me once, shame on me. Fool me twice, you suck—" He grabs my shoulders and spins me. I'm ready to whoop his ass when I see a very familiar and gorgeous figure headed my way. "It's him." I turn around and smack his arm again. "Did you have to man-handle me in front of my man?"

"Says the crazy woman attacking me." He turns around and waves. "I'll see you later, Trin. Sorry you can't take a joke."

"Later, Mason, sorry your momma named you after a jar."

He laughs, despite it not being the first time he's heard that one. He's a good guy, that Mason.

So here's my dilemma: I'm here, but I'm not here. And now that dreamboat of a man I'm here for, but not supposed to be here for, is headed toward me. Is this a good time to remind myself that everything usually makes more sense in my head? Probably not.

I brush off my sandy shorts and walk toward the water's edge. I keep walking, pretending to dip my feet. As he nears, I offer a small smile, followed by a small wave. Pathetic? Probably. But it's all I got, folks.

Instead of waving back—or heaven forbid, *smiling*—he surprises me by slowing to a stop next to me.

"Hi," I say.

"Hi," he mutters back.

I'm trying not to look at him. Really I am. But considering he's not wearing a shirt and beads of ocean water are drizzling from his perfect pectorals, down his eight pack abs, to where his black board shorts rest low on his hips, it's awful hard not to. If it means anything, I'm real proud I'm not wiping drool from my mouth.

He frowns as his eyes scan me from head to toe. "Why are you dressed like that?"

"Oh, cause it's hot and it's summer."

I can tell he's working not to roll his eyes. "Don't you have a uniform to wear?"

"I would if I was working, but I'm off today."

His brows furrow tighter and he angles his chin. "Then why are you here?"

"I'm in charge so sometimes I have to come in on my days

off to make sure everything's okay. It may not look it, but Irun a real tight ship."

His gaze skips to where Sean and Craig are trying to impress the new girls with their chicken arm farts. "You're right, it doesn't look it."

I make a mental note to kill them later and I shrug. "Just boys having fun."

Without looking at me, he motions ahead with a tilt of his chin. "I'm headed that way if you want to come. Unless you have to keep working on that tight ship of yours."

By now Sean and Craig are pumping their arms to the tune of *Mary Had a Little Lamb*. "Nah, I'm sure they'll be fine without me."

I follow when he pushes off, both of us fall into that nice steady pace we developed. I wait for him to say something. When he doesn't, I race ahead to catch the wave sweeping and kick up water to splash him. He's come to expect only smooth moves and maturity from me so I can't exactly let him down.

"Something on your mind?" he asks, ignoring the water trickling along his firm and ogle-worthy abs. His tone sounds annoyed, but the tilt to his lips suggests otherwise.

"That was something the other night wasn't it?" I say, resuming my pace beside him. "Obnoxious New Yorkers always coming down here causing problems."

"They weren't from New York," he tells me.

"Jersey?"

"Nope."

"Canada?"

He presses his lips tight. "They were from Texas. I caught sight of their license plate right before they sped off."

I blow out air. "Well, that explains it. All the crazies are from Texas."

"I'm from Texas," he rumbles.

I bat my hand in true "pa-shaw" fashion like I didn't just insult him and everyone he knows. "Oh, I'm sure you're the exception. You, your momma, your daddy, your brother—"

"I don't have a brother." Again the edges of his mouth

curve.

"Sister?" I offer.

"Three," he admits.

"Okay, I'll make the exception for them, too—and maybe a couple of first cousins." I scissor out my hands. "But I draw the line at second cousins twice removed. They're always a freaky bunch."

"Is that right?" he asks.

"Yes. Like I said 'dem Texans are nuts."

For once I shut my mouth, even though I think I may be entertaining him, however mildly. We hit the end of the beach and turn around. He stays quiet, but by now it's been like ten whole minutes since I said anything, and if you've been paying attention you know that's a lot for someone like me.

"So you're from Texas," I say.

"That's right."

"Did you play football?" I ask. "I know football's real big there."

Although it's a fairly simple and not very personal question, he seems hesitant to tell me. "You can't be a country boy in Texas and not play ball," he finally answers.

"Were you the quarterback? I can picture you as a quarterback." I toss him a wink. "A mighty, *mighty* quarterback."

And lookee here. There's that almost grin, again.

"I was a first string lineman," he admits.

"Oh, yeah?" I ask. "Hmm. I bet all the pretty girls were just lining up so you could deflower them, huh?"

His head ever so slowly rotates my way, but then he catches himself resumes his attention ahead. "No. I think the quarterback took care of all that."

It occurs to me then how much I love messing with him. "Did it bother you, not having all those girls to deflower? You can tell me seeing how we're BFFs and all."

He smirks, but mostly I think to squelch his widening grin. "Believe it or not, I didn't care," he answers.

He slows to a stop as my post comes into view. But I'm not ready to let him go.

"We can keep going if you'd like," I offer. "I don't have anywhere to be." He frowns, appearing either confused or unsure so I add, "Besides, that man in my bed is shackled good and tight, he's not going anywhere till I set him free." I throw out a hand. "Don't worry. I left the remote in his hand and plenty of water so he's fine."

The way Callahan straightens, makes me think that maybe I pushed the joke too far. But then he shakes his head. "There's something wrong with you," he mumbles.

"I think you might have mentioned that once or twice," I remind him.

I wave to my boys as we sprint past the station, ignoring the growing twinge in my thighs. But the further we run, the more that twinge develops into a steady burn. I was always a runner, and participated in cross-country all through high school. I kept up my stamina by running every other day while I was in college, but after Hunter and I broke up, I hiked up plenty of miles dealing with the stress and the depression that followed—so many in fact, I was able to participate in my first half marathon this past Spring.

I pride myself on keeping fit, but by now, Callahan and I are a few miles in, and in my haste to meet him, I never bothered with breakfast. So instead of teasing Callahan a little more, like I'd really like to, I focus on steadying my breathing and pushing through the ache.

"You all right?" Callahan asks.

"Yes. I've gone longer."

We glide across the sand, our strides purposeful and even, both of us working harder to maintain our pace. He seems to want to ask more, but doesn't.

When I'm sure he won't ever speak again without being prompted he asks, "How long?"

"Twelve miles." I crinkle my forehead. "We are talking about running, right?"

He loses his footing, but then catches himself, and semi-smoothly resumes his gait. My muscles are tightening so bad I should focus on breathing. But watching Callahan lose his footing *and* his composure is too much to resist. No. *He's* too much to resist.

"Ever have a one-night stand?" I ask.

"What?—*Jesus.*"

I breathe deeply so I can keep talking because hey, Trinity Summers is on a roll.

"I won't think less of you if you have," I tell him. "You're young, these things happen."

He says nothing so of course now I have to. "So the times that you have, were they like a lot? Or was it more like one here, one there—Oh, but don't tell me if it involves more than one girl, or a man, or crazy shit like on a roller coaster. That sort of thing is personal."

"*And this isn't?*" he fires back.

"I'm just saying—"

"All right, you want to go there. Have *you* ever had a one-night stand?"

He means to shut me up. If so, he needs to invest in duct tape. "Yes. Twice. But it's not really my thing."

"You've had one-night stands?" He emphasizes the first word, but the rest is distinctly quieter.

I smile thoughtfully. "I had a bad breakup last Christmas. Afterward . . . I don't know, I was sort of lost, and maybe a little desperate. So, I did." I look up at him. "What about you? Have you had your share of hook-ups? Or are you more the committed type?"

He returns to his more solemn demeanor, making me think I somehow hurt him by asking—and I absolutely want to kick myself for it.

I start to apologize only for him to interrupt. "I had a couple of steady girls in high school. Nothing real serious. After I enlisted, I didn't have the time or opportunity to meet anyone."

"That makes sense." I wait then say, "What about when you weren't in active duty? Or when you got out?"

He thinks about it. "That's when I had my share of . . . interactions."

"Oh," I answer, giving away the sadness I suddenly feel.

Aside from caressing his face, I haven't really touched

Callahan. Not like I've wanted to. It bothers me to learn there've been plenty of women who have stroked a lot more than his beard. It's not that I'm surprised. Not by a long shot. That doesn't make the news easier to swallow.

Callahan isn't a good-looking man. Nope, not at all. Callahan is hotter than fried chicken sizzling in Hades. The waves of his dark brown hair have lightened significantly over the past few weeks, giving his ravishing blue eyes an extra sparkle. His thin beard crawls along his jaw, up and over full lips that can alter him from rugged hunk, to sexy god when they pull back into a grin.

"Have there been many of these interactions?" I ask, my voice so quiet it surprises even me.

"No," he admits before cutting his eyes my way and offering a smile that flips my heart. "It's not really my thing either."

Ah, and there's my smile, too. "Good," I say.

He slows to a stop when we reach a path lined with palms and mangroves to our right. "This is where I get off," he tells me.

I wipe some of the perspiration from my brow and peek down the path. A ranch, covered in weather-beaten grey shingles, rests further back among the ancient trees. The trim and newly erected deck are painted in a fresh coat of bright white, and the roof and windows appear brand new. I take my time admiring the work he seems to have put in, permitting my breathing to relax.

"This is old man Callahan's place," I say after a moment. "I take it you're related?"

He nods. "He was my uncle. I was named after him."

"Now that I know where you live, I figured as much."

He crosses his arms, appearing to look at the house without really seeing it. "Did you know him?" he asks.

"Only a little bit," I answer. "I'd see him around town now and again. At the post office or supermarket." I speak slowly, watching his chest rise and fall as his breathing starts to settle. "He was a nice man, gentle. But mostly kept to himself. Were you close?"

"When I was younger we were." He bends when something catches his attention in the sand. He lifts a small rock with a sharp tip. I barely catch sight of it before he flings it into the dense brush. "My daddy wasn't around much so my uncle tried to be there for me as much as he could."

Like so many times before, Callahan's face gives nothing away. But his stance when he said "daddy" stiffened in a way I've never quite seen. "I'm sorry," I say quietly, feeling the depth of my words down to my bones.

He cocks his head, frowning slightly as if expecting me to press for more information. But while I want to know everything about him, I'd never force him to share something he's not ready for.

"My parents divorced when I was a few months old," he admits, watching me closely. "With only girls in the house, my momma felt I needed a strong male's influence. So she asked her brother to step in and be the man my father never was."

Just when I think Callahan can break any more of my heart, there goes another chip. My daddy is my hero. He's always been there, ready to catch me when I fell and cheer me on when I got back up. But now is not the time to tell Callahan as much, not when he still seems hurt by the father he never quite knew.

"I'm glad your uncle was there to guide you," I say.

"I am, too," he murmurs. "But our time together was always limited. He'd visit every summer, holidays; things like that. But his home was here, and ours was in Texas." He shrugs. "When I was trying to decide what to do with my life, he's the one who convinced me to go into the Army. We lost touch after I finished boot camp. I think the last time I spoke to him was about a year before he died."

I close the space between us, unable to stomach the sadness in his voice and place my hand carefully on his arm. "You must have meant a lot to him for him to leave you his home."

He watches my hand as it slips from his arm. "I suppose," he says, returning his attention to the house.

I'm not sure how many times the waves crash behind us, or how many gulls soar over our heads in their mad rush to fish. But it's not until a dragonfly zips between us that Callahan once more speaks. "You seem worn. If you want, I can give you a ride back to your post."

"You're not going to ask me inside for breakfast?"

His head jerks back to face me. "*What*?"

I regard him with a pensive expression I have to work hard to muster. "It's the Southern and hospitable thing to do," I remind him. And if that's not bad enough, I add, "After all, I did save your life."

Again he simply stares, disbelief spreading along his manly features while that grin I can't suppress around him warms my cheeks. I wait, taking in the way his expression alternates from "this girl is crazy" mode to "maybe she should have just let me die".

He whirls away, storming toward the house. "*Fine*," he says.

Chapter Eight

Trinity

Rather than skipping ahead and into his house, I follow behind him. It is his home and far be it for me to impose. Plus, it gives me a chance to ogle the muscles along his broad back and the way his bitable butt cheeks clench and unclench with each step. With all the strength and will I possess, I resist the urge to tackle him and have my way with him. I'm a Southern lady, after all, so I keep my dirty thoughts inside my head where they belong.

We step through the clear glass doors off the deck and into a large open family room painted light beige with a white trim. I pause to take everything in. The furniture is minimal, but comfortable and practical, giving the room a modern décor and an earthy feel, all while complimenting the original structure. Freshly sanded wide plank floorboards greet my feet as my stare travels to where a thick shaggy rug lies between a flat stone fireplace and comfy-looking brown couch. Despite the multiple tools lining the far wall, the dustpan filled with wood shavings in the corner, and all other evidence of his ongoing renovation projects, Callahan's house is clean and homey.

"This is really nice," I say. "You've done such a beautiful job bringing it back to life."

"You've been in here before?" he asks.

"Just once with my momma. We stopped by with a few casserole dishes when we heard your uncle was sick, but only stayed long enough to bring the food in." I smile softly. "He was sweet, but he didn't seem up for company and we didn't want to impose."

I point ahead to the open kitchen. "I remember there was a wall there before, separating it from the family room. I like it better this way. There's more light."

"Yeah. Me, too," he admits, growing quiet.

I'm not sure what Callahan's thinking, all I know is that he seems so sad. Maybe he misses his uncle, or maybe it's more than that. I scan the area, searching for something to draw his attention away from his thoughts and hopefully onto something better.

My eyes fall on a guitar perched on top of a brown and cream striped recliner. "You play?" I ask.

"I never had any formal training, and I don't know how to read or write sheet music." He steps toward it. "But I do know a few songs I learned by ear."

"You learned by ear?" I ask.

His focus hones in on my face, but then he looks away. "That's right."

"Well then consider me impressed," I say. I laugh, mostly to myself. "I can't read or write music either, but my brother taught me a few songs I can play well enough."

His brows knit together. "You play, too?"

"Just a couple of songs. Don't ask me about chords or anything technical. I never committed to learning so there's a lot I don't know."

He nods like he understands, stepping around me and into the kitchen. He opens the door to a stainless steel refrigerator. With a smile that doesn't quite want to leave me, I watch him fumble through the contents.

"You want some sweet tea?" he asks.

"Ah, sure. If it's not too much trouble. I don't want to be a bother."

It's my last comment that momentarily freezes him in

place. I cover my mouth as I slip onto a bar stool at the raised granite counter, doing my best not to full-out laugh. In an effort to settle, I skim the ceiling. Wires hang through the holes drilled directly above me. "What's going on up there?"

"Drop-down ceiling lights," he answers. He walks around the counter and places a glass full of iced tea in front of me, taking a seat to my left. "But I can't put them in until I'm done rewiring the house.

"Mmm."

I lift the glass and take a big sip. As I swallow, all forms of death find their way into my stomach.

"The room's too dark come sundown," he continues. "So I figure—" He does a double-take when he sees me. "What's wrong?"

I sprint to the sink and blast the water, trying to rinse the poison he's given me from my mouth. Despite my valiant efforts, I can't cleanse my tongue of the wickedness plaguing it. Callahan rushes to me, gathering my ponytail as I cough and gag.

"You okay?" he asks. "You sick?"

I glance up to where the glass remains perched on the counter, its contents appearing to mock me. "What did you give me?" I point to the glass. "What was in that?"

Callahan lets my hair slip from his fingers. "Sweet tea," he answers, frowning. "You didn't like it?"

No. It was brown-colored evil. Of course, I don't tell him that. "Um. It was filling."

"Filling?"

He returns to the fridge and pours an extra-large helping of that crap into a large glass. "You know what your problem is?" he begins.

I have taste?

"You blow things out of proportion," he says, lifting the glass. "Every time. All the time."

I bat my hand out. "Oh, that's just not true."

He scowls and takes a big gulp. That scowl vanishes about the same time that tea comes right back up. Now I'm the one smacking his back at the sink as he coughs and spews.

"God damn," he says, reaching for a paper towel to swipe at his mouth. "What the hell did they put in that piss water?"

I try not to laugh, but it's hard.

"Christ," he says, wiping his mouth harder. "I paid six whole dollars for that shit."

"Now, Callahan, what kind of self-respecting Southerner doesn't make his own sweet tea?"

"The kind who never learned how," he admits. It's only when he turns to face me that I realize he's smiling.

"How about I make us some? You have tea bags?"

"You want to make me tea?" he asks, like he doesn't believe me.

"I don't want to make you tea, I *have* to before that stuff kills you," I say. "You're welcome by the way."

He smirks, but doesn't say much, motioning to a set of double doors. I bounce inside a large pantry stocked with enough food to survive two zombie apocalypses, and possibly an alien invasion. "Oh. This is nice."

"Better to be prepared than not," he says.

I step out with the tea as he places a pan onto an electric stove set behind the raised counter. The stove is nice, modern, and barely looks used.

"I'm going to make some eggs," he says. "You want some?"

I drop the box of tea bags on the counter and lean against it, examining him closely. "How about I cook for you?"

"First you want to make me tea, now breakfast? What's next?" he asks, meeting my eyes in a way that halts me in place.

"Whatever you want," I answer quietly.

It's not what I planned to say. It just came out. Yet it's only when he straightens that I realize I crossed that fine line we've been straddling between somewhat friends and maybe something more. For a long few seconds neither of us move. I wait for him, hoping he'll kiss me, or at the very least lean in and meet me halfway. But like a giant piece of granite he stays in place, even though his breath grow more pronounced the longer our stares remain locked.

When I can take it anymore, I push off the counter, using my hip to nudge a wedge between him and the stove. I want to feel close to him. I want him to touch me. But I want him, to want it, too.

Without meaning to, my backside ever so gently brushes against his front. A soft sigh escapes his lips, and I bite back a groan, my heartbeat quickening as the two of us stand less than an inch apart.

Callahan curls his body forward, his breath a warm whisper across my bare shoulder as his hands glide down my hips. For a moment, I think something is about to happen. Something good, sexy—something that will allow my moans to escape. But as his hands ease away, I realize I may already be too late to act.

He's still close though, his breath continuing to tease my skin. I lift the pan and pretend to inspect it as if his reaction and our brief contact haven't sent my desire for him racing full speed ahead. "This is a nice pan . . . Calphalon?" I ask, my voice gaining and odd quiver.

"Yes." His voice is low, harsh, which does nothing to soothe my perky female regions.

It takes me a moment to form my words considering talk is the last thing I want to do. "Can you get me the eggs?" I finally ask. "Some butter, maybe spices you like?"

He swallows hard and edges away, gathering a bowl, whisk, eggs, and butter and placing them along the counter. He stays silent, keeping a very respectable distance much to the dismay of my very unrespectable thoughts.

The last things he sets down are salt and pepper. "I don't have much in terms of spices," he says, that tone of his oddly clipped.

What remains of my ardor quickly vanishes when I turn and face him. Instead of drawing closer, and meeting me with a kiss I so need, he backs further away—like he can't put enough space between us—like he doesn't even want me here.

"Do you have any cheese?" I manage.

He returns to the refrigerator and pulls out a block of

Cheddar and Colby Jack. Again, he's not saying a word. It's like he suddenly doesn't know how to act around me, or if he should even bother.

For all I thought he might be interested in me, I'm not so sure anymore.

"How about some orange juice?" I'm mostly asking to keep him talking. To remind him I'm still here with him, and that just because he's alone doesn't mean he has to be lonely. "It'll go nice with the eggs."

He shakes his head, but doesn't verbally respond.

"Oranges?" I ask, feeling and sounding desperate.

He motions to the bowl overflowing with oranges. I rub my face, trying to shake off the misery digging a hole into my gut. It's clear Callahan wants me gone. But I can't bear leaving him. Not like this.

"Tell you what," I say, dropping my hands away. "How about you shred me some cheese and I'll make you some fresh squeezed juice. You'd like that, wouldn't you?"

"You don't have to." He lowers his chin. "You don't have to do any of this, Trin."

I'm not sure what he's thinking. I only know that I've lost some serious ground between us and it's killing me. Callahan is more damaged than I originally thought. He would have to be given the way he's afraid to get too close to me.

Taking careful steps so as not to overwhelm him, I inch closer and place my hands over his. "I want to. Will you let me do something nice for you? Please?"

"All right," he mutters. It's what he claims, but it doesn't stop him from stepping further away and out of my reach.

I watch him fumble through the drawers for a juicer and a mandolin, disheartened by his withdrawal. He's no longer making eye contact or speaking. And while he sets up beside me and begins his task, he feels so far away.

My mind insists that I shouldn't push, so I don't, busying myself by making the fresh squeezed juice I promised.

After years of cooking with my momma, I'm used to working fast and am comfortable in the kitchen. It doesn't take me long to slice the oranges and pluck the seeds free from their centers. Callahan only speaks when he sees me ring the orange halves around the juicer, but even then he doesn't face me.

"Do you want me to do that? You look like your struggling."

He may not have been watching me directly, but it's clear he's stolen at least a few glances my way. "It's okay. I'm tougher than I look."

He continues grating the cheese, acting once more like I'm not standing directly beside him. I frown, determining he responds better to my asinine and obnoxious self than to my sweeter half.

All right. So be it, Batman.

I peer at the mound he's created. "That looks good. Thanks. Would you mind getting some glasses? It won't take me long to finish breakfast."

Without so much as a sound, he washes his hands and reaches for two tumblers from the cabinet closest to the fridge. The juicer comes with its own pitcher. I top off the rims the moment he places the tumblers on the counter.

"Thank you," he says almost inaudibly.

I smile brightly. "No problem. Here, have some juice. Go on now," I prompt. "After that run you're probably thirsty."

He rounds the counter and slides onto the stool, appearing to ignore me as I fill the teapot with water and place it on the stove. When I'm done, I crack six eggs into the bowl and whisk them along with some salt and pepper. He tries the juice and seems to like it. But I wait for him to lift his glass again before speaking.

"Thanks for being honest with me," I say.

He stops with the rim just below his lips and lowers his eyelids, like he's afraid to ask, but then he does. "About what?" he says.

He braces himself, as he should. "Oh, you know, about your one night stands filled with sin and debauchery."

"There was no debau—"

"It was right nice of you to be so up front with me. But you know what?"

He slumps in his seat. "Oh, God, what?"

"I realize I haven't been honest with *you*. At least not completely." I add another egg to the bowl, ignoring his call to Jesus to help him. "The first guy I had—you know after that break-up I told you about? He was a nice boy—cute, too, bless his heart." I stretch out my hands. "Thing is, he wasn't built like a stud if you know what I mean."

"Trinity—"

"Not even close. I can't even tell you how embarrassing it was—for both of us, if you must know."

By now Callahan's rubbing his face like he's in pain. Poor thing must have a headache. I sprinkle some cheese into the eggs and mix everything as I continue. "I mean, I didn't even know it was inside yet." I lift my head to find him glaring. "You know what I mean by 'it'?"

With an agonized breath he opens his mouth, closes it, and finally mutters, "*Yes*, Trinity." He snatches his glass and takes several big gulps.

"Good," I say, nodding. "It would have been rude to say *dick*."

I whip around, trying not to lose it when he starts choking on his juice. And while he probably thinks I'm certifiably insane, I'm having fun trying to draw another laugh out of him.

Call me crazy, but this rather, um, inappropriate conversation chips away at that miserable tension until there's almost nothing left. I open his cupboards, fighting hard to keep my smile from shifting into laughter as I search for plates and prep for round two.

I take my time, giving him, and me, a second to settle before I pull two white plates from the cupboard and flounce to his side. I dismiss his scowl like it's not even there and motion toward the glass doors leading out to the beach. "You want to eat outside? It's pretty out."

"Why the hell not?" he asks, his irritability causing his skin to flush.

Without another word, he takes the plates and gathers a couple of paper towels and utensils. I watch his fine ass—because hey, *it is*—twitch ever so nicely in those low-slung board shorts as he crosses the room and steps onto the deck.

He bends to set the table, those chiseled abs curving oh-so perfectly. The moment he's done, he arranges the chairs so we both face the ocean. Hmm. Maybe he doesn't want to look at me while we eat.

Nah. That can't be it.

I pour the eggs into the pan and crank the stove. "You want toast with your eggs? I yell out.

"Yeah. I'll get it."

He sweeps back in and grabs a loaf of bread from the pantry. "How many pieces do you want?"

"Just one please." In the time it takes him to toast and butter the bread, the eggs are done cooking. I follow him out with the pan and pass out our breakfast.

He's lifting his fork to try the eggs when I say, "Now, the *next* one night stand I had wasn't much better." He drops his fork down with a *clang* and leans back in his chair, slapping his hands over his face.

I take a bite out of my food. Yum. Pretty good if must say. "Bless his heart too, he tried. But his moves—you know what I mean about 'moves'?"

He lets his hands drop. "Yes, Trinity."

"Oh, good. It would have been awkward to explain." I point to his eggs. "Aren't you hungry?"

I can't quite make out what he's thinking, on account he's back to glowering at me. Either way he leans forward and shovels a forkful of eggs in his mouth. He pauses, slowing to chew in a way that makes me think he's enjoying the taste.

I wait for him to take another two bites, and one from his toast before continuing. "Anyway, like I was saying. His moves were all spastic. Like he was having a seizure or something. So being a teacher and medically trained—"

"You're a teacher?" He says the words in that slow, deep way of his that always somehow manages to cut me off.

"Yes, sir. Double majored at Princeton in Spanish and Early Childhood Education—I just love kids, don't you?—In fact, I'm scheduled to take my boards in two weeks."

"*You* went to Princeton."

I nod and pour him more juice. "That's right. I'm not all good looks and charm. I'm also what some might call a genius. Well, I don't know about that seeing how I have to work real hard to get the grades I do—but enough about me. Now, getting back to 'seizure boy' as my friend Becca—You know my friend, Becca? Lovely girl—likes to call him. I'm like trying to shove him off me and call 9-1-1 and save his life. Kind of like how I did for you the other night, but then he starts grunting. And I realize oh, he's not seizing. Even though he's doing this—" I put my fork down, lift my hands up and make jerky motions so he understands. "It's just his, well, *moves*, that he apparently thought were pretty awesome. Me, not so much. More like a horny jack rabbit with a—"

"Seizure disorder?" Callahan offers (rather testily, I might add).

I lift my fork and point it at him. "*Exactly*. Glad we're on the same page, here. What's wrong? Don't you like the eggs?"

"The eggs are good," he snaps. "In fact, they're the best damn eggs I've had in a long time."

I swallow and reach for my orange juice. "Then why are you looking at me like that?"

"Because *you're* sitting here with *me* talking about having sex with *other men*."

"Would you prefer I talk about sex with other women?"

His jaw falls open like it did when I accidently shoved my finger up his nose. "You've had sex with women?"

"Oh, no. Not at all." I polish off my juice. "But if I had, and that's what I was talking about now, I bet you wouldn't complain." I smile sweetly. "Now, you go ahead and finish your eggs before they get cold."

Once more, Callahan stares at me, stunned. At first, I'm not sure if he's going to swear, or accuse me of being crazy, *again*. But then I see it, the edges of his mouth lifting slightly and those startling eyes weld onto mine.

I return his smile, but I don't allow our stares to linger. I turn around, and face the ocean, well aware that this time, he's looking at me and not away. It's then I start to believe that I might stand a chance with Callahan. Goodness knows I want to do a lot more than just make him smile.

Chapter Nine

Callahan

How the hell did this happen? I'm standing in front of a set of tall wood doors outside of Trinity's house wearing my best pair of jeans, and the newest T-shirt I own. She invited me for supper after making enough sweet tea to last me a week. I glance at the bottle of wine in my hand, thinking it was a mistake. Mistake to buy it. Mistake to be here. And so were the flowers I bought. Thankfully, I had enough sense to leave them in the truck.

Too bad that sense was nowhere in sight when I agreed to supper.

The door swings open and one of her friends appear, the stocky one who's built more for football than he is for lifeguard duty.

He leans forward, shaking my hand. "Hey, Callahan. How you doing?"

"I'm all right," I answer slowly. It shouldn't surprise me, he knows my name, but it's still odd to hear it coming from his mouth.

"I'm Mason." He looks down at the bottle I'm holding. "Now that'll score you some major points." He calls over his shoulder. "Trin, your man's here!"

Her . . . man? The hell?

Another half-naked guy appears, the tall, lanky one who's always flirting with the waitresses. He lifts the wine from my hand. "*Hey*," he says, examining the bottle. "That some classy shit there. Hey, Mace, 2014 was a good year, wasn't it?"

"It was, Sean," he says, rubbing his jaw like he's trying not to laugh.

Sean throws open the door the rest of the way and calls out louder. "*Trin*, you coming? Callahan's here."

I step back, frowning. Both talk like they've been waiting on me to show up. When Trinity asked me over to thank me for breakfast (although she made it) I thought it would just be me and her. And when she told me she lived on Sugar Cane Road, I thought she lived in a house similar to mine—like the ones I'd passed on my way in—not a house big enough to have its own zip code.

Laughter erupts from the level below. I didn't expect all these people—I expected—hell, not these young men looking back at me like they know something I don't, that's for damn sure.

I'm ready to tear on out of here when I see her skipping up a set of stairs that lead down to another level. "Curtis, check on the burgers, will you?" she tells the guy hanging out near the top. "Lianna, could you and the others take down the salads in the fridge?"

"You got it, Trin," they say.

She bounces toward me, her dark hair sweeping behind her as she walks. She's in tiny white shorts fringed at the bottom and a red bikini top that looks way too good on her. She smiles brightly when she sees the bottle and takes it from Sean's hands.

"You brought wine? Oh, that's so sweet," she says.

She snags my elbow, her hold soft yet firm enough to keep me from hauling ass back down the driveway. "I didn't know this was a party," I mutter.

"Oh, it's not—not really. Every Sunday the gang usually heads up here after work. It's close enough that most people just walk."

Which explains why I didn't see any cars. She leads me down the marble, that's right, *marble* steps of the curved staircase.

"Hey, Callahan," one of her other friends says as he makes his way up the steps.

He stops in front of us. "Trin, can I borrow your car?" he asks. "Looks like we need more beer. Oh, look at that, *wine*." He pats my arm. "Nice move. Classy."

"So I hear," I tell him.

He cocks his head and frowns. I'm not trying to be an asshole. But I'm also not volunteering to be anyone's friend.

"Hale," Trin says, luring his attention. "My keys are on the hook in the kitchen—the one by the door. Take Tony and Jonathon with you, they offered to pay, and it is their turn."

"Sure thing, Trin," he says. He jogs up the steps, but not before shooting me one last look over his shoulder.

She sighs and even though voices trail from upstairs and downstairs, for the moment we're alone on the steps. "I was hoping you'd be okay with everyone being here."

She knows I keep to myself so yeah, I'm wondering why she wants me here. Am I someone she wants to get to know more? Or am I just another pal to hang out with?

Her dark hair slides along the wall as she leans against it and plays with the bottle in her hands. A few people carrying bowls of food pass us before she speaks again. "I know you're not what some refer to as a people person," she says. "But you might have noticed I am."

"I might have noticed."

She laughs and turns her head to the side, her grin fading as she continues. "My friends mean a lot to me, and this is our last summer together before we move on with our lives. I can't ditch them for a guy." She faces me, smiling slightly. "No matter how much I like him."

I'm surprised in a way she put it all out there. My first thought is to set her straight and tell her there's nothing between us. But seeing how I can't stop thinking about her, and how bad I wanted to kiss her in my kitchen *and* when I drove her back to her post, I don't say anything.

I wasn't supposed to fall for a girl. Especially one who can't keep her mouth shut for two whole minutes—who talks about one night stands like I'm one of her girlfriends—who pushes her way into my life and takes on men ten times her size to protect *me*—a man who's shot and killed, and . . .

"What are you thinking about?"

I can't tell her, so I switch it up so I don't have to. "Just wondering why I'm here. Is it to get your friends' approval?"

"No, not at all. More like their blessing."

She smiles, causing that sprinkle of freckles on her nose and cheeks to arch. Damn, she's pretty. Who am I kidding? Trin's beautiful.

I swallow back the need to kiss her again. "I don't know if you'll get what you want."

She makes a show of trailing her gaze from my face down my body. "Oh, I don't know . . . You're here, aren't you?"

Can't say she's wrong about that.

"Come on, I'll introduce you."

She wraps her arm around mine. Like a tamed lion, she leads me downstairs. I don't fight free of her hold which is odd, and even stranger yet, I don't want to.

The lower level has a pool, patio, and barbecue area with walls that open up into a large backyard where a volleyball net's been set up. The foundation of the house is all dense slate which is probably why I couldn't hear the group when I first pulled in.

Trin's friends: Hale, Sean, and Mason, make it a point to hang out with me, sticking with me even when she flutters off with Becca or when her hostess duties demand her attention.

They're good guys, especially Hale who seems to have moved past the dick way I treated him.

He nudges me and motions to where Trin's appeared with an old guitar. "Come on. It's show time," he says.

I hesitate, thinking he means for me to entertain them until I see everyone gathering around the fire pit and Sean reach for the guitar. "All right, what'll it be?" he says.

About six people shout out requests. I sit and take another sip of my beer. Trin takes a seat next to me, catching me off guard when she wraps her arms around mine and rests her chin on my shoulder like it's the most natural thing in the world.

"You having fun?" she asks.

"It's all good," I say.

It's then I notice that guy—the one who's been checking Trin out every time she passes—take a seat across from us. He flashes another approving smile as his stare travels down her body (yet again) like he can't wait to get his hands on her.

It's clear he's into her. It's also clear that by now, I want to beat his ass.

Men are possessive. It's an innate trait that's withstood the passage of time. Tonight's no different, especially with this woman latched to my side.

"Who's that?" I ask her.

The guy looks away when she glances ahead. "Hmm?"

"The guy in the red shirt," I say, loud enough for him to hear me, and let him know that I know he's looking at her even when it's obvious she's with me.

"Oh. I think his name is Davis. One of the new girls brought him. He's her cousin or something. Why?"

I take another pull of my beer. "Just asking."

Sean begins to strum the guitar. He's good, real good, playing a nice rendition of *Give a Little Bit*, that old Supertramp song. For a bunch of twenty year olds, they know all the classics. Maybe because they're the ones best played on a guitar. Everyone joins in, except for me. I'm too captivated by Trin singing next to me. Her voice is sweet, tender—very unlike that awful way she was belting out that rap song the other day on the beach.

Three Dog Night's *Never Been to Spain* is next. Trin knows that one, too, stopping between lyrics to grin up at me.

Sean continues to play, taking requests, but then people start taking turns singing by themselves.

"Hey," that Davis guy calls at the end of a Brad Paisley song. "Mind if I have a go?" He's asking Sean, but looking at Trin.

Sean shrugs. "I don't give a shit."

He sends the guitar around the circle so Davis can have it. I don't realize how tight I'm balling my fists until my short nails dig into my palms hard enough to leave marks.

Now, not only does he pick Toby Keith's *God Love Her*, he pisses me off by singing it well—and singing it to my girl!

Okay, not *my* girl. But damn it all, she's sitting right next to me.

Trin doesn't seem to notice, but Hale, Becca, Sean, and Mason, all exchange glances, not missing how I'm ready to pound the guy for being a disrespectful son of a bitch. He finishes to— get this—*applause* from the rest of the group.

With a wink, he stretches his arms out and offers me the guitar. "Want to give it a try there, partner?"

I didn't come here to sing or fight, and while I'm leaning more toward the latter, I can't disrespect Trin's place. I yank the guitar with enough force to jerk him forward and meet him with a grin that's nowhere near friendly. "Sure. Why the hell not?"

Trin relinquishes her hold and adjusts her position so she can see me better. I pause, taking in her encouraging smile, and how it lights up her face.

'Cept as I fumble with the strap so it rests over my lap, and place my fingers on the right markers, I'm beginning to think I'm in way over my head. Not only because *she's* watching, but because everyone's watching right along with her.

I do my best to ignore the whispers behind me, and the mutters from Davis who's started laughing. For some reason playing something I learned by heart so many years ago is a lot harder than it should be. That said, I've taken long enough and need to get started. So I focus on the prettiest girl here. The one sitting directly in front of me, whose eyes remind me of a warm autumn day.

My fingers begin to move long before I'm fully prepared, strumming the first chords of Kenny Chesney's *Anything But Mine*. Maybe I could've picked a better song, one that wasn't about summer love. But like I said, men are possessive and I'll be damned if I let a guy in plaid shorts and boat shoes show me up.

I start off slow, allowing the melody and my courage to build. With my next breath, I open my mouth and sing the first verse. *"Walking along beneath the lights of that miracle mile, me and Mary making our way into the night..."*

Sounding more Chris Young because of my deep voice, I capture the right rhythm and make it work. Everyone falls perfectly still, including Trin who's no longer smiling. Her pink lips form an oval like she can't believe I'm doing what I'm doing. Maybe she likes it. At least, that's what I hope, because right now, I'm singing it solely to her.

The last time I sang in a group was for my boys back in Iraq, back in our tent to try and drown out the distant blasts, and make like we didn't have to meet the enemy head on the next morning, all of us pretending like we didn't have to kill yet again and that'd we'd all return the next night in one piece.

Each pass of my hands, and each press from my fingers, stirs one of many painful memories I've tried to forget, forcing me to avert my gaze from Trin's. It doesn't seem right to feel what I'm feeling when I look at her—not when the memories that have plagued my dreams and woken me from sleep flash across my mind as clear as glass in the early morning sun.

The excess emotions firing through me range from good, like when I catch Trin's stare, to not so good, when I think back to how many didn't make it back from that raid. But everything I'm feeling, I feel it down to my heart, using it to fuel each verse. I finish the song, not bothering to look up until my fingertips finish plucking that last note.

When I'm done, there's no applause. Not for me. There's only dead silence. Trin, of course, is the first to speak.

"Oh, my God," she says. "That was *amazing*!"

"No shit," Sean says. "I think my panties are wet."

Heat creeps up my neck and face as everyone busts out laughing. I quickly pass him the guitar and get rid of it. As I turn back, and Sean starts playing *Thunder Road*, Trin flops onto my lap. Her hands wrap around my neck as mine snake her waist.

"Thank you," she says, greeting me with that smile I now know all too well.

I nod because it's all I can do.

And because there're too many people around for what I really want to do to her.

Chapter Ten

Trinity

I was worried when Callahan arrived that he wouldn't even make it through the front door. He surprised me by staying and by *singing*. I couldn't shake that goofy grin off my face, convinced no man alive could be more beautiful than him. God, it wasn't just his voice, or his command over the guitar, it was the way he played down to his soul, exposing his vulnerability as well as the strength he carries like a shield.

He smirks, while the rest of us laugh as Sean explains the disastrous night that made up his latest hook-up.

Sean spreads his hands, holding tight to his beer. "I swear that broomstick was this long. Cindy Anne starts screaming at her momma to stop and to let me get dressed, but that woman is possessed by hate—"

"And the fact you were having sex with her daughter on her and her husband's bed," Mason reminds him.

"Yeah. That, too. But anyway, that's how I got this."

We all groan when he drops his drawers and points to the welt on his right ass cheek.

"Aw, Sean," Becca says. "You need to invest in man-scaping tools and weed-whack some of that shit."

I think we're having a good time, but as the night goes on, his attention seems to fade away. "I should go," he tells me.

My hands fall away from him. "Why?"

"It's late," he says.

It's not that late. But I suppose for someone who's not used to being so social, this is a lot for him.

"Okay," I answer, wishing I didn't have to and forcing the next few words out. "I'll walk you out."

Instead of cutting through the interior which would be quicker, I take the long way through the yard and around the house, hoping he'll follow me. Just because I don't think I should stop him from leaving doesn't mean I want him rushing out.

He stays by my side, keeping a leisurely pace, but careful not to get too close.

We reach the end of the driveway where he's left his truck. I shift back and forth on my feet as he positions himself beside the driver's side door, struggling to find the right words to say.

"I know parties aren't exactly your thing," I say. "But I hope you had fun."

Okay. Not exactly the right words I think I need. But they're true enough.

He watches me, falling back into the deadpan silence I hoped was far behind us. Ordinarily, I'd make an obnoxious comment to stir a grin or maybe even a chuckle. But it doesn't seem right at this moment. So instead of tapping into my playful side, I search my heart, hoping it will speak better than my mind.

I take a step forward, keeping my voice light. "You know, I was hoping you'd kiss me tonight, especially after you sang me that beautiful song." I clasp my hands in front of me, feeling suddenly shy. "Am I crazy for thinking you might?"

"No. Not at all," his deep voice rumbles.

I raise my head slowly, shock hitching my breath. Callahan edges back and opens the door. Instead of climbing in, he stretches his long body across the seats, slipping back out with a spray of gorgeous wildflowers.

"You brought these for me?" I ask, barely able to get the words out.

"No." The corners of his mouth lift. "They're for Sean seeing how I make his panties wet."

I start to laugh, but it doesn't last, because the way Callahan is looking at me is very different from the way he was looking at me seconds before. This expression is the perfect blend of sweetness and ardor, just as it was when he sang to me.

He doesn't know that the song he chose is among my all-time favorites. Nor does he realize how his deep soothing voice and the gesture affected me. I want to tell him, but I'm not sure how to express something that touched me so deeply simply with words, especially now that the sadness he stows deep inside of him, finds its way to the surface.

I take a risk, and ask him what I've wanted to know since I first saw him. "Are you okay?"

When he doesn't answer, I'm not sure he will. Yet when he does, I feel it like a pull, drawing me closer.

"Not always," he admits quietly.

I purse my lips, struggling to stay strong for him. "Do you hurt?" I ask.

His stare travels down as I inch to his side, close enough that the leaves from my flowers sweep against his chest. "Sometimes," he answers.

I tilt my chin and meet his face. "Are you lonely?"

He lifts his head slowly, pitching me with such an intense stare, it holds me in place. "Not when I'm with you," he whispers.

He moves forward, sliding his right hand behind the curve of my neck to cup the base of my skull. His other hand winds carefully around my waist. As I try to remember how to move, he skims my jaw with his thumb and lowers his mouth to meet mine.

At first his lips scarcely touch, trailing over me so softly I can barely sense the contact. The care he uses is sweet, subtle, but carries enough fire to warm all the right places and make me crave more. Yet what he's doing feels so right, and so pure, I don't force it, allowing him to lead us.

My lips follow his, brushing lightly, teasing gently, fitting perfectly. It's only when his tongue probes forward and the tip flickers over mine that everything changes.

And dear *God*, there's nothing pure or tender about what happens next.

Callahan devours me, fueling a frenzy within me and inciting me to ravish him just as hard in return. I moan and whimper, my heart racing hard enough to fill my ears with its beat. This isn't a kiss. Oh, *hell* no. This is our tongues having sex!

He grunts, whirling me around and pressing my back against the truck door. My legs fasten around his waist as he hoists me onto his hips and deepens our kiss.

"Trin?"

Something hard presses against my belly.

"Trin?"

My lids flutter when he slips his tongue inside my ear.

"Trin?"

My hands yank up his shirt, traveling upward to smooth over his hard chest and graciously erect nipples. But when my teeth find his neck, and he swears, I just about rip his clothes off.

"Trin? You out here?"

Callahan breaks our contact and lowers me to my feet, stepping on my abandoned flowers as Sean appears with Mason.

"Trin?" Sean calls out, yet again.

I stomp forward and throw my hands out. "*What*? Tell me what is so important you have to interrupt quality face sucking time?"

"Can we have the wine?" Sean asks, looking at Mason who's doing his best not to crack up.

"Sean!" I yell. "Did you even have to ask? Drink the whole

thing for all I care."

"Thanks, Trin," he answers all excited-like. "Later, Callahan."

"Night, Callahan," Mason says, no longer able to hold back his laughter.

I turn back to Callahan who, like me, is panting. But very unlike me he's chuckling as he rubs his jaw.

"Sorry," I squeak.

"It's all right," he tells me. But then he says the last thing I want to hear. "I should go."

We're not going to have sex against your truck? It's what I think—and after that kiss no one can blame me. But contrary to popular belief, I don't always say what I think.

"You don't have to," I stammer.

"It's late," he says.

"Oh." *Let me rephrase that, how about we have sex against your truck?* "Okay."

He stares at me for a beat then bends to retrieve my flowers and passes them to me. The daisies are broken and the peonies have seen better days. And yet I'm so touched by the sweet gesture from a man who's so hard and almost impossible to get to know, I find it hard to keep my voice steady. "Thank you, Callahan. They're lovely."

His features soften apologetically. "They don't look quite like they did in the store."

"I don't care about that. It's the nicest thing anyone's done for me in a long time," I tell him truthfully. "Thank you for thinking of me."

Again he watches me. I'm hoping he'll change his mind and stay. But he doesn't.

"Goodnight, Trin," he says quietly.

I find a way to smile despite my disappointment. "Goodnight, Batman."

He laughs and hops into his truck. I edge away before I strap myself to the hood, seeing how I err on the side of classy. Mostly. Sometimes. Who am I kidding? Classy left the minute my tongue wanted to make babies with his.

I clutch the bouquet as I make my way down the driveway. That kiss—that toe-curling, mind-blowing, nipple saluting *kiss*. If Callahan can fire my engine with his lips alone, what's he going to do when we—

He rolls down the window and calls to me. "Trin?"

I whip back, albeit a little too excited. "Yes?"

He hooks a thumb behind him. "Your house is that way."

Yes it is. "Oh, I was just going to check to see if we got mail." Because it's Sunday after all, and everyone knows mail always comes on Sunday.

His smirk tells me he doesn't believe me and why would he? Especially since I'm now laughing as my face burns. He chuckles and shakes his head, popping his truck in reverse.

The electronic sensor picks up on the vehicle's movement and triggers the gate to open. As he passes, he offers me a wink and a grin I feel straight down to my feet. I watch him, wishing he was taking me with him and knowing it won't be long before he does.

Chapter Eleven

Trinity

Insecurity is a big old bitch, who whores around and likes to have puppies. I used to be fairly confident and pretty well-adjusted thanks to my parents' constant support.

Everything changed when I found Hunter in bed with Blakeney. I started to doubt everything and everyone, convinced that Happily Ever After was simply a dream never meant to come true.

Yet for all the hurt Hunter and Blakeney caused, I haven't thought about them in a long time, especially since meeting Callahan. He's the wakeup call I needed to prove life can and will go on for the better—the much better. That kiss alone me was something I've never quite experienced.

Too bad it came to an abrupt end.

Not only did he not show up to run with me the next day, he completely disappeared. When I didn't see him on Monday, and he never popped in on Tuesday, I drove to his place after my shift. His truck was gone, and his place was locked tight.

He didn't own a cell phone. At least not one that I'd seen, and he hadn't given me a number where I could reach him. To make things worse, Hunter texted today, pretending like nothing bad had ever come between us.

Hey, Trin. It's me, Hunter. I swung into town for the 4th. I'd like to see you and catch up. Been missing you.

Yet I haven't missed him. I didn't bother to tell him, choosing instead not to respond. It bothers me that I never confronted him, or Blakeney. Not that they gave me a chance.

"Whatcha thinking about, Trin?" Hale asks.

"Not much, just tired," I answer. I try to smile, but this is one of those grins I only barely manage.

From the back, Becca, Mason, and everyone else who tagged along crack up over something Sean says that I miss.

Hale, it seems misses it, too, the music pumping from his stereo and the wind whipping in from the open windows making it too hard to hear what's going on behind us. "You can't be tired," he tells me. "The night's too young and so are we."

He's right. But after a rough day at the beach involving a too drunk husband, and a very distraught wife, topped with Hunter's text and Callahan's absence, it's all I can do not to beg him to drive me home. For the first time in a long while, Your Mother's is the last place I want to be. But I can't let my friends down. These weeks are flying by way too fast, no matter how much I need them to linger.

"I know. But it's been a long day, you know?" I say.

"I hear you," he says, making a face. "But some loud music and dancing may be exactly what we both need." He pats my knee and backs his Tahoe into a spot in the far right corner of the lot.

For all he's trying to lift my spirits, it seems he needs his lifted as well. I didn't miss how bummed he seemed when Becca opted to slip in the back with the rest of the crew instead of joining him in the front. But Hale, being Hale, still manages to flash me a smile.

I slip my feet back into my flip flops as he sets his SUV in park. And while I showered and changed back at the beach, I'm not at my best given how weary I am. Everyone piles out, ready to cut loose. I'm not in as big of a rush.

Hale notices, creeping up to me when I hop out of his SUV. "What's bugging you, Trin?"

"A lot of things. Like I mentioned, it was a long day."

"It was," he agrees, watching everyone sweep through the front entrance before Hale and I can even make it halfway across the lot. "'Cept you handled it well like always."

"I hope," I say. "Some things are real hard to see. Even if we helped that woman today, it's not over for her unless she leaves that idiot. I offered her my number and told her to call me if she needs a friend."

Hale stops in front of me and shakes his head. "Trin, why'd you do that? You can't help someone who clearly doesn't want it. Did you see her arms? Some of those bruises were old, but even more were fresh. She's not in the right frame of mind to accept help."

"Maybe not today. But it's always nice to know at least one person cares about you."

His grin lights up the space between us despite the encroaching night, and almost as much as the short blond curls on top of his head. "Do me a favor, will you?"

I tilt my head. "Sure. What?"

"Don't ever change, sweet thing."

He flings his arm around me long enough to kiss the top of my head. He's trying to be kind, but the brotherly love he shows me pangs at my heart. "What am I going to do without you, Hale?" I ask.

He shrugs, laughing. "Probably save the world like you've always planned."

I smile like he intends, thanking him when he opens the door for me. We're greeted by Santana on the jukebox and the escalating voices of our friends. I'm not expecting Callahan to be here.

Just like I'm not expecting to find him alone with Becca.

I ground to a halt when I see her beaming up at him, and him leaning across the bar to speak to her softly. Both look in my direction when they realize I'm standing there, Becca's smile fading as she takes in my face.

No, that doesn't trigger a bad memory or anything—or cause my heart to fall to the pit of my stomach. Nope. Not at all.

I keep pace with Hale as he heads in, catching enough in his expression to know he's not happy either.

"Hey, Trin," Callahan calls quietly.

Maybe it's the day, or the mere inches that separate him and Becca, or Hunter's recent text—whatever it is keeps me walking to the rear deck without a word. And while Becca has saved me a spot next to her like she always does, I follow Hale and sit between him and Mason.

I feel Hale's attention on me, and while he seems bothered, mercifully he doesn't say anything. I clasp my hand over my eyes, trying to shake every negative emotion digging its way through my skin. Not that it works. Right then and there, it's all I can do not to run out of here.

A few minutes later Becca—gorgeous, leggy, blond Becca— returns with four pitchers gripped tight in her hands and plastic cups tucked beneath her arm. She sets everything out and makes a bee-line to me, crouching between me and Hale.

"Now, how are we going to go beer for beer, if you're not sitting beside me?" she asks.

I try to smile and say something polite, because I don't want to believe that she can hurt me like Blakeney did—and I don't want to upset her because I'm upset, or accuse her of something she hasn't done. But I can't even speak. I was blind once, and more than a little naive. Am I still that same foolish girl I've been too many times?

Sadness creeps up on Becca's stunning features when I don't answer, dulling them in a way I can't stand, but can't help then. She strokes my hair away from my face. "Trin, you know I'd never do anything to hurt you."

My eyes prickle with impending tears. Blakeney had once said something similar. Sisters before misters, right? Yeah, not so much.

"Who wants a shot? Trin's buying," Becca yells. She straightens to her full height, a right proud grin spreading along her face when everyone cheers. "Go on," she says. "Don't want to keep these fine people waiting."

When I don't move right away, she bends and whispers, "Besides, Callahan misses you. He called me to the bar and asked me where you were the minute he saw me. No, hi. No, how you doing? Nope. Just 'where's, Trin?' in that Green Bumble Bee voice of his."

I think she meant Batman, but thought Green Hornet, and became all sorts of confused. I laugh without meaning to and stand, pulling her into my arms.

"I'm sorry," I whisper.

She hugs me tightly. "You know I love you. No matter what."

"Love you, too, Becks," I tell her.

She kisses my cheek and pats my ass as I walk off since that's the kind of friend she is. A real one. I start to feel better, especially when Callahan glances up and the corners of his mouth curve in that "almost smile" of his.

It's probably why I don't notice Hunter right away, or Blakeney, even though they stop directly in front of me.

Their sudden presence strikes me across the face like a slap. They exchange glances, but it's Hunter who's the first to speak. "Hey, Trin," he says. "We were hoping to find you here. Can I buy you a drink?"

"Buy me a drink?" I repeat, unable to get past the fact that he's actually standing in front of me after all this time.

Never once did Hunter try to reach out to me—not to apologize, not to check in to see if I was okay, not even so much as to wish me well. Until he texted me today, it's like I'd stopped existing to him—like I'd somehow wronged him *and* her—and I wasn't worth wasting any more time on.

We never broke up. We never had it out. We simply stopped being a part of each other's lives. I was certain he'd call—after the two years I gave him, he owed me as much. And I certainly wasn't calling him.

But he never did, and neither did Blakeney. Not when I needed them to.

Blakeney offers me an apologetic smile that may appear genuine to some, but certainly not to me. "We were hoping we could talk to you," she says.

She's is in a short white skirt that shows off her legs and a coral tank that highlights her white blond hair and dazzling teeth. Hunter is in his signature Polo shirt and cargo shorts. If I were to take an objective step back, I'd peg them among the most striking and elite of the privileged youths who frolic along the Carolina shores in the summer, and ski down the Swiss Alps in winter. But right then and there, I can't be objective. Nor can I get past the shock and sting their presence evokes.

And apparently, I'm not alone.

Becca is suddenly there, and so is everyone else. "What in the *hell*?" she snaps.

Both Hunter and Blakeney right their stances, but hold their ground. Hunter's eyes cut to my boys. "Hey," he tells them.

"Hey?" Hale answers back, laughing. "You talking to me?"

"That's right," Hunter replies.

"In that case, *fuck you*," Hale says, no longer smiling.

"You have a lot of nerve being here," Mason says, the muscles along his hefty shoulders tensing.

Sean steps forward, hovering over Hunter as he offers to kick his ass.

Blakeney trains her tightening stare to my right where Becca is leaning close. It's Becca's way of letting me know she has my back, and that she's seconds from clawing Blakeney's eyes out.

"We're here to talk to Trin, *alone*," Blakeney tells her.

"Don't you think you've done enough *alone* with this limp

dick—Oh, wait, it's not so limp is it? Giving how you straddled it more than once when your best *friend* wasn't around."

Blakeney's stare sharpens with rage, but when she returns her attention to me, her voice is soft. "Please, Trin. Just give us a moment. *Please*," she says.

I take a small breath, knowing this moment has been coming for far too long.

"Okay," I mutter at the same time Becca insists I don't owe her a damn thing, and may or may not have called her a whore.

I take Becca's hand and squeeze it. "I'm all right," I assure her, even though we both know it's a lie. "I'll just be a moment."

My friends don't seem happy. Not that I blame them. We always swore we'd protect each other from harm, and we always have, as much as we could. Just last summer, someone had to rip me off Becca's boyfriend when I found out what he did to her. And if Hale, Mason, and Sean had found out what happened, I doubt that piece of trash would still be alive.

For a long time no one moves, but then Hale clears his throat, drawing everyone's attention. "All right, Trin. If that's what you want. Come on y'all. We're here if she needs us."

As my friends edge back, warm fingertips trail down either side of my arms. I crane my neck, unsure who's touching me.

Callahan stands directly behind me. He was with me this whole time, and I didn't even know it.

He glides his hands down, stopping above my elbows, keeping his voice low as he stares Hunter down. "You sure you're all right?" he asks. I nod because that's all I can really do then. "I'll stay close," he promises.

He's not only trying to reassure me, that rumble in his voice is directed at Hunter as a warning. Hunter keeps his attention trained on Callahan as Callahan returns to the bar. Blakeney's focus is on Callahan, too, except she's eyeing him in a whole different way than Hunter.

Really? *Really?*

She catches me watching her, and offers me a smile which I've seen a thousand times, and which I now recognize as phony. Keeping her smile, she motions to the small empty booth behind her. "Shall we?"

"After you," I say.

She slides into the booth that will keep her back to the glaring group also known as her former friends. For as tough as she always acted, she can't handle their scrutiny. At least not now. I slip into the opposite side, staying close to the edge so Hunter knows he's not welcome to sit beside me. The last thing I need is to be boxed in by these two. As it is, despite the open walls, I feel the room closing in around me.

Blakeney smiles. "You look good, real good, Trin."

"Yes, you do," Hunter agrees, nodding approvingly.

He takes me in, letting his stare linger as it passes along my body. To be honest, I don't care if he likes the way I look or not. But Blakeney does, her lips pressing tight the longer he examines my features. A year ago, I may not have noticed her reaction. But knowing what I know now, I'm more aware of subtle changes in her expression and posture.

If I wasn't so blinded by what I believed was love and true friendship, maybe I would have suspected something sooner. Maybe. Like I said, I notice a lot more now.

For starters, unlike me and Becca, Blakeney always strove to be the center of attention. She laughed at all the right moments, moved her hips as she walked just so, and knew what it took to snag a long glance her way. Me and Becks, we just did our thing. And come to think of it, that seemed to work out fine. Or so I thought.

"My momma was telling me you did a half marathon in the spring," Hunter says. "I bet you had to train real hard—"

"What do you want?" I say, causing Hunter to straighten. While he doesn't scowl, my no nonsense tone does catch him off guard.

I fold my hands in front of me, waiting for them to tell me

they're engaged or even married. It wouldn't surprise me. They make the perfect couple after all.

"We're here to apologize, Trin," Blakeney begins. "About everything."

My spine stiffens. Okay, wasn't expecting that one.

Hunter starts to say something, but Blakeney's clasp to his arm quiets him. She notices my stare shift to where she's holding him and pulls her hand away. She probably thinks it bothers me to see her touch him. Yet it doesn't. Unlike the day I walked in on them.

As I sit here now, watching them, the hurt I felt that day fills me once more. These were two people I trusted with my love—two people I'd given my life for. That heart I wear on my sleeve didn't appear overnight. They knew as much, and didn't think twice about slapping it out of my hands.

Despite how close we were, Hunter and I didn't see much of each other when we returned to college our senior year. I was struggling to complete my undergrad requirements at Princeton, and he was finishing up his degree at NYU. He was supposed to pick me up on his way home to Kiawah for Christmas. But having missed him so bad, I couldn't wait to see him, and took the train to surprise him the morning after my last final.

I used the key he'd given me and very quietly snuck into his apartment, and into his room. Blond hair poked out from the top of the thick comforter I'd bought him as a gift. I thought it was him, until I pounced and someone else startled beneath me.

Blakeney—the same girl who I'd shared countless memories with—the same girl who was texting me pictures of bridesmaid dresses to wear at my wedding!—was in bed with the man I'd planned on marrying.

"We're going to make beautiful babies together," Hunter had told me just the week prior. "All you have to do is say yes, and come graduation, we'll have the biggest wedding Kiawah Island's ever seen."

It's what he promised. But he never meant it. Not when my friend was staring back at me with those wide pretty eyes that used to sparkle every time she saw me.

I couldn't move or sense anything around me. Because this wasn't supposed to happen. These two people I loved with all my heart couldn't do this to me. But as Blakeney gathered the covers around her bare breasts, and pushed away the messy strands of her bed-tousled hair from her perfect face, I knew how wrong I was.

I crawled away and stumbled onto the floor, her stare glued on mine as she frantically shook Hunter's shoulder.

He rolled onto his back. "What, babe?—Oh, *shit*," he said, sitting up with a jolt.

I broke down, barely able to think straight. But I managed to ask what I needed to know. "How long has this been going on?"

Neither spoke. Hunter simply watched me, not bothering to explain or even apologize. By then, Blakeney was crying, too. She stayed in the bed, making no attempt to stand, or reach for me, or, or—

"*Trin*," she simply said, half a second before I bolted from the apartment.

"Trin?" Hunter says. His voice is soft, but bringing me back to the moment in one forcible pull. "Say something, will you? It's been too long, pretty girl."

"Pretty girl", huh? Well, based on the way he's taking in my face and a whole lot more, maybe he means it. Not that it matters anymore.

That familiar twinkle lightens his green eyes, making it clear he remembers more than our talks. I gave this young man everything: my affections, my attention, and handed him my virginity without much thought, convincing myself he was the one. But as I see him now, I don't really notice his handsome face, don't care much for those long lean muscles that bulge his arms and shoulders, and could care less about that twinkle. To be honest, he can shove that twinkle clear up his ass.

As much as I thought I loved Hunter, I know now what I felt was about as real as he had been. And he was a phony, lying snake.

"We want to do right by you, Trin," he says. He chuckles. "Blakeney and I aren't even together anymore. We haven't been for a long time."

To me it makes no difference one way or another so I don't respond. "We are real sorry," he adds.

"About which part?" I ask.

My question seems to catch them off guard so I continue. "Is it the lying?" I ask, looking at Blakeney. "Like when you used to tell me you didn't know what I saw in him. And that I was too good for him. And the way you'd make fun of how his hair always had to be just right. Metro-bitch—that was your nickname for him, right? Even though I told you not to call him that."

My, doesn't this seem to surprise Hunter. But no, now it's his turn to get my attention. Fair is fair after all. "So when you told me you didn't like Blakeney, and that she was dumber than a box of bent nails pulled from the gutter—and about as warm as a field of corpses—I defended you by the way, Blakeney—and that her boobs were as fake as she was, were you lying then? Or were you just trying keep me in the dark?"

"*Trinity.*" Hunter attempts to interrupt, but I don't let him.

"You're not answering my question," I point out. "Is it the lying? Or are you trying to apologize that it took you this long to say something—*anything*?"

I don't want to admit that my phone never left my side for weeks as I waited for him and her to call—to phone and tell me something that could explain why they did what they did—instead of allowing me to beat myself up and blame myself for something I wasn't responsible for.

The flowers I was sure would arrive never came. Nor did the knock on my door and the pleas for forgiveness. They didn't bother with an "I'm sorry" then. So I think I have a right to question why they're saying it now, and to what their apology actually pertains to.

"Is the apology for the sex? Believe it or not, I can look past it," I admit. It wasn't all that memorable, after all. At least not between me and Hunter. "It's the lying. It's everything you both had to do and say to be together. *That's* the hard part. I understand making mistakes. I've made my share, including trusting the two of you."

My last comment is like a verbal punch they weren't expecting. Their expressions steel, even though I keep my face and tone fairly neutral. My words aren't meant to burn, or challenge them to a fight. I'm being honest with them, and myself, betraying me is the best thing they could have done. It proved how little I'd meant to them and that my heart belonged far away from them.

"So you won't forgive us." Hunter's voice is terse, but I can sense a hint of disappointment.

"I forgive you," I say. "I forgave you a long time ago."

They gape at me, stunned, before smiling with as much genuineness as they're capable of. Blakeney's eyes glimmer with what may be the start of tears. She reaches out and clasps my hands. "Thank you," she says. She searches my face, taking her time. "God, I've missed you, Trin."

Hunter leans in. "Maybe with time, we can all be friends again. It would be nice to hang out, don't you think?" he asks.

He adds what appears to be an inviting wink, like it will somehow seal the deal. His smile loses its luster and does Blakeney's when it occurs to them I'm not smiling back.

"I didn't say anything about being friends," I say quietly. "I can forgive you, because I want to be a good person. But being a good person doesn't make me a doormat." I slip out of the booth and stand. "Y'all have a good night."

"I expected more from you, Trin," Hunter says, halting me before I take my first step.

"Judging by your 'come fuck me eyes' I figured as much," I answer sweetly.

His jaw drops, but he doesn't try to deny it.

Despite my light tone, and despite that it was a right good comeback, I have a lot of emotion I need to release. But I won't release it in front of them. No. These two have seen the last of my tears.

I head straight back through the double doors leading out to the deck. Hale snags my wrist as I pass him. "You all right?"

I grin although he can see right through it. "I'm fine. Just going for a walk."

He raises his brows. "Now?"

"I need a moment," I admit.

My splintering tone is subtle, but he hears it anyway. He releases my hand. "All right," he says. "Don't be long."

I nod the way women do when they're trying to keep from crying and walk cautiously past him, ignoring how everyone at our table trains their eyes on me. As casually as I can, I hop down the rear steps and onto the beach. The moment I feel the grains of soft sand slide between my toes, I can't seem to move fast enough. I slip off my flip flops and shoot toward the left, keeping the ocean to my right. If I keep going, I'll eventually reach Callahan's place. And if I walk far enough, I'll reach the post where I keep watch.

Those old wounds tore right open when I saw them, even though I thought I was long past the way they'd treated me.

The cool Atlantic water splashes along my legs. In an effort to relax, I pause to take in how the moon's reflection dances along the waves. It's beautiful, breathtaking even. The problem is, I'm so full of pent up emotions, lovely imagery does nothing to settle my nerves. Nor does the soft summer breeze sending my hair sailing behind me offer reprieve.

Blakeney never saw my pain when the boys ignored me to seek out her and Becca. For all the times I wiped her tears, she never seemed to notice mine. She didn't care that I was always the one without a date. In fact, if it wasn't for Hale asking me to prom, I wouldn't have gone at all. Something

Blakeney never stopped to consider.

Hunter . . . when it comes to him, I feel more foolish than brokenhearted. At least now. He made me feel special, that much is true. But when I think back, it was always when he thought his pretty talk and that wink he practiced in front of the mirror every time he fussed with his hair, would get him something in return.

To him, I was that cute, polite young woman from a good family he could bring home to his momma—the smart one who smiled and said all the right things. Much to his delight, I was also the woman who never denied him sex, driven to please him anyway he wanted.

I roll my eyes. Too bad that pleasing wasn't reciprocated.

A thought occurs to me as I thread my fingers through my hair. Regardless of what they did, and how badly it affected me, something really good came of it.

I met Callahan.

If I was still seeing Hunter, I never would have flirted with him, much less kissed him. In fact, I would have missed out on every moment I've shared with him.

How is it possible I'm only meeting this amazing man now—when I have such little time left?—And how is it fair that I'm getting to know him here, when I could be halfway across the globe in another two months?

I glance over my shoulder. Your Mother's is roughly the size of an M&M from where I stand, and if I'm right, I've already passed Callahan's place. I didn't realize how far I'd walked until now. While I think I should head back, my skin continues to prickle with too much negative energy, and way too much angst.

It was an awful day that had taken a turn for worse. But as the waves continue to drench my shins, I'm reminded that my days on Kiawah are numbered. I kick at the water, wanting desperately to shake my sadness away in order to return to Callahan and my friends with a smile. I hope he'll tell me where he's been. So then maybe I can admit to him how much

I missed him in the time he was gone.

I strip out of my clothes and toss them far from the water's edge. With a determined sigh, I race into the ocean and dive in, ready to cleanse my body of all the lingering pain that soils it.

What I never imagined as I broke through the surface and pumped my arms along the waves, was that the pain I'm feeling would be *nothing* compared to the agony that ultimately followed.

Chapter Twelve

Callahan

I don't know who this dipshit is, or the blonde he sauntered in with who flashed me a plastic smile. But I heard enough from Trin's friends, and recognized the hurt in her eyes to figure out what went down between them. It's one thing for someone you care about to cheat on you. It's another thing to have that someone cheat with a person you think is your friend.

My hands stay busy mixing, but my eyes are trained on Trin. I'm waiting for this idiot to raise his voice, or do something to upset her. It won't take much to set me off, not after the past two days I've had, and especially not when it comes to Trinity.

Trin's one of those rare and genuine young women with a smile so sweet you'd think she was made of honey. She shimmied, that's right, *shimmied* her way into my life. But for all I didn't initially want her, found her annoying, and tried to push her away, all I could think about from the moment I left was getting back to her as quick I could. I needed her smile, and that compassion she offers so freely. Needed it bad, considering the news I received the night I left her.

It doesn't seem right to feel this way about someone I've only known about a month. She's different than the women I'm used to. There's no denying she's beautiful, and kind. But it wasn't until I kissed her that I realized how damn sexy she is. It was like something smacked me upside the head and yelled, "Wake up, son. This girl's smoking."

I pour another few shots as I watch her speak to the Stepford twins. I can't hear what she's saying, not with this crowd. But that edge of steel flickering in her expression assures me she's not about to let them push her around.

Either way, they better not try.

"Hey, hot thing. How about another refill?"

The brunette who's been hitting on me all night shakes her empty glass in my face. I take it, dump the contents, and pour another few fingers of scotch over ice. I pass it back to her without bothering to meet her face. She slips me a hundred with her digits scrawled on it.

"Keep the change," she tells me.

She leans over the bar, pretending to act more drunk than she is as I head toward register. "You going to tell me your name, cowboy?" she asks. Her fingers trail down her low cut shirt, giving it a hard yank to the side.

I don't bother to look at what she's flashing, slapping the change down in front of her. "No ma'am. I'm not," I answer.

I start to move toward the next customer when Trin passes in front of me. Her walk seems off, like she's working to slow her steps and not run. I lean over the bar to make sure she's not crying, and that she makes it to her friends okay.

Hale stops her. I can't see her face, but I see his just fine. He frowns, his expression is split between worry and anger. I think he's trying to coax her to sit beside him, but instead of taking a seat, she takes off.

That asshole and the blonde leave their seats, rushing to catch her. I don't know what they're up to. All I know is that Trin's upset because of them, and that's enough for me.

I stomp down to the end of the bar and hop over, stepping in front of her ex before he can reach the double doors leading out to the deck. "If she wanted you with her, she wouldn't have left. Stay away from her," I warn.

"Who the hell are you?" he snaps back.

Becca shoves her way in front of me. "Trin's new boyfriend," she answers for me. That statement doesn't bother me, even though it's not true. But I have to work not to grimace when she doesn't stop there. "And unlike you, he has a tremendous dick."

Heat fires his face, and probably mine, too. Christ Almighty, is it a wonder she's Trin's best friend?

Dipshit is pissed, and looking to take it out on a Becca. I lug her behind me and into Hale's arms, knowing he likes her, and that he'll keep her safe.

The moment she's out of the idiot's reach, he turns his anger at me. "*You're* Trin's boyfriend?"

In truth, I don't know what I am to her, but I'm not letting him know that. "That's right."

"A bartender," he says.

"I'm a *soldier*," I fire back, ramming my fingers into his chest hard enough to make him stumble. "Special Forces, former Ranger, and someone capable of beating your ass if you ever hurt Trin again."

"This here *bartender* as you called him served his country for eight years," Hale says. "Show respect, *son*."

Mason and Sean take Hale's lead and run with it. They don't have to raise their voices much, seeing that by now the music's stopped and the entire bar is watching us.

Mason points at Trin's ex. "While you were scrolling through Instagram on your iPad, Callahan here was shooting down our enemies to give you that privilege and freedom. The *hell's* wrong with you giving a man who's bled for our country a hard time?"

"You should be thanking him!" Mrs. Brewster shouts, to which every last patron yells in agreement.

The idiot lifts his hands, trying speak and soothe the now fuming crowd. But no one is listening. "To disrespect Callahan is to disrespect America," Sean says, talking over him. "You trying to disrespect America?"

"Kick his ass, Spanky," old man Perrington yells.

Jesus.

The blonde starts up with Becca. By now I know Becca well enough to realize this is mistake. "It didn't have to be this way," the blonde says, angry tears streaming down her face. "You were my friend, too."

Hale and I barely catch Becca in time when she hurtles herself forward. "You stopped being my friend when you screwed over the best person I know!" Becca yells. "Trin trusted you and you treated her like she was nothing. All because you couldn't handle *one man* looking at her instead of you!"

Hurt and something else flashes in that young woman's face. Becca nailed her with something a lot of people can't handle, *truth*. She whips around, the prick she came with shooting after her, but not before Becca screams, "You ever come in here again, you'll be leaving with fewer teeth!"

At this point, Sean's leading the crowd in *God Bless America*. Although it should be funny, it isn't. If that duos' presence fired up Trin's friends this bad, I can only imagine what they did to her.

"Trin's been gone a long time," I tell them. "We need to find her."

"I can cover the bar if you want," Mason offers. "I can't mix drinks, but I can pour beer."

He knows I want to go after her so I don't hesitate, and take him up on the offer. The rest of us hit beach, splitting up and taking off in a sprint.

Sean and I cut left, we're running pretty fast and calling her name. But even though he's a lifeguard and in decent shape, he's winded not long after we pass my place. I slow to a stop to give him a moment to breathe. By the looks of it, I'm not sure how much longer he'll last.

"Sean, head back to Your Mother's. Maybe Trin's already there. But in case she's not, I'll keep heading this way."

He shakes his head. "Hale and Becca would have called if

she's there."

"Not if they're still out looking for her," I tell him.

"Good point," he says. "But let's make sure." He fumbles through his shorts. "Shit, I forgot my phone. You have one?"

"Not on me." I place my hand on my hips and think things through. "Remember that overturned rowboat we passed?"

"Yeah?"

"A few yards to the left of it, there's a break in the trees that leads to my house. Go back to the bar in case Trin's returned. But if you find her before then, and if she's hurt or something, take her back to my place and use my phone to call for help."

He frowns. "Shit. You don't think anything happened to her, do you?"

I hope not, but that's not what I tell him. "Just thinking like a soldier, is all."

Sean seems satisfied with my excuse and edges back. "Okay. But she wouldn't have gone all the way to her post. So if you hit that section of beach and don't see her, head on back."

"I will."

I take off running again. There are a few couples walking along holding hands, but no Trin. When only about half a mile remains between me and her post I pause and look around.

"Damn it. Where are you?"

I turn back toward Your Mother's, out of my mind with worry. I don't think I jog more than a few yards before I see a familiar figure break through the water's surface. With the poise of a mermaid, she flips her hair back, sending it soaring over her head in an arch to smack against her shoulder blades as the waves sweep against her tiny waist in their rush to return to sea.

Moonlight drenches her skin with its glow as she abandons the ocean, her head high, her small, lean muscles gracefully moving her forward, and salt water trickling along her curves. Without realizing, I'm almost to her, knowing who she is, and drawn by her magnetic pull.

"Trin?"

She whips around, my eyes widening when I realize only a tiny pair of black panties and bra cover that sweet, *wet* body.

Holy shit.

"Callahan?" she asks.

I jerk my head to the side, feeling myself get very hard, very fast.

She hurries toward me. "What are you doing out here?"

"Shouldn't I be asking what the *hell* you're doing?" I snap.

She stops in front of me. "Did you just growl at me?" she accuses.

"*No.*" In her defense, given what's trying to punch a hole through my jeans, I'll admit, my voice is pretty damn strained.

"You did so just growl at me. What's your problem?" she asks, crossing her arms.

"What's *my* problem?" I turn to face her, but after another look at well, *everything*, I realize it's a mistake. Again, I avert my gaze. "You're the one standing in your panties, soaking wet—" I grimace. Talk about the wrong thing to say. Now I'm ten seconds away from busting through my zipper. "—while me and your friends have been worried sick looking for you."

"I only went for a swim to clear my head."

"In your panties?" I ask.

She pauses. "You like saying that word, don't you?"

"Trin—"

"I mean that's like the second time you've said it."

I don't have to look at her to know she's smiling, but I do. Great. Now she's cold, and I don't just know that because she's hugging herself and shaking. Two of the stiffest, most tempting nipples I've ever seen are protruding against the lace of her bra, demanding I step in for a closer look, begging me to touch, insisting that I lick, and pleading for me to suck—

I curse out loud and rip off my shirt, offering it to her without looking. "*Here*, take it."

"Oh, you don't have to do that."

"Trust me. I do," I say, growling yet again. Hell, wonder why?

"I'm serious," she insists. "My clothes are right over there."

I make the mistake of looking up in time to see everything the good Lord gave Trin bounce perfectly as she runs along the sand. She stops and scans the beach, then jogs further up, the globes of her ass stretching against the tiny piece of fabric barely keeping her covered.

Jesus H. Christ.

Just ahead of her, what appears to be a pair of college-aged boys are walking toward her. Both stop dead when they see her, one of them flat out pointing.

Oh *hell* no.

Trin turns around when she sees me charging toward her. "I can't find my clothes. The current must have taken me further down—*hey*."

I shove my shirt over her head and yank it down past her ass. She squeals as I throw her over my shoulder and storm in the direction of my house.

"Spanky, put me down this instant."

If I don't shake the image of her in those barely-there clothes—or the way things bounced as she ran—by the feel of it, I may very well be living up to that nickname several times tonight.

She wriggles against me, likely trying to break her arms free. "I mean it, Callahan!" she yells.

"Zip it, woman," I tell her.

She stops wiggling. "Did you just tell me to zip it?"

"Yup," I answer.

"Well, that's rude."

I huff. "Says the woman running around in her—"

"Panties?" she offers. "You were going to say it again weren't you?"

"I was going to say skivvies," I fire back, lying through my teeth.

"No," she drawls. "I don't think you were."

For the love of all that's holy. Her arms are practically tied, she's draped over my shoulder, and she's still talking like she's standing right in front of me. Does this woman ever shut up? No, of course not.

"Hmm. You seem to be walking funny," she points out. "Everything all right down there, big boy?"

I know she's playing with me and having fun doing it, but my steps slow anyway and I mutter a curse.

"What's wrong?" she teases. "You sound ah, frustrated."

Here's the thing. I'm not quite sure if she knows I'm harder than that stand of trees we pass as we head toward my back door, or if she's pretending like I could be. One way to find out.

I set her down in front of the sliding glass doors. She hurries to thread her hands through the shirt holes, freezing in place when I lock my eyes on hers and my right hand cups her face.

With my other hand, I push the strands of her wet hair behind her shoulder, taking care to be gentle while I continue to hold her stare. "Maybe I am frustrated," I say, my voice rough. "But there's this little brunette who I bet can help me out with that."

At first she doesn't say anything, but when she does her voice barely registers. "Who might that be?"

I move in close, real close, like I'm about to kiss her. Trin lifts her chin higher, closes her eyes, leans forward, and —

I drop my hands so quick, Trin stumbles forward "I don't know her name," I tell her, clasping her elbow to steady her. "She's back at the bar." I turn and head into the house. "Let's get you some pants so we can head back and I can find out."

The door slams shut as I reach the small hall leading to my bedroom. Quick steps echo behind me half a second before a couch pillow nails me in the back of my head. I turn around, laughing my ass off.

Trin's standing in the middle of my living room fit to be tied. "You-you—"

"Panty-loving stud?" I offer.

"That's not funny," she says, stomping her feet.

Damn, she's cute.

I stroll up to her, grinning. "Now, Trin, what's got you all worked up?"

She crosses her arms. "What do you think?"

"Can't say I know," I say, stopping directly in front of her.

"Yes, you do," she tells me, her voice quieting. "You know I really like you."

I straighten. It's one thing to suspect it, but it's a whole other thing to hear her say it.

She shifts her gaze to the floor. "I don't—" She lets out a breath and meets my eyes. "It would kill me to see you with someone else. But if that's what you want, don't expect me to sit around and wait for you."

I catch her elbow when she tries to leave, realizing what an ass I am. I wasn't thinking about her ex, or how he cheated on her with her friend, or hell, how they both showed up tonight. The way she came out of the water, looking like she did, wearing what she was, all I thought about was her, and how much I wanted to touch her. But she hasn't forgotten them or how they made her feel.

"I'm sorry," I say.

Her face crumbles a little. "It's okay if you're interested in someone else. I'd rather know now than—"

I pull her to me. This time when I lock my eyes with hers, I mean to do more than tease. My stare flickers down to where my erection is trying to tear its way through my jeans. "Does it look like I'm interested in anyone else?"

Her eyes widen. "Oh, my . . ."

I'm not sure who moves first, but we're suddenly on each other, kissing like this is our last goodbye. The shirt she's no longer wearing falls to the floor as my hands slide beneath her panties to cup those silky round globes. I wrench her up and carry her to the couch, lowering her on top of me in a straddle.

Her mouth tears away from mine to find my throat, licking and sucking, making me want to do the same except not to her throat.

I strip her out of her bra, my lips latching onto a very stiff nipple.

"Oh, *God*," Trin gasps, clutching my head.

My teeth graze over the point until I pull it deep in my mouth and flick it with my tongue. Her other breast, it needs attention, too. I reach between us, rolling the nipple with my fingers.

Trin bucks against me, grinding her hips. We're moving fast, rough, *hot*—both of us loud and getting louder. God *damn*—I'm so into her, and the way her body reacts to mine.

Everything is going well, until it's suddenly not. Her movements slow and something changes in her demeanor when I try to tug off her panties. I'm not sure what's happening, but I know something's wrong.

I lean back to get a better view of her face. She averts her gaze, her racing heartbeat pounding against my hand as I pass it along her sternum. Trin's . . . *scared*. For as much as she's played and teased, I know that much is true—just like I know that I'm the cause.

So instead of pulling off her panties, and taking her to my room where an unopened box of condoms sits in my drawer, I yank the edges up and drag her to me for a long deep kiss.

At first, she startles. I take my time, stroking my tongue over hers until she relaxes and returns my kiss with equal heat. My palm smooths over the soft skin between her breasts, feeling her heart settle so I know she's more turned on than frightened.

"Better?" I murmur against her ear.

She moans when I tug on her lobe. "Sorry," she manages.

I trail kisses along her neck. "Don't be," I whisper.

She groans when she slides over my thick erection. "Do you like that?" I ask, nipping her chin.

"Yes," she stammers.

"Then that's what we'll do."

My fingers grip her hips, and my mouth returns to play with her nipples. The tilts of her pelvis are slow at first, but it's not long before her speed increases.

I'll admit, rubbing like this fully clothed isn't something I've done since I was sixteen. But I like how she feels on top of me, and I love how she responds. Her hair bounces against her shoulders with how fast she's working me, and her grunts grow fiercer with each pass. Between those lust-filled cries and her reddening face, I know she's peaking. I help her go faster, desperate for a scream that will signal her release.

The moment I hear it, my head lolls back and that familiar tightening claims me. *Fuck.* This might not be full out sex—not with three layers of clothing between us—but it feels real damn good. I come with her riding me hard.

She slows her movement as I finish, her breathing as crazy as mine.

"Shit," I say, lifting my head from the couch and glancing down. Her panties are stretched and my boxers and jeans are soaked. While I don't think there's anything to worry about, there's something I need to know. "Are you on birth control?"

"I am," she confirms, easing my worry with her words and voice. She pauses, then carefully says, "My last check-up states I'm clean, and I haven't been with anyone since. What about you?"

"My blood tests have always been clean," I assure her. "The last one I had was in March." I slide my hands along her hips. "And it's been a long time since I've been with anyone, even like this."

She smiles in that soft way of hers that doesn't quite show her teeth. "Good," she says.

I kiss the spot between her breasts when she cradles my head against her. Although her breath has begun to slow, her heart is beating wicked fast.

"Were you scared?" I breathe against her skin.

"Yes," she admits. "This is sort of all new to me. I thought I . . ." She clears her throat. "I thought I'd had orgasms before. But based on what just happened, it's pretty clear I've been missing out." She bites on her bottom lip and adds. "Is this normal?"

I chuckle, tickling her skin with a few strokes of my beard. "No. But like I said, I haven't been with anyone in a long while. I usually last—"

"Please don't tell me about being with anyone else."

I tilt my chin, meeting the sadness dimming her pretty brown eyes. "Trin, you don't have to worry about other women." I hesitate, but then add, "You're all I ever think about."

Her voice quiets. "You're all I ever think about, too."

Good.

I pull her against me, covering her with a blanket before reaching for my house phone. "Here. You better call your friends."

Becca picks up on the first ring and she's so loud I have no problem hearing her. "Hello?"

"Hey, it's me," Trin tells her.

"Where the hell have you been?"

"I went for a swim to clear my head. Callahan found me." She takes a moment to smile at me. "I'm with him now."

"You're kidding." Her voice drops. "Did you show him your titties?"

Seeing how Trin doesn't answer right away, for Becca, that's as good as hearing, "yes".

"Holy fuck. You did didn't you?" she squeals. "Hey, Trin's over at Callahan's showing him her titties."

"No, shit," Hale calls from a distance.

Trin covers her face when she catches my grin. "I have to go, Becks. Look, I'm sorry I worried you."

"Aw, sugar, you can make it up to me by telling me all the dirty little details later. Bye now."

"It was your idea to call her," she insists when I start

laughing.

I stroke her hair when she settles against me, trying to warm her rapidly cooling body.

"Where were you?" she asks. "You were gone a long time."

She means when I took off without telling her. "I had some things to take care of," I admit.

"I was worried."

It's what she claims, and I believe her. But while she's not demanding more of an explanation, she does want to know why I left as abruptly as I did. I don't really want to talk about it, but it's because it's her that I can. "A buddy of mine from the Army died."

She lifts her head so she can see my face. "Oh, no. I'm so sorry."

I shrug like it doesn't affect me even though it damn well does. "The funeral was yesterday in Oklahoma. I left as soon as I heard to get there in time and drove all night to get back."

"Were you close to him?" she asks cautiously.

"I served three tours with him," I explain, my mind drifting away from her and back to my time back in Iraq. "During one of our raids, he was in a Range Rover that was struck by a missile. The rest of the boys inside were killed. He was considered lucky to have survived." I huff. "I'm not so sure he'd agree. He lost his left arm and part of his face, also suffered permanent brain damage that affected his nervous system."

"That poor man," she says. "How did he die?"

I play with the strands of her damp hair, but I can't look at her when I answer. "He killed himself, Trin. He couldn't handle what happened. It wasn't just the combat, his disfigurement, or even his girl leaving him when he came home. It was all of it, and more. No one would give him a job or a chance. He lost everything back in Iraq, including all those men who died when that missile hit, and what did he get in return? Absolutely nothing."

We wait in silence for a while. When I finally bring myself to look at her, I see nothing but tears pooling in her eyes. "I'm sorry for your loss and for everyone who loved him," she tells me, swallowing hard. "But most of all, I'm sorry for him, and what he must have gone through."

My attention travels to the ceiling when that all that anger that flared at his funeral returns full force. "I know suicide is the worst kind of sin," I say. "A straight ticket to hell. But I refuse to believe in a God that wouldn't show mercy to someone like Billy. Someone so good, but so sick with grief, he sought peace the only way his beaten soul thought he could get it."

I don't realize the extent of my emotions until Trin's fingers splay on either side of my face and she kisses my eyelids. Her touch is warm and delicate, something I could have used when I watched Billy's parents drape their bodies across their son's casket.

Christ, seeing them like that, and all those familiar faces breaking down like they did, it brought everything back in one cruel blow, triggering a slew of vicious memories and further riling all the ones that have been eating me alive.

"I believe your friend is in heaven, and whole, and loved," she says, her own tears falling. "I'm only sorry he couldn't find that peace here on earth."

My arms wrap around her as she settles against me. "Thank you," I whisper, not realizing how bad I needed to hear those words until they fell from her lips.

In the quiet that passes, I'm sure that she's fallen asleep until she shifts her weight, and that gentle stare finds me once more.

"Callahan?"

"Yeah?"

"When I asked you if what was happening was normal, I didn't mean what you thought I meant. I was speaking of what's going on between us." She sighs. "It's hard to describe—and maybe it's too soon to tell you. But what I feel when I'm with you, I've never felt with anyone else." Her voice is so quiet it seems to drift away. "I just wanted you to know that. It's one of the reasons I was so scared when you touched me."

I don't respond, keeping my jaw closed tight. Mostly because I feel exactly the same way, and because it scares the hell out of me, too.

Chapter Thirteen

Trinity

Callahan kisses me again. It's so sweet. No, *he's* so sweet. And even though I want to know what he's thinking, I don't ask, choosing instead to melt into this kiss.

The door swings open and good ol' Sean walks through—like I'm not making out half-naked with Callahan.

"Oh, *shit*," he says.

Callahan clutches me to him, trying to shield me, as he covers my back with that small throw.

"*Sean*. What are you doing here?' I ask, fumbling with the blanket and trying to gather it around me.

"I found these," he says, tossing me my clothes. "I wasn't sure what happened to you and ran back here to call for help." He smirks. "But looks to me you have all the help you need."

"I told him to call from my place," Callahan admits. He rubs his jaw, pausing when Sean makes no effort to leave. "Sean, now that you know Trin's safe, how about you head back to the bar?"

Sean laughs like the thought hadn't even occurred to him. "Sure. I can do that." He starts to leave, but then adds, "By the way. Nice rack, Trin. They ain't so tiny, after all."

"Get out of here, Sean!" I yell. By then he's already out in the back, but that doesn't mean I still can't hear him crack up.

Callahan's light touch lures my attention back to him. "Is it wrong that I'm glad he hadn't seen these until now?" he asks, passing his hands over my breasts.

I watch the way his fingertips trace along my small curves. "It's not like that with him, or Mason, or Hale. We've been friends forever and nothing more."

"I wasn't sure," he says. "I know you're a tight bunch."

"We are, and I'd do anything for them. But they're my brothers, and I'm the little sister they've always watched out for."

I enjoy the quiet between us and the way Callahan continues to play before he finally drops his hands away. "I have to head back. I left Mason covering my side of the bar."

My eyebrows lift to the ceiling. "You left Mason in charge? That boy can't do more than pour beer."

He laughs. "Yeah, he mentioned that."

I start to rise, both of us laughing when we realize we're a little stuck. "I'd better get cleaned up."

"Me, too," I agree.

Callahan appears with a new shirt and a pair of jeans moments later, stopping when he sees me dressed. "Thank Christ. I was worried you were going back out in your underwear."

I glance at our linked hands as he leads me out. "Now, why would I go and do a thing like that?"

We step onto the sand and follow the path out to the beach. "You're acting like I didn't catch you skinny-dipping," he tells me, that testiness returning to his tone.

"I wasn't skinny dipping. It was dark, and my panties and bra are black. Anyone who saw me probably mistook it for a bikini."

"No, they didn't," he mutters. "What you were wearing isn't anything close to what decent folk wear swimming."

"You calling me indecent?"

"Yup," he answers.

The couple I passed on my walk stroll by. I was alone then.

I'm not now and it feels amazing. "So you're saying I shouldn't wear things like lacy panties and bras in front of you—"

"Trin."

"Or like thongs or edible panties and such?"

"*Trin.*"

"Do you like cherry or strawberry?"

"*Trin.* I have to get back to work!"

"I meant on your ice cream. Get your mind out of the gutter, soldier."

I try to storm off like I'm offended only for Callahan to wrap his arms me and lift me in the air. I squeak as he nibbles my neck.

"You really know how to drive a man crazy, you know that?" he murmurs against my ear.

"Is that good or bad thing?" I ask. I laugh when he doesn't answer. "Sounds like it's a good thing to me."

He lowers my feet to the ground. This time he's the one eyeing our intertwined fingers. "How did this happen?" he asks.

"You holding my hand?"

He quirks his eyebrow. "Among other things."

I shrug. "It was bound to happen."

He shakes his head and chuckles as we resume our pace. "Was it?"

"Oh, yeah. I mean we've been going steady for like three whole weeks now."

Callahan almost grounds to a halt at my comment, but then pushes forward. It's similar to people who are walking along, and suddenly remember something they forgot, but then say screw it anyway, and continue on their merry way.

"Something wrong?" I tease.

He regards me out of the corner of his eye and pretends to scowl. "Going steady for three weeks?" he repeats.

"Mmm-hmm," I say.

"Christ," he mumbles back.

"You're cute when you're all broody, Batman."

"I wish you wouldn't call me that."

My focus trails from his face and way down south. "You're right. You're definitely more like Thor, God of Thunder. After all, isn't he the one—" I pretend to fan myself. "*Whoo*, with the giant—"

"*Trin!*"

"I was going to say hammer. See there you go again, taking a perfectly innocent conversation straight into Smutville. Shame on you; trying to corrupt an innocent little thing like me."

He throws his head back and laughs, but then pulls me against him. I wind my arms around his neck, slowly losing my smile. For all I joke, I mean it when I say that I'm scared. I've never experienced this connection and draw I feel with Callahan.

His heart makes mine shatter into a million pieces all the while melting what remains, and his soul, while bruised and battered, holds strong in spite of the blows it's taken. Given what he's survived and endured, I'm in awe of him. That doesn't mean the pain he buries deep isn't something I long to spare him from.

The kiss he meets me with reignites my smile. I confess, that while it was his appearance that first made me want to know him, it's the man beneath all this muscle that makes me want to keep him.

I stiffen. The thing is, I won't be able to keep him long.

"Something wrong?" he asks.

Now doesn't feel like the right time to tell him I'll be leaving in September. In fact, it feels very wrong. I trust my instincts, hoping they won't steer me someplace neither of us wants to be.

"Just thinking about you," I answer him truthfully.

"All right," he says, taking my hand and leading us down the beach.

He quiets, growing almost tight-lipped. I'm not sure if it's because he doesn't believe me, or because he's having reservations about being with me. But as we reach the steps leading up to Your Mother's, I realize now isn't the time to ask, even when his hand slips away and he steps aside.

"After you," he says.

I tell myself there's no need to get upset—that he's not snubbing me and his reaction is only related to his need to return to work. But like I said, insecurity is a real bitch. I slide my discarded flip-flops back on and walk ahead toward the inside bar, not at all ready to leave him.

Poor Mason is beside himself, standing with his hands out as he tries to talk down a crowd of irate women demanding he make them some Hurricanes.

"Beer!" he says. "I can only pour beer. Doesn't anyone want beer?"

The women are screaming at him, making it clear that no, they don't drink Bud, Heineken, or anything in between. Mason's hefty shoulders slump when he sees Callahan.

"Thank God," he mumbles.

Callahan inches in front of me, appearing more than ready to put some space between us. I think I should say something clever—something to lure his grin before he leaves me. And maybe if it wasn't for Hunter and Blakeney showing up earlier, I could come up with something decent to say. Instead, I remain quiet, doubting everything he could feel about me, despite what happened at his place.

Callahan on the contrary has plenty to say, except he doesn't exactly use words. He hauls me to him, graciously and very vigorously reintroducing his tongue to my tonsils.

My spine bends backward with how hard his body and mouth press against all my right parts, and my foot is doing this jerky-twitchy thingy. I'd like to say I wrap my arms oh-so gracefully around his broad and manly shoulders, but they're too busy flailing like I'm falling from the sky because *yes*, it's *that* kind of kiss.

He pulls away and grins. "I have to get back to work,

baby," he says, loud enough for everyone to hear. "If you stick around until closing, I'll take you home."

I try to be all smooth-like and mature because that's the kind of gal I pretend to be. But there's no pretending. Nope. Not after that deep and very necessary exploration of his tongue.

Instead of "yes" or "sure", something like "yush" comes out of my mouth. He chuckles and releases me slowly, but not before shooting me a wink that no one misses.

I may or may not have Beyoncé strutted back to my cheering and *woot-woot-woot-ing* friends. But I do refrain from high-fiving them. After all, I am a lady.

Like Callahan promised, he drove me back to my place following closing and clean up. He pulls into my driveway, but doesn't punch in the security code when I offer it. "You don't want to come in?" I ask.

He runs his fingers along his steering wheel. "I better not. It's late and I haven't slept much these past couple of days."

I didn't say we were going to sleep. In fact, I'd planned to do anything but. I want him with me, and while he's been a gentleman—especially after recognizing how scared I was earlier—I'm hoping he'll change his mind and make love to me all night.

Yet as I watch his eyes grow distant, I'm reminded how rough these last few days have been for him. He does look tired, and more than a little sad.

I click out of my seatbelt and turn to rest my head against the seat. "How do you sleep?" I ask.

He swivels to face me, the change in his expression alerting me that he understands what I'm really asking. "Not well," he admits.

"Has it been like that since you've been back from war?"

"No, longer. I haven't had a good night sleep in years," he says. "When I first joined, the excitement and thrill of being part of the U. S. military kept me up. They reel you in, those recruiters, emphasizing all the lifetime benefits, building up the honor of serving and protecting your country, and making like you'll be a hero and someone who'll always be respected. 'You'll be a part of history, son,' one of them told me."

He leans back a little, as if wondering if I'm listening. It's only when he sees that I'm hanging on his every word that he continues. "That excitement turns to fear real quick when you realize you could actually die. And that respect? It may come good and strong from those people who appreciate your sacrifice. But it doesn't erase all those haters calling you a murderer to your face—or those screaming mobs yelling at you in a language you can't understand, and in a country that's not your own."

My eyes widen, but I'm quick to control my shock and anger. Callahan's expression remains neutral, and though the pain is evident by the rigidness in his posture, he keeps his voice low and steady. "You wonder if you'll be good enough. And when you are, you're given more opportunities to kill, put in situations that seem more suicidal than strategic, and sent on special assignments that the last team didn't come back from. So then you stop wondering, because you know you're good, and wonder instead when your luck will finally run out and whether you'll be the next one sent back home in a box."

He looks in the direction of the house. "Trin, given what I've seen and done, sometimes I don't know how I'm still here in one piece."

But he's not. For all he looks whole, his soul is busted up something awful.

"I don't know either," I tell him. "I'm just glad you're here with me." My eyes sting, but I manage a smile. "I can't imagine ever not meeting you."

Callahan cocks his head slightly, his stare softening with

enough kindness to cloak the ire and pain that lies beneath. He unsnaps his seatbelt and leans forward.

"Come here," he says, reaching for me.

Our lips part when they meet so our tongues can immediately play and explore. This kiss isn't like the heated ones before. It's slow, reassuring me that he's safe and that I shouldn't be afraid.

I slide my hand up, digging my fingers through his thick silky waves while his arms circle my waist. He holds me tenderly and so close I feel his warmth and the thud of his beating heart. For a moment, I fool myself into believing that I'm the one reassuring him. Maybe I am. So I give more of myself to our kiss, hoping he'll take a part of me with him so he's not so alone.

His hands slide over my waist to grip my hips before gradually loosening his hold. I watch him edge away, struggling it seems to let me go.

"I think I should leave," he says.

As much as I want him to stay, I don't ask him to. He needs space. I can see it, and sense it. I'm only hoping he doesn't pull completely away. "All right. Goodnight."

I reach for my purse and start to climb out when he says, "Wait. Don't leave yet." He hops out of the truck and jogs around the other side to open the door for me, offering me his hand to help me down.

"I want to make sure you get inside," he says.

He keeps my hand in his and leads me up the long driveway. "You let me walk up by myself the other night," I remind him.

He offers me a one shoulder shrug. "That's different. You weren't walking into an empty house."

He glances up, taking in the house when we reach it. "Can I ask you something personal?"

"You can ask me anything," I tell him truthfully.

He laughs a little. "You said your parents did volunteer work."

"That's right. They did so for years, and they still do locally."

"How is it that they came to live here?"

It's not the first time someone asked me this question. As a child, it made me uncomfortable. I had friends who didn't have much. And even though I did, it's something we never flaunted.

My parents bought us only what we needed, not just what we wanted to have. They kept my brother and I humble by taking us around the world and showing us what poverty really was, introducing us to those who didn't have much, so we'd see firsthand what it was like to be hungry, sick, and alone. They taught us the importance of compassion and how we should spend our lives demonstrating it to everyone we meet.

"Trin?" he says.

"Sorry," I say, pausing as we reach the bottom of my front steps. "My father comes from what people refer to as old Southern money. There's a lot of blood attached to those dollar signs, and even my granddaddy admitted he's not proud of how the family fortune was built." I push a strand of my hair behind my ear, feeling the brunt of what I'm telling him. "No one has ever come out and fully explained, like I said, there's a lot of shame. But it's understood that good people broke their backs to make my great granddaddy rich."

A lot goes unsaid in my words, but Callahan seems to understand. "It's not something many southerners with our degree of wealth discuss. And many like to pretend it didn't happen. But we know it did, and I'm not going to lie."

He nods like he understands. "All right," he says.

"What's your family like?"

He motions toward the large front doors. "Not like yours," he says.

The way he responds makes me think that his family is another sore spot in his life. After baring his soul about his experiences in the war, it's clear that he's already shared more than he's comfortable with. So instead of pressing for more, I lift up on my toes and kiss his cheek. "Okay," I whisper.

He smiles, sweeping a finger along my jaw. "Are you going to be okay by yourself?"

No. I'd rather be with you. Again it's what I think, but don't dare say aloud. I motion up the brick steps. "The alarm's set, and you may not believe it, but sometimes even I need some peace and quiet."

He chuckles. "You're right. I don't believe it."

I laugh, lifting my arms to embrace him when his hands reach around to stroke the small of my back.

"Do you want to go out to dinner tomorrow night?" he asks. "Maybe catch a movie?"

"Callahan Sawyer, are you asking me out on a date?" I say, trying not to gush and failing miserably.

His lovely baby blues twinkle. "What if I am?"

"Then I'll have to say yes," I answer.

"In that case, I'll pick you up hereafter your shift." He pauses, and then adds. "I didn't own a cell phone, but I bought one earlier today. I'll give you the number so you can call me to let me know when you're ready."

"Okay. Sounds good." I pull out my phone from my purse and send him a text so he'll have my number, too.

As soon as I'm done, he leans in and offers me a very small, but very alluring kiss. "Goodnight, Trin."

"Goodnight, Callahan," I respond, struggling to pry my hands off him.

Somehow I manage and hop up the steps, resetting the alarm after I slip inside and lock the door.

I hurry to the upstairs balcony to watch him leave. Anyone else passing him on the street wouldn't notice the darkness he's experienced, and how it squares his shoulders, tightens his stance, and evens his stare. At least I don't think so. But I see it, and maybe know it a little better now, too.

I only hope I can help him through it, and that he'll somehow use me to be his light.

Chapter Fourteen

Callahan

Boom.

"Yeah. Get some!"

Boom.

"Run, Cal, *run!*"

Boom.

"It's an ambush—Retreat. Jesus Christ, *retreat.*

Limbs fly. Maris's blood soaks my shirt. They're dead. All of them.

I curl inward, gathering the pillow around my ears. I tell myself they're just fireworks in the distance—that I'm *not* back in Iraq. But between Billy's death and all the blasts lighting up the sky, all I hear is enemy fire and all I see are my friends lying in pieces.

My breath is too fast to register, my pulse too quick to trace. I clasp my wrist, focusing on counting each beat. One-ten. One-twenty. One-thirty.

"Cal, help me. I don't want to die. *Help me!*"

"We're counting on you, Ranger."

Sweat soaks my sheets. I go back to counting my heartbeat. One-forty. One-fifty. How fast is too fast?

Fear rattles my body, making me convulse.

"Callahan?"

They're dead.

"Callahan, are you in here?"

I know they're dead.

"It's me, Trinity . . ."

God, please let me die with them.

"Oh, Jesus," my angel whispers. "Sweet Jesus."

The slamming of a door, the trample of steps rushing forward, and fingers sweeping along my sweat-soaked brow. "I'm going to take care of you. You hear me? You're safe, and-and strong, and you're going to be fine . . ."

I wrench away. She's wrong, dead wrong.

Another blast. Another death.

Something crashes to the floor. "Shit—I'm sorry," Trin says. "I'm so sorry."

The sound of pouring rain drifts in, growing louder, filtering the next blast. I don't know what's happening. Something pushes into my ears.

"Hey—*hey*. It's okay. Don't fight me. They're earplugs I bought to cushion the sound."

I shake my head, not understanding. Not caring to either. I need to run. Need to get the boys out. Need to carry Lewis. He's not moving. Christ, why isn't he moving?

I push up from my bed only to be wrenched back down.

Lips find mine, warm and sweet. I welcome them, taking the kiss deep and digging my fingers into hair as smooth as silk.

The mouth and body I crave and need withdraw abruptly. I haul both back, but again I'm denied.

"Later. I promise," she tells me. "Right now let me help you, okay?" She struggles to catch her breath. "I'm going to try to put these plugs in again, all right?"

I don't respond, waiting to understand. Something soft forces its way deep into my ear canal. This time I don't fight it.

"That's it," she says, her voice is muffled and the sound of pouring rain dims. "Just like that."

Next explosion. Next death. They're weak, those sounds,

but I jolt with each one.

"Lewis is dead," I tell her.

She pauses and smooths my hair. "He's at peace, Callahan. I swear he is."

Something in her voice makes me believe her. "Shhh," she says. "One more. One more and we're good."

Pressure against my ear, and the world fades. I remember a body curling around me. I remember hands stroking the length of my spine. I remember shaking. Why was I so cold?

Life ends.

But *she* is with me.

Chapter Fifteen

Trinity

My head was still spinning from my morning with Callahan when I arrived at the beach. But reality hit me the moment I saw how bad the waves were and found my team struggling to save a couple of swimmers who were caught in the riptide. With four lifeguards down, I ended up jumping in the water with my clothes on to rescue a little boy. It's not the first time I'd saved someone from drowning, but this little boy, whose face was so white with fear, hit me especially hard.

I didn't notice Callahan arrive. My team and I were too busy trying to make sure everyone was safe and accounted for. But there he is, waiting patiently while the sheriff, the owner of Magenta Groves, the EMTs and I conference to discuss everything that happened. Like the rest of my team, I pushed myself to my breaking point. But it was saving that little boy drifting away that well-neared choked the life out me. I'm tired and want nothing more than to leave with Callahan. But I try not to let it show as I listen to each man speak.

The sheriff nods. "The other beaches pulled their swimmers out when they got wind that Magenta Groves was closing shop. Just so you know, your executive decision likely helped save a lot of lives all over the island."

I smile at Hale since it was his call. "I'd expect no less

from my second in command," I tell them.

With the owner's permission, Hale and I step away.

"So, I'm you're second in command?" Hale asks, smirking in that way that makes all those pretty gals chasing him swoon.

"Of course," I tell him. "And after today, I think you deserve a promotion and a raise."

"A raise, too?" he says.

I pat his back. "That's right. I'm going to make sure you get that buck fifty an hour extra if it kills me."

He laughs, but then glances up when one of the ambulances pulls away. One of the men, he and Mason pulled out is stable, but given his age, they're taking him to the local hospital to make sure he's okay.

"It could have been bad," Hale says, his humor fading as the ambulance disappears. "Real bad. It didn't take long for those waves to go from bad to worse, and for the riptide to drag people under."

"I know." I look to where Callahan is sitting on the sand. To any outsider, he looks like someone simply taking everything in. But I recognize that detached stare in his gaze, similar to the way I'd found him last night. The two men sprawled along the sand just moments ago, along with the little boy being cared for must have triggered more of those terrible memories.

"Lewis is dead," he called out last night when his PTSD hit him hard.

Had he carried Lewis's body out from the ambush he spoke of? The way he seems to stare out into the distance, makes me think he's carried his share of fallen friends.

I shudder. Today might have been something out of a bad dream for me. But for years, war had been his everyday nightmare.

Hale nudges me with his elbow. "Why don't you check on him?" he says. "I'll go around and make sure the team's getting the stragglers off the beach."

I pat his arm appreciatively. I didn't realize how lost in my thoughts I was until Hale touched me. "Thanks, Hale."

My feet kick back the moist sand as I ease down to Callahan's side. He frowns when he sees me and wraps the large blanket folded at his side around me. It's one of those we use for emergencies, I wonder briefly which guard he asked for it, but I'm so touched by the gesture, I don't wonder for very long.

"You look cold," he points out.

"I'm all right." It's what I claim, but when I feel the warm skin of his shoulder press against my cheek, I realize how chilled I am in these soaked clothes.

His hand skims down my arm and over the quickly forming goose bumps. The days have been so hot. But beneath the overcast sky, I feel that same bitter cold I felt when I went after that little boy. I saw him out there, but the current was taking him out to sea so fast, it took me a long time to catch him, and another few minutes to find him when the ocean dragged him under.

The sand was kicking up from the bottom, making it hard to see. But God led me to him, and gave me the strength I needed to get him to shore. He was there for us all of us, helping us save everyone we needed to despite our low numbers.

"You followed me here," I say, pointing out the obvious.

"I couldn't stay in bed without you," he says, his words warming me in a way this blanket never could.

He gathers my body around him, like I'm not soaked to the bone, and like it's the most natural thing in the world. "I also didn't want to leave you out here on your own. If things got bad, I wanted to be around to help."

The deep thrum in his voice causing me to melt further against him. "Thank you," I tell him.

In the quiet that takes us in like the breeze skimming across the sand, I remember how it felt to lay against him all night. I draped my body against his. Not only because of my need to feel close to him, but because he seemed to drift away. I don't want to admit how much he scared me, or how I worried he'd run out into night. But I can't ignore what I saw, or pretend his reaction was no big deal.

"Last night was really hard on you," I say, wondering if he can even hear me with how softly I speak.

"Yeah," he offers, but not much more.

"Is it always that bad around fireworks?" I press.

"Don't know," he says, appearing to hesitate to even answer that much.

I feel him trying to put some space between us, so when he rests his cheek against my head, I'm grateful for the closeness it seems to bring us.

"It's the first time I've heard any real explosions since I've been back," he admits, the roughness in his voice and his sudden response taking me by surprise. "I don't think they would have been as bad, but things have gotten worse for me since learning Billy died." He huffs. "For all I know, maybe it still would have been bad, even if nothing had happened to Billy."

"Have you been to counseling?" I ask.

He shrugs. "I tried it, briefly. But I couldn't keep going. I wasn't ready to talk—to put it all out there. All I wanted to do was to forget."

"But you haven't forgotten," I say carefully.

"No. You don't forget things I've seen," he says. "Those memories etch into your bones and become a part of you."

"I'm sorry," I say, wishing I could say something better.

My arms fasten around his waist. I want to take away some of that pain and ease his suffering. But I know I can't, so I wait, resting my head against his chest. It's my way of reminding him he's not alone, and maybe to remind myself he's also with me.

He pauses then angles his head, examining me closer. "You all right?"

I nod quickly, but then pull up the edge of the towel to

cover my face when a lump claims my throat and my eyes burn with impending tears. Callahan draws me closer, speaking low against my ear.

"What's wrong?" he asks. When I don't answer he says, "Tell me why you're crying, baby."

Something about the way he calls me "baby" is so comforting that after a moment, I'm able to rein in my emotions to some respectable degree. But I'll admit, some of that fear I felt escapes my eyes and trails down my cheeks.

I use the towel to wipe my face and sniffle. Crying is not something I do often. But when it happens, it's like my soul is bleeding tears. I don't like this feeling, and every last emotion that comes with it, and I especially don't like it now. Everyone's okay, I remind myself. Everyone.

It's not the first time I've had a post-rescue breakdown. But the situation today, coupled with the night I spent with Callahan makes my fears more brutal and raw. I think it's because my vulnerability appears to dismantle more in his presence. It's not a bad thing, I reason. It's simply the way he affects me. Everything around him—all these emotions—be it sadness or joy I feel to the extreme when he's near. Yet I wouldn't want it any other way.

With Callahan with me, my world is simply better.

Feather-like kisses sweep along my temple. "I don't like to see you cry," he tells me.

"Sorry, but I'm not always as happy as people think," I confess. "And sometimes, I really get sad."

He waits for me to say more, and I don't disappoint him. "I don't have to tell you that there's a lot bad in the world," I begin. "Through actions of others, or sometimes like today because of chance. I've had a lot of good, and smiles, and have laughed more times than I've cried. But some people haven't been as blessed." My gaze falls to my feet where my toes are digging into the sand. "I can't explain it, but when I see others hurting, it breaks my heart."

"I think I understand," he says.

Maybe he does.

He smiles softly in the quiet that follows, only to ultimately close his eyes and take a breath. When he opens his eyes again, I watch his stare grow distant. He's no longer with me, not fully. He's remembering, be it because of what he saw here today, or everything he's experienced over these last few days.

Watching the way he withdraws, destroys me. Yet there's nothing I can do right now to help him.

I kiss him briefly, wanting my lips to linger, but knowing that now isn't the time. "I still have to finish up here," I tell him. "Why don't you head back to your place? I'll be there as soon as I'm done."

He nods and doesn't argue, which pains my insides even more. I still don't know Callahan well. What I do know is how much I want to.

And how fast I'm falling in love with him.

I remain at the beach a lot longer than I intend. By the time I pull into Callahan's gravel driveway and skid to a stop, it's almost dark. I don't mean to run, but I do, anxious to reach him.

The house is dark when I hurry in, exactly like it was the previous the night. This time, instead of that horrible silence I encountered yesterday evening, the sound of pouring rain blasts from his bedroom. He's listening to the CD I purchased him, even though there's no noise in the distance. I don't know what he's doing, I only hope that it's helping.

"Callahan?"

I stop short when I find him sprawled across his large bed. His arm is draped over his face and the opened container of earplugs is on the nightstand to his right. I don't think he can see or hear me, but somehow, he realizes I'm there.

He drops his arm away and sits up, his eyelids heavy from more than just the lack of sleep. Callahan is a man exhausted by life and all he's endured in its grip. I sit beside him and pass my hand along his bare chest.

"Hi," I whisper.

My voice is so low, I'm not sure he can hear me with all the white noise despite that I notice he's not using the earplugs I'd brought him.

He brushes my hair from my shoulders. "Hey," he says back.

"Did you have dinner?" I ask.

"No," he replies. "It's been a bad night."

Because of those awful memories, he doesn't add. "Are you hungry?" I ask.

He nods, and rubs his face, searching for something to say. But he's already shown me enough.

I lean in, offering him a brief kiss. "I'll make you something to eat. Why don't you lie back and try to relax?"

When he doesn't move, I press my hand against his shoulder. He clasps it, his face on mine as I edge him down to the mattress.

The way he holds my hand against his shoulder, I think he means for me to join him. But then it slips away. I watch him as I back away. Something in his leaden stare telling me that despite the white noise CD, the voices of his demons continue to whisper.

I head into the kitchen and wash my hands, then fish around for something to make him. I settle on grilled cheese and tomato soup given that it's fast and easy to prepare. It's cold in the house with the A.C. blasting, but I think the hum from the motor is the reason it's on so high.

I make several sandwiches and cut them up into tiny triangles that he can dip into the soup. It's not much of a meal, but we both need to eat, and I need to get back to him.

When I make it back to his room, he's covering his eyes again, but appears more restless, clenching and unclenching his fists like he's raring for a fight. I reach to stroke his foot so he knows I'm back, but end up startling him instead. He jolts and kicks out, striking my packed tray.

The soup sloshes against the sides of the bowls. I barely keep everything from spilling. He hurries to his feet, trying to help me steady the tray.

"Sorry," he says.

He's breathing fast. It's not as bad as last night, but it's far from the slow methodical breaths he usually takes. It scares me. *He* scares me. I don't want him to fall back into that darkness I found him in—that terrible place where he sees his friends dying around him.

I place the tray on the dresser and face him, his hands gripping my hips when mine glide along his chest. My stare latches onto his. But the way he takes me in, I'm no longer certain that panic and trauma are what's escalating his breathing.

My focus trails along every inch of his form. A small scar mars the spot below his right nipple. I'm not sure if it's an old wound from Iraq or something from childhood. Right then, I don't care and bend to trace it with my tongue.

His breath catches. In my exploration I see another scar. This one's thinner, longer. It must have been painful, whatever caused it, but it doesn't detract from his beauty nor does it discourage me from tasting it. My tongue continues to discover him, going down until I'm almost to his belly button.

Callahan's hands slide along my curving spine, stopping where my T-shirt has ridden up to rest against my lower back. When his fingers skim the edge, I'm certain he means to pull it over my head, and strip me out of it. As scared as I am, I won't stop him. I want to lie naked beneath him and have him push inside of me. Just like I want his hips to pound and grind with each thrust.

The thought of him pumping into me makes me dizzy with desire and sends chills streaking down my limbs. Is it normal to be drawn to someone so sexually? I'm not sure, but I don't care. All I know is that I need him.

No one's ever evoked such primal need like Callahan. I envision myself spreading my legs for him, him sliding in, and working me until I cry out with pleasure . . . just as I did this morning when he roused an orgasm with his long, thick fingers.

I continue to kiss the planes of his hard stomach. I'm past his navel, and want to go lower. Yet instead of freeing me of my shirt, he clasps my elbows and guides me to him, stamping his lips on mine.

His kiss is desperate and needy, the kiss of a man who's dying and wants to be saved. I return his affection, circling his neck—wanting to be the one to spare him from his pain and lure him away from his past. With the weight of my body, I press against him, falling with him and onto the bed. I lift off enough just to rid myself of my shirt. But when I dip my head to renew our kiss, he turns his head away.

"What's wrong?" I ask, panting softly.

He doesn't answer. I stroke his soft hair, letting my fingertips skim down to his beard, hoping to speak to him with my touch.

Instead of allowing me to soothe him, he rams his eyes shut. The movements of his chest so pronounced, they lift me with him.

"Callahan," I say. "Please talk to me."

Slowly he turns to face me, the fire lighting his irises so intense, my hand freezes in place. "I want to make love to you," he rasps. "All night if you let me."

I nod, barely able to control myself. "It's what I want, too."

I bend forward to kiss him, only to have him jerk his chin away from me. I don't understand what he's doing, or why he appears so torn. Can't he see how bad I need him?

He shakes his head, clenching his jaw tight as he speaks. "Not like this, Trin. Not the way I am."

I try to reach for him only to pull away before my skin

makes contact, my hand shaking with how much I desire him.

Callahan grasps my fingers, bringing them to him, his eyes closing as he runs his cheek along my knuckles. "I want you so bad," he breaths against my skin. "And I want it to be good. Right now, I'm not okay. Do you understand?"

I don't answer because I know how bad he hurts. Yet that doesn't stop me from wanting to give him pleasure. It's what his body demands of me, and the one thing I can do to make him feel better . . . if he'll just let me.

"Trin," he groans. "Don't cry, baby."

I don't realize that I am until the first tear escapes. He sits us up, carefully holding my face as he presses small kisses to my eyes, the tip of my nose, and lips. "Let me get through tonight, and the next time we're alone, I'll prove to you just how bad I want you . . ."

Chapter Sixteen

Callahan

I wake sometime around ten. My first instinct is to reach for Trin. But she's not here. My bed feels strangely barren without her. I rub my eyes, but then drop my hand irritably against the mattress.

Once again I'm in my self-imposed isolation. But that sweet little thing has more than proven it's no longer where I want to be.

Annoyed and pissed at myself, I shift out of bed. The more I think about last night, the more my fury builds. I hate how there are days where I think I'm all right. Not great, but functioning and doing well enough. But then that darkness creeps up on me, reminding me it's still there and threatening to kill me where I stand. Maybe it was Billy's death that started it all. Or maybe it was fireworks. Whatever it is, I'm tired of it.

I'm so screwed in the head I couldn't give Trin the one thing she wanted. Hell, the one thing we both wanted.

The last thing I remember was holding her close as I did my best *not* to remember. Despite the CD she'd brought me, nothing could drown out the explosions ingrained in my memories. They banged around my skull like falling bowling balls, keeping me from touching her like I wanted to.

The blasts I heard were reminiscent of the day that missile struck the Range Rover Billy was in. The damn thing detonated right in front us. If it hadn't been for Darton at the wheel of our vehicle, we would've hit our fellow Rangers head on and joined them in the afterlife.

Darton maneuvered our SUV behind a crumpled old structure, shielding us from incoming fire. We split up, hitting the ground running. Some ran to pull Billy out and sort through the unmoving bodies trapped inside. The rest of us were supposed to cover them. Instead we lost our shit. We didn't fire, we didn't cover. What we did was shoot anyone stupid enough to cross us.

I killed eleven men in under thirty minutes. One after the other like some kind of twisted carnival game I couldn't possibly win, but continued to play. Nothing stood in my way. No mercy, no conscious, *nothing*.

I aimed. I fired. I sent those bastards straight to hell. And considering what I did, and how I did it, I know one day I'll meet them there.

I lean against the dresser and grind my teeth. Last night was four kinds of fucked up. A mix of beauty and ugly. Peace and violence.

Trin stood before me, her body pure and untouched by the trials and vices of life. But I couldn't taint her with the sin I'd committed and was reliving. I didn't want to see her perfect face, while the imperfections of my life poked at my soul and reminded me of the deeds I'd done. And I didn't want to touch her with those same hands that aimed that rifle and took all those lives.

Not then.

She cried, like she thought I didn't want her. But she's all I ever wanted, even though I never knew it.

I flop back down on the bed and adjust the pillow behind my head. Despite our rough night, I can't help laughing when I think about how she used to bug the ever lovin' shit out of me. And how the day she first ran with me on the beach, I actually tried to run *away* from her.

My smile vanishes. Now all I want to do is run to her, lift her in my arms, and not think about ever letting go. When she's not with me, it's like something important is missing from my life, like air—no, not air, more like sunshine. She's my brightness, my light, even though I never intended her to be.

I tuck my hands behind my head, staring at the silver ceiling fan I installed the previous week. I'm not sure what's happening between me and Trin. I just know it extends past the way we've kissed and touched. While I wasn't prepared to feel what I'm feeling, or how quickly it's happened, I can't deny what this woman means to me.

Christ. Whatever this thing is that Trin and I have, it's serious. I may not have wanted it, looked for it, and tried to shove it away. But it's definitely something I don't want to be without.

And I plan to show her tonight.

"Here you go, Mr. Perrington." I slide the crazy old coot his shot of Captain Morgan so he can take his "vitamin" as he calls it.

He raises his glass and grins. "Much obliged, Spanky."

I cringe at the name, but don't correct him. If he keeps taking that damn blue pill and meeting up with the widow Levine like he's been doing, the poor bastard doesn't have a lot of years left.

My hand snags a beer mug to fill. I'm waiting on Trin. I sent her a text telling her to stop by after her shift. Aside from a reply back saying she would, I haven't heard from her.

We ate the grilled cheese she made last night in bed. I focused on chewing and sipping the soup so I wouldn't have to look at her small sad face. Every few breaths, I stole glimpses her way. She didn't take my rejection well, even though I tried to cushion it for the both of us.

Sean slides into the empty bar stool beside old man Perrington and places a set of empty pitchers in front of me. "Thanks, Callahan," he says when I set them beneath the tap to fill. "How you doing, Mr. Perrington?" he asks him.

"Real good," Mr. Perrington answers, smiling when the widow Levine saunters in wearing her best Sunday dress. He slips off the stool. "I'm going to get me some tonight."

Yes, he is, based on that limp that has nothing to do with his bad knee. He shuffles toward the widow Levine who's pretending not to notice him.

"Remind me never to ask him how he's doing," Sean says. He makes a face. "Now all I can picture is loose skin flapping in the wind when he fucks her."

This time, I'm the one making a face. "Come on, Sean. Did you have to share that?"

"Just get me a shot of whisky so I can clear all that creepy Grandpa sex out of my head," he says. He reaches for the shot I pour him, but pauses before taking a sip. "You don't think he goes down on her, do you?"

"Christ, Sean," I say. "Just drop it already."

"Cause she's had like seven kids," he says, ignoring me. "I hear she was some kind of dancer in her day, but I don't think that shit stays the same after seven kids no matter how good you can tap dance." He tosses back the shot and glances at Mr. Perrington again. I make the mistake of looking up in time to see the old timer's hand disappear under the table and widow Levine jerk up, giggling like a naughty teen.

Sean and I exchange glances. "I'm going to need another one," he tells me.

Hell, I might need one, too.

He looks at me again. "Do you think she—"

"Sean, just shut up already. I don't need another visual." I point to one of the waitresses. "Go and talk to Loretta over there."

He frowns. "Don't you mean Lindsey?"

Whatever. "Sure. Talk to her. I'm sure she'll keep your mind off things."

Like Sean, Lindsey likes to talk, excessively. She's also been getting too close and searching for any excuse to hang out with me behind the bar. I don't want Trin to think she has anything to worry about because she doesn't. I meant it when I told her I only think of her.

I'm only wondering what's keeping her. Her team's already been here an hour and she's still not . . .

Becca saunters in, dressed in a way that causes a few locals to whistle when they spot her. She looks nice, but she's not who keeps my interest. Trin trails in behind her, showing me what's kept her.

Normally, she bounces in wearing her lifeguard bathing suit and a pair of shorts, or sometimes shorts and a shirt if she squeezes in a shower before she leaves work. Sand typically coats her feet or her hair's still damp from freshening up. It's never bothered me, nor detracted from her beauty. But tonight . . . tonight I have to say she's more than beautiful.

Her hair's extra shiny and falls loose around her bare shoulders. One of those black strapless tops wraps around her breasts, riding up enough to give me a peek of her waist. A long colorful skirt flows behind her, falling just above her black sandals and freshly painted toes.

Where Becca's met with wolf-whistles, Trin's met with "oh's" by the local women, and "don't you look pretty?" from the men.

No, she doesn't look pretty. My girl looks exceptional—sexy and innocent in one alluring package. Lord help me, I can't tear my eyes from her as she makes her way toward me.

She takes a seat in front of me, but doesn't quite look up, not right away. When she does, I catch a small trace of a blush.

"Hi," she says, smiling lightly.

"You took a shower," I say, like a dumbass.

She laughs into her hands then drops them down. Maybe it's me, but it's like she's suddenly shy or something. Why is she acting shy around me now?

"I was trying to look nice for you," she admits.

"You always look nice," I tell her. I mean what I say, but somehow she seems disappointed.

She turns her head from side to side like she's trying to think of what to say. What the hell? Trin *always* has something to say. I'm guessing I'm supposed to say something about her clothes.

"It's a cute dress," I offer.

Apparently that wasn't it. Whatever's left of her smile is now long gone. "Thanks," she mumbles. Her focus drops to the bar. "It's actually a skirt. I . . ." She lifts her gaze. "I know last night wasn't good."

"It wasn't," I agree. "But it had nothing to do with you."

"I shouldn't have cried." It's what she says, but her eyes shimmer anyway. "I know that didn't help, and probably made it worse for you. I'm sorry. I just—"

Lindsey, taps my arm. "Excuse me, darlin', coming through."

I glance at her as she flounces by, annoyed. She could have slipped behind me. There was plenty of space. When I return my attention to Trin, her stare drifts from me to Lindsey and then back.

I frown, not sure what's bothering her. "What is it?"

She starts to tell me when Lindsey passes. This time, she slaps my ass with her tray. "Sorry, not a lot of room back here," she says, laughing.

Her flirting needles me. But what she did was meant to bother Trin. It doesn't take a scholar to recognize she's upset now. She straightens in her seat, pretending to play with her hair so she doesn't have to glance directly up.

I tickle her chin. "Hey. You all right?"

Instead of answering, she lifts her stare, watching as Lindsey stomps away in a huff. But I don't care about

Lindsey. I only care about this sexy little kitten in front of me who clearly has no idea how bad I want to carry her out of here and into my bed.

"Tell me what you were saying," I ask Trinity, softening my voice and folding my arms across the bar.

The corners of her soft pink lips lift a little. "I was trying to tell you that I really like you," she admits. "And I wanted to show you by dressing up."

She doesn't think I see her. Or notice that she's made an effort. Maybe it's because she's not used to the attention she deserves.

When she walked in, the locals and tourists were blown away by Becca, like always. But everyone saw Trin as pretty and sweet when she intended to be more, at least for me.

Tonight, she wants to be more than that cute young woman everyone gravitates to dance and laugh with. She wants to be seen as more than everyone's pal. But to me, she's already that, and more.

She smiles a little and glances down. "I wish I knew what you were thinking," she says.

"Come here, and I'll tell you," I say, my voice gruff.

Her lips separate ever so slightly. She's surprised and maybe a little nervous about what I have to say. Regardless, she leans forward when I do, meeting me halfway. My hand cups the back of her neck and my deep voice lowers to whisper in her ear. "Your hair's shiny and you smell good. I like the skirt. But the way you look right now makes me want to rip it off you and yank your panties down with my teeth."

I smash my lips against hers, slipping my tongue in briefly to play. Before I finish pulling away, I peg her with a look and grin that lets her know I intend to make good on my promise tonight.

Chapter Seventeen

Trinity

If I was wearing socks, Callahan would have knocked them right off with that kiss. But his words? Sweet baby Jesus in the manger playing with a rattle, considering how his tongue just made friends with mine, my mouth feels awfully dry.

He holds my stare and releases me slowly, but maybe it's not slow enough. I slip off the stool and crash to the floor the moment he let's go. I hop up in the time it takes him to leap over the bar. Let's just say there have been more graceful moments in my life.

He clasps my elbow to steady me. "You all right?"

"Oh yes, fine. Totally fine," I say, slapping at my skirt like my butt doesn't feel like it's been spanked with a two by four.

He tilts his head and smirks. Yeah. He knows what he's doing to me. I only wish I could do the same to him back.

"Callahan, think you could leave your girl and do your job?" Lindsey barks.

"I gotta go," he says quietly, reaching down to play with my hair.

"All right," I tell him, wishing I didn't have to stop looking at those pretty eyes.

The strands of my hair slip through his fingers as he walks away, passing Lindsey without bothering to acknowledge her. It's a sweet gesture meant to assure me, but I have to say, I'm really starting to dislike that girl.

For the most part, I've done my best to ignore her, the other waitresses— and every other woman who struts in here seeking Callahan's attention. And considering how many there's been, I think I've done all right. Yet for all I think Lindsey is trashy, I can't deny that she's pretty—beautiful even. Aside from Becca, she's probably the most stunning person here.

I can't say I don't see her as competition because I do. She wants Callahan, and even though he doesn't seem to want her, he didn't want me either. At least not at first.

Becca hurries to my side when she catches me heading toward our table. "What happened?" she whispers. "You were supposed to go for sensual and smooth. Not Bridget Jones meets Aquaman or whatever the fuck works here."

I grin, keeping my voice to a murmur. "He told me he wants to pull my panties off with his teeth."

This time Becca's the one stumbling. She laughs as I right her and throws her arm around me. "Trin. Holy shit!"

"I *know*. Why do think I fell off the stool?"

"Okay. You're forgiven." She leads me away from our group and to the end of the deck. Almost in perfect sync, we lean our arms on the banister and pretend to look at the beach. "So you're going home with him, right?"

"I want to," I admit.

She tilts her head. "So what's wrong? You scared?"

"Yeah. I am."

"Why? It's not your first time," she reminds me. "And you were so willing last night."

"Last night, I was scared, too, despite how willing I was," I confess. I adjust my arms over the railing. "Besides, it is going to be my first time, with *him*."

"But you know what to do, right?" she asks.

"In theory. I mean, I'm no virgin. And I'm not going to pretend like I didn't have sex with Hunter for two years. But Callahan is a man capable of making me orgasm with our clothes *on*. He knows how to make me feel good. I'm not so sure I can do the same for him."

"Trin, you gave it right back the other day when you pulled down his shorts. You told me so yourself."

I laugh. "No, more like you dragged it out of me."

She bats her hands. "Oh, details, details."

Which was exactly what she had demanded. I didn't share much, but she understood what I'd done well enough.

She twists her back and leans against the railing. "What is it about him that worries you so much?"

I stare out to the ocean, trying to word my thoughts so they actually make sense. "For starters, I thought I knew and felt passion. When I've had sex in the past it's been . . . nice."

"Nice?"

I raise my eyebrows. "You've described it the same way."

She fixes me with one of her slyer grins. "I'm a southern lady. 'Nice' is the polite way of saying I didn't fall asleep or think about what I was going to buy online during the experience."

"Yeah. Tell me about it." I roll my eyes, remembering, but then I pause, thinking about my brief yet very intimate experiences with Callahan. "I'd never describe what's happened between me and Callahan as 'nice.'"

"No?" she teases.

Oh, no. "But as amazing as it was, I couldn't help but think of Hunter."

"*What*?" she practically screeches. "Why on earth would you be thinking about Sponge Bob when you're getting naked with Hercules?"

I nudge her. "I didn't. But afterward, I couldn't help it . . . just not in the way that you're imagining."

"Then kindly explain. Because when it comes to Callahan and Hunter there simply is no comparison."

She's right. To a point. "Becca, look, as much as I don't want to, I can't help wondering if I'd been a better lover, Hunter wouldn't have looked elsewhere."

"Trin, Hunter is an asshole. Instead of looking at you, the way he should have, he was always preoccupied making sure everyone else was looking at him. He's an arrogant son of a bitch who felt he could have anyone. If it hadn't been that slut Blakeney, it would have been someone else."

"Maybe. Maybe not, Becks. But there's a difference between getting someone off, and rocking someone's world. You've told me so yourself. Hunter most certainly didn't rock my world, county, or even as much as my zip code. So how can I be sure he didn't feel the same way about me?"

"Callahan intimidates you, doesn't he?" she asks gently.

"Yeah," I answer quietly. "I don't want to embarrass myself."

"Are you planning on juggling sex toys while dressed up like Elvis?"

I laugh. "Ah, no. That wasn't the plan."

"Then you won't embarrass yourself," she tells me.

"I'm not so sure."

She pushes my hair back and considers me. "Trin, you're one of the most fearless people I know—whether you believe so or not. What is it about Callahan that has you all aflutter? And don't tell me it's the sex, because I know you well enough to know there's more to it."

"Callahan's special, Becks. I think . . ." I nibble on my bottom lip, wrestling with whether I should come clean, and more than a little nervous to do so.

"You think what?"

Becca is my best friend in the whole entire world—The one person who completely gets me. Even still, it's hard to say the words, but I manage to meet her square in the face when I finally do. "I think I'm in love with him."

Her eyes widen briefly, but then her expression changes to one I can't place. "You only just met him," she says, looking away from me onto the sand below us. "And you're only now getting to know him."

"I know what I feel," I insist, recognizing she's trying to

talk me out of things, and downplaying my emotions. It upsets me because I know what Callahan means to me and because she knows I don't use that word lightly.

"I'm not simply attracted to him. I know that's how it started, but it's not what it's become. I *need* him, Becca. Need to hear his deep voice, and feel his warmth when he tucks me against him." I clasp her hand, speaking gently and trying to get her understand. "He shares his soul, knowing I'll listen with my whole heart. And when he kisses me, I never want him to stop. It's like something's missing when we're apart. Something I can't stand being without."

She turns back to meet me eye to eye, her features more solemn than I've seen in a long time. "Then I think you're in serious trouble, Trin—Hear me out," she says, quickly when I try to argue. "You may think you're falling in love with him. But that man's already there. You don't see the way he looks you, the way he takes you in like no one else matters. And that night of the brawl, he wasn't just angry some guy had touched you. He was genuinely scared something could happen to you." She purses her lips as if afraid to continue. "Men, they don't behave like that over someone they know in passing. They get that way over the women they love."

I cover my mouth, a little shaken by what she has to say, and how she phrased it. It's one thing to think someone likes you. It's another thing for someone who knows you—as well as Becca knows me—to flip it in a way that demonstrates what you've failed to see.

She sighs, her beautiful face heartbreakingly sad. "Trin, you're leaving in September. Now's not a good time to fall in love," she says.

"I—"

She shakes her head, cutting me off, and returning her attention to that sea none of us ever want to know life without. "Don't tell me you won't go, because you will. It was always your plan to travel the world and help those in need. It's what your parents instilled in you, and what you were born and bred to do." She swallows hard, surprising me by wiping away a tear. "You're not going to give up helping villages full of people to help one man, no matter what you feel. I know you better than that."

I lean in close and wrap my arms around her. "Why are you crying?"

"Because I wish you were that selfish, Trin—to stay behind and be with all of us who love you. But you're not. Why do you think this summer is so important to us? Why do you think we're working for a few dollars an hour instead of using our hard-earned degrees to make real money? We want to be with you, Trin—me, Hale, Sean, and Mason—the five of us together one last time."

"You act like we'll never see each other." I say it to make her feel better, but it's a fear that's crossed my mind too many times. Growing up often means moving on, and far away from those who know and love you best.

She wipes another tear. "You may not be going to war, girl, but that doesn't mean it's not dangerous. Something can happen to you out there. Something bad. But that won't stop you, will it? You'll still go."

"I *have* to," I say, my tone splintering. "Look, I've always had my heart set on volunteering all over the world—just like my parents did. But I'll admit, now that I've met Callahan, it's like my life is imploding around me. I don't want to go— not like I did before. But I can't back out. There're people with worse problems than me who need help."

"So you'll go?" she asks. "No matter who you leave behind?" She shakes her head again when I don't answer. "Trin, if that's the case, I don't know what to tell you."

I rest my cheek against her shoulder. "I'm sorry."

"Sorry for what? Leaving us? Or leaving him?"

I'm seconds from losing it, and barely manage to answer. "All of it."

She sniffs, squaring her shoulders as she tries to rein in her emotions. "Have you even told him yet?"

My hands slip off her shoulders. "No."

"*Why?*"

"Becks, I'm the only one he has to talk to. And he's been through a lot. If I tell him I'm leaving, he'll close up. I have to be there for him for as long as I can."

"Until you up and leave him," she says, slowly.

I don't answer, not right away. Mostly because she's right. "Do you think I shouldn't be with him?" I finally ask.

"I don't see how either of you will be able to stay apart. Not given what he means to you, and what you seem to mean to him." She embraces me, holding me tight. "Trin, I don't know what's going to happen. All I can tell you is I don't think it's going to end well. For either of you."

Chapter Eighteen

Callahan

Jed flips over the last chair so the afternoon crew can clean the floors before they open the bar. The only chair still perched on its legs is the one Trin's sitting on. I asked her to wait for me after Jed announced closing and she started to pile out with her friends. She seemed hesitant to stay, and for a moment, I wasn't sure if she would. But she did. And I'm glad.

Except for Lindsey, all the waitresses hurry out the second they're done counting their tips. Jed glances from Lindsey and Trin before meeting me with a smirk. I'm not sure what he's thinking until I see Lindsey walk toward the door. She stops beside Trin and turns around, smiling in a way I know means trouble.

"Hey, Callahan. If you ever want a real woman, instead of a little girl, be sure to give me a call."

I train my glare on her, pissed she's insulted Trin. "What the *hell*—"

"He has a real woman," Trin says sweetly, as if I didn't say anything. She rises, her smile fading when she pegs Lindsey with a hard stare. "Watch your mouth around me, and your hands around him. He doesn't belong to you."

I'm already to them, but something in the way Trin's watching Lindsey flat out shows that my girl's not playing around. Lindsey sees it, too, and backs away. Trin keeps her attention on her and all the way out the door until she speeds away in her rusty pick-up.

Trin's riled. And even though she has nothing to worry about, I have to admit her claim over me gets me hot.

Jed moves forward, chuckling and starts to lock the front door. "I'll take care of it if you want to head out," I tell him.

He turns to Trin and smiles knowingly. "All right, fine by me."

I lock the door behind him and switch off most of the lights, except for the ones over the dance floor. Trin, so confident seconds before, seems skittish.

"Do you have a lot more to do?" she asks.

"Just one more thing," I say.

I move to the jukebox, scanning through the songs until I find one that works and fish out a dollar. The first chords from Jason Aldean's remake of *Heaven* ring out as I make my way back to my girl.

"Will you dance with me?" I ask her.

Ah, and there's that smile I've missed all night. "I'd love to," she whispers.

My arms immediately circle her waist. I bend forward so she can slip her hands around my neck. Listening to the lyrics, and how the acoustic guitar builds the melody, I want so bad to kiss her. But as our bodies settle in closer, I know once I start, I won't want to stop.

We sway back and forth. I'm not much of dancer, but the beat and everything about Trinity seems right. We fall into a perfect, natural rhythm. And while her sweet perfume, and how soft she feels, only make me want to pull her closer, I keep my hold gentle. At least at first.

Halfway through song, I draw her closer and curl around her, using the whiskers on my chin to tickle her bare shoulder.

I mean to tease her, and make her laugh. Instead she sighs softly, her small frame melding with mine. As close as she is, I can feel her heartbeat, and how fast it's racing.

"Do I scare you?" I ask.

She takes her time answering. "Yes."

"I'd never do anything to hurt you," I promise against her skin.

She moans barely above a breath, moving her lips close to my ear. "It's not what I'm afraid of."

"Then what is it?" My hand travels up beneath her hair, to trace slow circles between her shoulder blades.

She shudders, her cheeks flushing with heat. "*That*," she says. "You make me feel so good. I want to be able to do the same to you."

I take in her delicate features, how they're intermixed with that same desperation and longing she met me with last night. "I don't want you to be afraid of anything. Not with me."

She glances down briefly. "Can I ask you something?" I nod. "Will you let me know if I do something wrong?"

"What?" I can't believe what she's asking. I can practically *taste* how bad I want her.

Her lashes flutter and she draws in a breath of air when my short nails settle over the base of her skull. "I want you to tell me if I do something you don't like," she repeats, her voice quivering.

"Trinity, there's nothing you'll do that I won't like." I choke the words out, because it's taking all I have not to strip her out of hers clothes when the song ends and our bodies still against each other. "Come home with me, and spend the night, and I'll show you how good we can be . . ."

I'm trying to be gentleman. I am. I start off by holding Trin's hand as we walk along the sand. But the closer we near my place, the more the space between us dissolves.

We both carry our shoes in our free hands, but my other hand—the one now snaked around her waist—is tightening against her hip. We're not speaking, allowing our bodies to feel that warmth and closeness surging from our close contact.

Trin leans heavily into me, her breast rubbing against my chest with each step.

The gesture might be purposeful. It might be accidental. Right now I don't care. I only know my yearning for her grows.

When she tilts her head, and I see my heat reflecting in her eyes, that kiss I've been holding back starts faster than either of us are prepared for. Our mouths open wide to receive each other, and steal a taste of what's to come. I bend her back with how hard I press against her. I'm being too aggressive. I know I am. Except when I try to pull back, her small nails dig into my shoulders, keeping me in place.

My lips leave hers to drag along her neck. She moans when my teeth find the base of her throat, similar to the way she did that morning I pushed my fingers inside of her. The memory of that day gets me harder. Damn. We're not even naked yet—or alone—and I'm ready to thrust inside of her.

It takes some effort, but gradually I ease away from her. Her breath, like mine, leave in a rush, making it hard for her to speak. "We have to get inside," she says.

"Oh, *hell* yeah."

I bend to retrieve my shoes. The moment she has hers, I snag her hand and we take off in a run. She laughs as she lifts her skirt and we sprint along the beach. Like a fool, I can't stop that grin the sound of her laughter invokes.

We reach my house and hop onto the deck, our laughter ceasing as we slip inside.

I toss my shoes aside. As I turn to lock the door and close the shades, I hear her sandals fall softly behind me. I walk away from the door to find her washing her hands in the kitchen. She seems nervous, maybe even a little frightened, so I wait by the door and give her some space.

It's only when she dries her hands that she glances up. With a shy smile, she leaves the kitchen, stopping in the center of the room to face me. As I watch, she crosses her arms in front of her and lifts the edge of her top.

Each pull of the tight fabric exposes more of her tan skin. I'm almost disappointed when she reveals the strapless black bra covering her breasts. Almost. No matter what, it's coming off next.

Her long hair falls along her back and shoulders in waves of silky black ink as she finishes removing her top. She meets me with another shy smile, pushing a strand of hair behind her ear. "Should we turn off the lights?" she asks.

I shake my head, drilling my stare onto hers. "No. I want to see all of you."

Her smile vanishes as a spark of desire lights her face. "I want to see you, too," she tells me, her voice soft and husky. She motions with a subtle lift of her chin. "Your turn," she says.

I prowl forward, stripping out of my shirt. It hits the floor as I reach her. Only inches remain between us. I can feel her heat, and hope she can feel mine.

"Hey, beautiful," I tell her.

Her gentle smile squeezes my heart. "Hey."

My fingertips trail up her arms while I take in every inch of her gorgeous features: those soft pink lips, the thick lashes veiling her brown eyes, and the damn cute freckles lightly sprinkling her nose and cheeks.

I lift a hand, taking my time to pass it along her cheek and down the base of her throat until it skims above her breasts. My focus never leaves her face, but hers stays trained on my motions. I know she's nervous and take care to be gentle.

"I want to touch you so bad," I tell her. "Will you let me?"

It's then her focus leaves my hands. "I want you to do more than touch me," she murmurs.

Her fingers hook the waistband of her skirt. My hands clasp hers, keeping them in place. "Let me," I say, leaning in close to speak in her ear. "I've been waiting to do this all night."

Her body trembles when I claim the curve of her neck with my mouth, drifting kisses down to the swells of her breasts. I reach behind to unclasp her bra, but not before I tug on each nipple through the fabric with my teeth.

The bra falls away and her head snaps back when I seize the first breast to suck. My tongue circles the stiff center while my hands get busy ridding her of her skirt. Trin stumbles backward with a grunt. My arms snatch her waist, keeping her from falling and keeping her close.

I edge her over to the back of the couch, my movements neither graceful nor slow—they're staggered, clumsy—so out of my mind with how good she feels in my arms and how she tastes on my tongue. My knees smack against the floor as my mouth continues downward until my hot breath releases against the crotch of her panties.

"*Shit*," Trin gasps, her hands shooting out.

My teeth snag the thin lace. Just as I promised, this is the way her panties are coming off. My fingers pinch the sides, helping me easily tug the tiny piece of fabric until it falls at her feet.

She watches me, barely breathing. She knows what's coming. And as I catch a glimpse of that sweet spot between her legs, I can't wait to start.

In one motion, I hook my elbows beneath her knees and stand, stealing a moment to kiss her as I settle her on the ledge of the couch. My teeth nibble her bottom lip as I slowly withdraw. "Keep your legs open for me, okay?" I rasp.

She manages a nod, but that's all she seems capable of doing. I reach for her fingers and pull two in my mouth. Her eyes round when I slide them out and flick them with tongue.

I kneel in front of her, taking her wet fingers and placing them where I need them.

"You want me to touch myself?" she stammers.

I squeeze my eyes shut and pause, my mind flooding with images of her reaching between her legs to please herself. "Only if you want to," I rumble.

Instead of waiting for a response, I slide her fingers further down and use them to spread her folds. Now that I see her—see her completely—no way in hell can I stay in control.

Trin screams in total bliss when I shove forward and devour her. My motions should be slow, gentle. They're not. My tongue and mouth are frantic, licking, sucking, *tasting*.

She writhes against me, grunting and swearing. If not for my arms fastened to her thighs, she'd fall off the couch with how hard she comes.

When her quivering ceases, I rise slowly, licking my lips. Her face is flushed a deep red. For a moment she simply stares at me, her expression split between shock and hunger. I can barely control my breathing, ready for more of her. But I need to know she still wants this—wants *me*.

Before I can ask her, her fingers clasp the waistband of my jeans and she hauls me to her for a long, grateful kiss.

Chapter Nineteen

Trinity

My lips seek out Callahan's, tasting every bit of me all over him. Something feral overtakes me, compelling me to consume what he took and more. He doesn't fight me, digging his fingers into my hair and allowing me to ravage his mouth.

I pry his zipper open, his breath hitching when I reach in and stroke. My movements quicken, using my toes to shove his jeans and briefs down. When the waistband of his boxers falls just above his knees, I slip off the back of the couch and take him deep into my mouth.

"Fuck," he says. "Oh, *fuck*."

He places his hands on either side of the couch, kicking away what remains of his clothes before curving forward to take in my motions. Maybe I'm supposed to turn away from his gaze, or close my eyes. Good girls don't watch, right? They don't lust after men. They don't do what I'm doing down on my knees.

If so, good girls are overrated and there's no Callahan in their lives.

This man—my *man*—enlivens every part me. I feel him and savor him down to my soul. The way he touches me, and how his face disappeared against me, demonstrates his desire, and incites mine. I surrender to our passion, dismissing any fears so I can take him without holding any part of me back.

My mouth seeks him deeper. I'm so captivated by the way he reacts to my pulls and suction, I can't help *but* watch, meeting his face with the full force of my ardor.

His hand strokes over mine as I work him. "Keep going, baby," he pants. "That feels so good."

I moan against him, his words accelerating my movements and spurring that clenching pain that yearns for another orgasm. My lips and hand continue to explore, and for a moment, I think he's going to let me finish him. But then he wrenches me up and places me back on top of the couch.

We move in perfect rhythm, like we've made love a thousand times, my legs falling open and my hands clasping his shoulders. I groan when he strokes me with his thick tip.

"You sure you want this?" he asks.

My lids squeeze tight as he makes another pass. But I meet his eyes to let him know I mean what I say. "Please don't stop," I say, my words releasing in gasps.

And he doesn't, gradually easing himself inside me with slow steady pumps. My body for all that it's ready to receive him is tight, given the time that's passed since my last lover, and Callahan's generous size.

My teeth trail behind his ear to tug on the lobe, only for my tongue to flick between kisses.

"*Jesus*, Trin," he mumbles.

He's not the only one making noise. As he advances, my whimpers grow louder, needier, the anticipation making me tremble.

He averts his chin, swearing. "Am I hurting you?"

"No." I sigh against his ear and swivel my hips. "Am I hurting you?"

He chuckles softly, his voice dripping with lust. "No. You feel so good. So right."

With one final push he's in. Then he begins to move. It's then he begins to thrust.

My spine bows as he slides in and out of me. Now, I'm swearing, begging him to go harder, and throwing my head back and screaming when he does.

My orgasm builds hard and peaks faster, crashing at once and building again. I'm not sure how much I can take, it almost feels too good. But I want this, and for him to never let me go.

Callahan whips me off the couch with my legs still pinned to his back and races us down the hall. If he intends to carry me to his bed, we never make it. Instead my back smacks against the door to the spare bedroom, his hips ramming into me and threatening to break the door off its hinges.

Between the steady beat, his thrusts, and those deep lustful sounds breaking through his chest, my desire for him spirals and I lose my mind. Heat and want surge through me sending wicked jolts of energy shooting down my legs. This time when I finish, he finishes with me.

He slows the pound of his hips, filling me as his chin tilts forward and his quick breaths tease my shoulder. He raises his head, the rise and fall of his chest matching mine, smiling gently and taking me in as if no one else matters.

I almost tell him I love him.

Because I do.

Yet even though there's no doubt in my mind, I can't. Not yet. So as he keeps us linked and carries us to his bed, I do my best to show him.

Again, I kiss him. Again I circle my hips against his lap, holding tight to him, and doing my best to stir his moans.

Callahan smooths his hands over my breasts, pinching my nipples. The sexy way he plays naturally increases the speed of my rocking pelvis. It doesn't take long for him grow and expand inside of me. He wants me again, and I so want him, too.

I press my hands against his shoulders, forcing him flat on his back. I then slide his palm down the curve of my waist to rest against my side, angling my body so my hair sweeps along his chest in time with the movements of my hips. This time, he's the one writhing beneath me. This time, I'm the one moving fast against him. This time, I'm showing him how badly I want him.

Chapter Twenty

Callahan

Trinity and I don't start dating. We become what I call inseverable. Unless she's on guard duty, we're always together, taking a run, working on my house, hanging with her friends, and yeah, making love all night.

I'm sleeping.

For the first time in years, I'm sleeping soundly.

There's shit I still think about. There are memories that haunt me, stirring when I least expect. But I suppose after what I'd seen and done, that darkness will always remain. The thing is with Trinity in my arms, the world doesn't seem as harsh as I remember, and when that darkness comes, this sweet thing is my resounding light.

"Would you ever think about travelling again?" she asks me one morning. "Outside the U.S., I mean?"

I shake my head though she can't see me the way she's tucked against me. "No. After eight years of living in a foreign land, I'm never leaving again." I pull her closer. "I'm finally home, and it's where I intend to stay."

"I understand," she whispers.

No. She really doesn't. If she did, she wouldn't sound so heartbroken.

I hate the sadness dulling her pretty face. So after a brief kiss to her lips, I ease away and reach for my guitar.

By now, I've sung to her in bed more times than I can count. It's something I can share that's a part of me, and the one thing I can offer that doesn't involve my hands gliding down her body.

Today I pick Rascal Flatts's *Take Me There* because I know the words, and I know she loves it. I keep the melody, but slow it down to accommodate my deep voice. I think I sound well enough, and I think she enjoys it. But this time, something's different.

Instead of that tender smile I've come to expect when I sing to her, tears well her eyes. "Callahan?" she says the moment I'm done.

Devastation splinters her voice, and the first of her tears spill down her cheeks. I perch my guitar against the bed and reach for her. "What's wrong?" I ask.

Her voice quivers as she struggles to speak. "I don't want to let you go," she says.

I still against her. "Then don't," I tell her.

I don't like how far away she seems. I want her to feel as close to me emotionally, as she is physically. So instead of letting her continue to speak words that don't make sense, I kiss her deeply.

With her body warm and naked against mine, it doesn't take me long to get hard, or for our hands to wander and play. I push inside of her, reminding her that I'm here, and that I'm not going anywhere without her.

She doesn't understand that the reason I'm finally "home" is because of her. For the first time in my life, I belong somewhere.

And that place is with Trinity.

Trin leaves her friends at the table and makes her way to the bar where I'm working, a big grin fixed on her face and a sparkle as bright as sunshine lighting her irises. She's already had a long day on the beach, and I'm scheduled until closing. That doesn't hamper her enthusiasm, or the smile spreading along my face. I've missed her all day, and I'm glad she's finally with me.

Neither of us slept much the night before seeing how we couldn't keep our hands, or mouths, off each other. I know she's tired despite the bounce to her step— I am, too. But it's hard being apart, so when we're together we make it count.

Last night she had friends over at her parents' place so I stayed there. Tonight, she'll be at mine.

I lean over the bar and give her a quick kiss, smiling against her lips when she laughs. "What'll it be, sweet thing?"

She taps her chin and glances at the ceiling like she's giving it actual thought—like she's not going to order four pitchers of Bud and enough Hot Damn shots to pass out to her entire crew. "How about a few bottles of Armand de Brignac? Oh! And your best cognac. Nineteen forty-seven was a good year, wasn't it?"

She throws back her head, laughing when I give her a knowing glance and start pouring the Hot Damn shots.

"Well, now see?" she says. "You dismiss my oh-so classy suggestions and leave me with no choice but to retaliate."

I tilt the bottle up so I don't spill and groan. "No, Trin. Not that."

She pulls a dollar bill from her pocket, wiggling it and her ass as she heads toward the jukebox. I know what she's going do. But when Blake Shelton's latest ends and *Gangnam Style* begins I know I've died and gone to hell.

I might have mentioned that if Trin's dancing, then so is everyone in the damn place—her crew, the Brewsters, Old Man Perrington, the Rossens—*all* the locals—even the tourists she coaxes onto the floor. Hell, even Lindsey joins in, taking her place beside Sean now that she's sunk her fangs in him.

I catch Jed's arm before he jumps over the bar. "Do *not*

encourage her," I warn.

"I can't help it, Cal," he tells me, laughing. "Your woman's too damn cute to resist."

He leaps over the bar, joining the line of people doing those God-awful moves. I continue to fill the pitchers and mutter a curse. Jed didn't mean any disrespect against Trin, or what we have. But his words are a reminder of how many men notice my girl. At first glance, they think she's cute, and she is. But for those whose stares linger, they see what I see, a beautiful young woman with an undeniable sex appeal.

The line dancing continues, the stomps to the floor rough enough to shake the boards beneath my feet. The men closest to her watch her tear it up, unable to look away. Two things stop me from launching over the bar and making a stake on my claim: One, they're keeping respectable distance. Two, Trin doesn't even seem to notice them. She's busy looking at me as she wiggles, and flashes me that grin she doesn't share with anyone else.

I wink her way and keep working, all the while making sure she stays safe. When the song begins to mercifully end, I see someone I don't recognize walk in. He's wearing a jacket, a baseball cap, and sunglasses, and keeping his head low. He doesn't want to be seen, and carefully makes his way around the group, going unnoticed.

My hackles rise, knowing he's up to something. I clutch the glass I just filled with scotch and make my way closer to where this guy is now leaning over the jukebox. He's young, and he appears slightly familiar. But his profile doesn't offer a decent view of his face, especially with those glasses and that cap. He smiles when he finds something he likes and slips in a dollar.

Trin's making her way back to me when Toby Keith's version of *Mocking Bird*—the duet he sings with his daughter —starts to play. She grounds to a halt, her eyes wide and frantic as she searches her surroundings. My eyes cut to the stranger, who's slipped off his jacket, hat, and glasses and is placing them across the bar.

Trin clasps her hands over her mouth and screams when she sees him. She's . . . *excited* that he's here. And this guy, instead of waving or saying, "Hi," is walking over to her, singing out loud to this song.

This idiot is singing to *my* girl.

And she's singing back!

They're dancing their way to each other, closing the space between them as they fucking serenade each other. This isn't a pal of Trin's. Any moron can see he's something special to her, and that he *adores* her. Now everyone's gathered around them, clapping to the beat and hollering in encouragement.

I don't realize how hard I'm squeezing the glass until it shatters in my hand. Scotch and ice drench my palm and arm. I fling the pieces in the trash, ready to bash this asshole's face in.

Hale's hard smack to my chest keeps me from hurtling myself across the bar. "Calm your shit," he says, laughing. "That's Landon, her brother."

My focus cuts from them and back to him. "*What?*"

"I said that's her brother." He peeks through the crowd, his smile widening. "And here come Owen and Silvie Summers." He claps my shoulder and takes a swig of his beer. "Looks like it's time to meet the family, Callahan."

Sure enough, Trin's losing her mind. She squeals as a middle-aged man with white hair and a round frame shoved into khakis and a polo shirt steps in to dance, shaking his hips like Elvis and holding tight to Trin's future self.

Silvie Summers is a little heavier than Trin, her long hair tied back in a braid and white instead of dark brown. But her face and that grin are proof enough that's her momma Trin's dancing with.

They finish the song, everyone cheering as Trin flings her arms around her family and showers them with kisses. As they calm, she says something that makes them glance in my direction. Owen's and Landon's grins fade.

Silvie is the only one who keeps her smile, leaning in to speak against Trin's ear. "That's him?" I watch her mouth.

Trin nods and herds everyone forward. She's still smiling as her family gathers in front of me. "Everyone," she says. "I'd like you to meet Callahan. . ."

Chapter Twenty-One

Callahan

I'm not mad at Trinity. Really I'm not. The best way I can describe what I'm feeling is ill-prepared. Upon learning her folks were here, Jed offered to have his friend cover my shift.

Next thing I know, we're having a late supper at her parents' home.

I'm not sure how the hell I ended up here. I was lured to Kiawah by the desolate silence and peace I thought it promised, wanting nothing more than to be by myself. Instead I fell head over heels for the loudest, craziest, most in-your-face human being on this Godforsaken planet. And here I sit now with her family. *Family.* Eating pot roast, potatoes, and fried okra while she and her kin go at it to see who could out-yell the other.

Trinity wins.

Of course.

She points to her brother. "Oh. The fertility dance. Now *that* was all sorts of ego crippling. Goodness, Daddy, how did Landon not land straight into therapy after that debacle?"

Owen, her father, pretends to narrow his eyes in anger as he points at her with his fork. "Your brother was inducted into that tribe by those men. That there is an honor, and he knows it."

Landon shakes his head. "No, he doesn't," he mutters.

Trinity laughs and pats my arm excitedly. "Picture my brother in a grass skirt," she says.

Landon groans and rubs his face. "No, please don't."

"With a giant wooden penis strapped to the front."

My head turns in Landon's direction, my neck so stiff and tense from the words that just spewed out of my girl's mouth, I swear everyone here can hear it creak. I don't think I want to know, and I'm pretty sure Trin knows as much, but of course it doesn't stop her from explaining.

"It's a dance they do in this one tribe," she begins. "A ceremony to celebrate the boys in the village becoming men by—"

"Dancing with giant dildos strapped to their fronts—yeah, yeah, he gets it, Trin," Landon says.

Their momma, Miss Silvie, shakes her head in what I initially mistake for disapproval. "Those weren't dildos," she corrects. "They were wooden phalluses. Huge difference. *Huge*."

Jesus Christ, help me.

"Did you feel more like a man after it was done?" Trin asks, unable to stop laughing.

"Bout as much as you felt like a woman after that fertility circle bullshit you took part in," Landon says before taking a long pull of his beer.

"Watch your mouth in front of your momma, boy," Owen says.

"Sorry, Momma," Landon says, with a smirk.

Trin turns back to me. To her credit, she's not any less affectionate around her folks than she is around her friends. I should be relieved that she's not shy about showing her family who I am to her. Instead, here I am feeling ill-prepared again. She winds her puny arms around one of mine, and rests her chin on my shoulder. I glance over at her daddy and brother. They're watching me closely. And to *their* credit no one's reaching for a gun. Now if roles were reversed, and this was my little girl, I would've shot me.

She giggles as heat pricks my skin. "Did I ever tell you about the time Momma and I had to help that woman give birth in a field?" she asks me. "And Momma had to break that poor woman's pelvis with a rock to get the baby out—"

"Yes. And please don't remind me," I mutter. That little story came out over a crab dinner I took her to a few weeks back. I was cracking one those little bastards open when she spilled the details like most talked about the weather. Let's just say I couldn't finish my meal.

To my relief, Owen and Landon groan along with me. "Yes, please don't," they both mumble.

"But my quick thinking saved them both," Silvie says casually. "It was either that or cut open her belly with that hunting knife—"

"Silvie, baby, don't," Owen says, waving his hands in surrender. "I can't go through that story again, sugar. I just can't."

"All right," she says. "But there's no miracle like the miracle of life."

And there's nothing like this family here on earth.

Owen, Landon, and I stand when Miss Silvie and Trin rise from their chairs and start to reach for our empty plates. She bats her hands when we try to help. "Now, you boys stop that. Trinity, help me get dessert together. It'll give your Daddy and brother time with Callahan."

Time to shoot him between the eyes.

"Yes, ma'am," Trin says, pulling the plate from my grip with a grin.

We lower ourselves back to our chairs, none of us saying anything even after Trin and her mama disappear into the kitchen. I can hear banging, the occasional word, and some giggling, but not much more than that as they skitter around cleaning up and preparing for dessert.

I wait quietly for her father and brother to speak. Turns out, I don't have to wait that long.

"So you work at Your Mother's?" Landon asks, making it damn clear he doesn't approve.

"Yes, sir." I call him "sir" even though he's probably my age. But that's what we do here in the south.

He watches me as he plays with the beer bottle in his hands. "You doing anything else?"

Do I have a decent job is what he means. "I'm fixing up my uncle's old place. I'm about halfway done." This time, it's my turn to take a swig.

"What happens after you're done with your uncle's place?"

"Don't know," I tell him truthfully. Before Trin, I couldn't think past the next day. Now? Hell, can I really blame the scrutiny crinkling the edges of her daddy's and brother's jagged stares? They don't know me. They only know I'm with their precious little girl.

Landon's focus wanders to Owen, pegging him with a look that clearly tells him it's his turn. I brace myself for the hard hand only fathers know how to wield, with their words or with their fists. I don't impress either of them. Not by a long shot.

I lift my beer to take another swig when Owen motions to the tattoo on my right arm, the one of the solider. "How long did you serve?"

The bottle doesn't quite reach my lips before I place it back on the table. "Eight years, sir."

Despite that I wasn't trying to hide my ink, and that I was sure Landon saw it, Owen was the one to ask about it. But there's something in my tone that appears to catch his interest. "Did you go in straight out of high school?"

I answer with a slight tilt of my chin. "I graduated, but missed the ceremony to get on the bus to boot camp."

"How many tours did you do?" Landon asks.

By now, Landon's tenor lacks the warmth it carried in his sister's presence. I don't know if he's in the process of judging me, or already has. This man—boy really—doesn't think I'm good enough for sister.

And maybe he's right.

The blood pumps hard in my ears when I meet him square in the eye. "Four," I respond.

His eyes widen slightly. "Shit," he says, drawing out the word.

There're lots of words for it. And that's one of them.

"Iraq?"

"Yes, *sir*," I answer Landon.

I wait for Owen to speak. For a long while his words don't come. And even though I steel myself for what he may ask, I know then I'll never be ready for all he has to say.

"Were you in Special Forces?"

He's been watching me closely. I felt the weight of his stare drilling into my skull throughout my interaction with his son. He didn't blink when he asked, and he doesn't blink as he continues. "I doubt that tattoo's just for show, boy."

I straighten a little more. "No, sir. It's not for show," I tell him.

I don't see Trin, or her Momma. But I feel my girl standing behind me. In their silence, I know they've heard our exchange.

As close as Trin and me have been, and after all that we've done, I've barely said a word about my time in Iraq. But here I am, telling the two most important men in her life more than I've dared to tell her.

'Cept there's no stopping now is there? The murderer is out of the bag.

"Were you a SEAL?" Owen asks.

"No. Ranger."

I know what he's doing….what they're both doing. They're trying to gauge just how dangerous I am. So I wait, unsure how much more they'll tolerate before I'm asked to leave and not come back.

Her daddy hasn't moved, and his expression is as hard and cool as cracked granite. "What was your specialty, boy?"

This time, it's my turn not to blink. "Sniper."

Silvie's sharp intake of breath robs the room of all sound, and twists the knife already lodged deep in my gut.

"How many confirmed kills?"

It's Landon who asks, but my focus stays on Owen. "A hundred and seven."

"All your own?" Owen asks, his face unyielding.

"Yes, sir," I say.

The quiet that follows lasts more like hours than minutes. My tightening muscles are screaming and threatening to tear clear from my frame. But it's when the air thickening the space between me and Owen, appears to freeze and lower the temperature around us, that I'm certain judgment's been passed, and that I'm no longer welcomed.

I start to rise, but Owen's words cement me in place. "I was a Green Beret. Got sent to Somalia on special tour to find some rebels." His voice grows distant. "Lost count after I fired those first thirty-five shots."

I'm hovering mere centimeters from my chair. Somehow, I find my way back down. Owen's cold exterior remains. Only his eyes are different. They're those same vacant, dead eyes soldiers get after serving too many tours, and the same eyes that stare back at me each time I dare to look in the mirror. But he continues, although he doesn't seem to be breathing, not anymore.

"We spent close to three months rounding them up," he says. "Some were just children, really. Children bred and trained to take lives. But that didn't make a difference." He looks at me then, the torment deadening his stare as palpable as his daughter's presence beside me. "We had a job to do. Didn't we, boy?"

My fists clench and I swallow the lump that's building. "Yes, sir," I say.

Chapter Twenty-Two

Callahan

I don't think this is Trin, or her brother's first time learning their father was a Green Beret. And based on the heaviness in the room, I don't think it's the first time learning the extent of his sins. We eat a homemade sweet potato pie in silence, with nothing more than the clinking sound of forks against the plates to break the quiet.

The minute we're done, Landon excuses himself to make a call.

I thank Silvie for dinner and help Trin gather the plates, my hands not quite steady as I load the dishwasher. She tries to catch my stare more than once, but each time I deny her the reassurance she seeks.

She wants, okay, maybe not wants—she *needs* to know I'm okay. That we're okay. But I'm not sure if we are. Not after learning I killed a hundred and seven people all on my own. Those same fingers that sweep over her body, pulled the trigger that abruptly ended a shitload of futures. And those hands that give her pleasure, caused a hell of a lot more pain.

Trin knows what I am now, knows what I did. I can't take it back, but then I never could.

The plate, the one I think I used, doesn't quite fit along with the rest. But I need it to.

I place my plate on the counter. Compulsively, erratically, I start rearranging the dishes. I move the pie dish, a lid, and a flat pan her momma used to fry okra. My hands move fast, snatching up her daddy's plate, her mother's, and everything else in between.

And it's still not enough. There's no room for me among the rest.

It. I mean *it* not *me*.

I take a deep breath, and release it slowly, knowing I'm seconds away from breaking every damn dish in this piece of shit appliance. That rage, the kind I've beaten down more times than I can count, hovers close to the surface. I can taste the adrenaline it stirs in the back of my throat and sense the fury of the beast I've become.

I need to get out, need to leave fast before I lose myself to that darkness—the one where the bodies of those I failed lie bloody and still.

"Here, baby," Trin says. "Let me."

Her voice is soft, patient. I stare at her outstretched hand for several painful heartbeats before I surrender my plate. She removes a lid from the rack and replaces it with the soiled dish I held for too long.

As easily as that, she makes a place for me.

I can't do much more than breathe, and even that much hurts. But her gesture is effortless. Her solution simple. Her voice relaxed. She's . . . *Trin*. Fixing everything as naturally as she fixes everyone with her smile.

That doesn't stop me from moving stoically away.

Landon's returned. Whoever he called, and whatever he or she had to say, pissed him off. But I don't ask why. Instead I shake the hand he offers, and thank Miss Silvie again for the meal and the hospitality.

There is though, one person I need to see before I can leave. And while I've only just met him, it's his words I won't forget.

Trin's daddy stands alone out on the terrace. Miss Silvie

stops me with a gentle clasp to my arm. She flashes that small smile all southern ladies somehow manage, even when they're hurting for those they most love.

"Mr. Owen needs a moment," she says. "You'll excuse him if he doesn't pay his respects, won't you, son?"

I nod, although the motion barely registers. "Yes, ma'am. Please tell him I said thank you, and good night."

"I will, son," she answers.

The wrinkles along the corners of her eyes soften as her hand slowly slips away. She steps out onto the terrace, where her husband is leaning against the stacked stone railing and staring out into the darkness. He's likely searching for the peace I've often sought, and I hope he finds it.

Miss Silvie takes her place beside her husband, not to speak, but to let him know she's with him. It's a sight to see, and a moment I don't remember my mother ever sharing or offering freely. But right then and there, feeling what I'm feeling, it's a form of beauty that's too painful to watch.

This time, it's my turn to walk away. I march down the hall, out the foyer, and through the main doors. By the time I slip behind the wheel, my chest is as rigid as titanium and my lungs raw with every breath I take.

I grip the steering wheel, trying to ease my breathing before I crank the engine. I can't drive like this. Not safely. So I take my time and concentrate so I can.

The apocryphal foot mashing my chest in, slowly releases its pressure. I rub it a few times, more to be sure I'm well enough to drive, before starting my truck with a roar. As I shift into reverse, the passenger side door handle slaps back.

Through the window, Trin stares back at me, her thin brows puckered. At first, her presence confuses me and I don't initially act. I'm not proud to admit this, but I wait before setting the truck in park and flipping the locks to allow her in.

She opens the door and hops into the seat, reaching for her seatbelt and snapping it in place. "You were leaving without me?"

She's not asking me, or yelling. She's genuinely dumbstruck that I'd take off without her.

I fiddle with the steering wheel. "I figured you'd be staying with your folks."

I don't miss the disappointment in her voice. "Then why didn't you tell me goodbye?"

Shame has me bowing my head. She doesn't deserve the way I'm treating her. "I'm sorry, baby." I sigh. "I'm tired. It may be too much for me to drive you back later, and no way in hell are you walking back alone."

"Why are you talking like I'm not spending the night? It's what we planned."

I swivel my body to face her. "Your parents are here," I say, slowly, leaving out the obvious.

"I know. We—I mean if you're up for it—are meeting them for brunch tomorrow."

I angle my body in the direction of the house again. "Do they know you plan to be with me? All night?"

"Yes. They know. Just like they know we've been sleeping together—why are you covering your face like that? Callahan, my parents aren't stupid. They know we've been doing it like horny rhinos beneath the hot Serengeti sun."

I finish running my hand down my face to find her laughing. "I told you, my family and I are close," she drawls. "Now, I did spare them the details. Especially about that night you lifted me up and pleasured me against the wall—by the way that was real hot, hon—Oh! And that time you bent me over the dining room table—you know the one we just ate on—and gave me like *four* mind-blowing orgasms. And, *hey*! Remember when we did it the shower? Goodness, we never did find that soap now, did we . . ."

She keeps talking, because she's Trin. The best I can do is pop my truck back in reverse and pull out of her driveway. It's a wonder Owen and Landon didn't each pick a ball to shoot off.

The closer we get to my place, the less she says. I park close to the back door, but I don't make an effort to move, and neither does she. Despite her animated voice, I know I hurt her when I tried to leave without her. I take her hand, watching it disappear within my grasp.

How did this little ball of energy come to be the most important thing in my life? More to the point, how does she sit beside me knowing all I've done?

"I'm sorry," I whisper. This time when I say it, she knows I'm apologizing for a lot more than walking out without saying goodbye.

"Do you want to talk about it?" she asks gently.

I tighten my jaw and shake my head. That shit in the kitchen. Lord, she has no clue how close I came to losing it. But I don't mention it, even though I think she may know a lot more than she lets on.

I lift her hand and kiss it, then slowly edge out of my truck. This time she waits for me to open the door because maybe she knows I need to make up for how I treated her.

She leans against me when I wrap my arm around her. It's a warm night. Beautiful, perfect, just like most nights here on Kiawah.

All the stars sparkling brightly above us, and the ocean's gentle purr, beckon us to walk along the shore. On another night, I'd surrender to its call. But tonight's not like all the other nights with Trin. Tonight she learned that the same man who gave her his heart, and who's holding her now, is a killer. And regardless of her smile, and the way she wraps her arms around my waist, it's a truth I can no longer spare her from.

We walk in the house and straight to my bedroom. I slip off my shirt and sit on the edge of the bed. This time, I don't touch or tempt. I lean back on my hands and wait. Now that she knows what I am, I have to be sure she'll still want the man before her.

I don't wait long.

Trin kicks out of her flip-flops and pulls off her tank in one smooth move. Her tiny denim shorts—the ones that drive me wild—are next, followed by her bra and panties. With her knees, she pries my legs open and stands before me. But it's not until she unbuttons my jeans and reaches for the erection her naked body stirred that I act.

When I take her, it isn't gentle. Not once I flip her onto her back and join her body with mine. My thrusts are hard, driving her up the bed. I don't know how many times she orgasms. All I know is that by the time I finish, she's thrashing, her nails raking my unmade sheets, and her hot body dripping with sweat.

She trembles, whimpering, her breaths more pronounced than mine. I look down at her, taking her in before seizing her mouth, my lips hungry for hers. She wraps her arms around my neck. But I can't stop the rock of my hips. Again, I'm hard.

I break our kiss and dip down to suck on her stiff nipple. She screams, jolting hard enough to break my suction.

"Don't stop," she begs me when I hesitate. "*Please*, don't stop . . ."

Chapter Twenty-Three

Trinity

I don't know how long we make love, but the birds are beginning to sing as we settle down to sleep. Callahan's head lowers to his favorite spot between my breasts while I drape an arm along his back.

As glimpses of sunlight trickle through the sheer curtains, I remember our plans with my folks. I cradle his head against me as I reach for the cell phone he left charging on the nightstand following round two, or three—I don't remember which. I only know we both had this overwhelming desire to feel close to each other.

Using pure skill, and one hand, I send Landon a text, letting him know we'll meet him and our parents for dinner instead. I don't manage much more than that. Instead I surrender to that blissful exhaustion sex with Callahan always brings.

Sometime around one in the afternoon, he stirs against me. I awoke only a few minutes before, but use this moment to stretch my arms over my head. The motion causes my breast to glide along his cheek and in an instant later, something hardens along my leg.

An anticipatory grin spreads along my face as his body drags along mine and my lady parts rejoice. He stirs again, tilting his hips. I'm not sure if he's completely awake, but I like what he's doing, so I don't dare interrupt.

What I do is moan, a lot, when his dense tip presses against my center and slides along my folds. Sweet mercy, he feels so good rubbing against me. I involuntarily squirm, my body ready to receive his. But it's not until his hand slides between us and he slips two fingers in, that I'm sure he's not going back to sleep.

He lifts his head, his lids heavy with sleep and lust.

My expression splits with agony and pleasure as his fingers circle. Agony because I want more than his fingers inside me, and pleasure because he knows how to work me into a frenzy.

He licks his lips, accelerating the movements of his fingers, wanting to watch me peak and lose control. Knowing so, and how hot it makes him, surges the spasms claiming and electrifying me. My orgasm hits me hard enough to buck my body, I'm still reeling from it when he hauls me to him and joins his body with mine.

He hooks my knees under his elbows, his face scrunching as he rams me, going deep. I'm no longer grunting, or whimpering, or even trying to be quiet, the lust Callahan invokes rattling me down to my core.

Callahan roars with his release, falling forward and folding my body. His hands splay on either side of me, his chest heaving with each breath. I meet his gaze, smiling softly as the fervor in his eyes dims, replaced by an adoration that flutters my heart.

"Hi, there," I say.

"Hey, beautiful," he whispers back, his warm smile lighting his blue eyes.

"Is now a good time to tell you I love you?" I ask.

My smile fades as his leaves him. He averts his head to the left. But the only thing there is a wall. "You may want to take that back," he says.

"I don't want to."

I barely get the words out before he carefully separates us

and disappears into the bathroom. I clasp my hand over my eyes, trying not to cry, but those tears silently push their way through.

My misery isn't caused by his rebuff—I *know* he loves me. He's never said it, but I feel it. Feel it every time he opens doors for me, pulls me close, and seeks me out to make sure I'm safe. His soft words, his gentle ways, his kindness—no man has ever been this good to me who wasn't blood.

I sit up and wipe my eyes, staring at the wetness they leave against my fingertips. No, these tears aren't for me. They're for him, because he can't believe I love him.

Before he can return, I dress and leave the room. I walk down the hall and into the spare bathroom. Without meaning to, I slam the door a little too hard.

Callahan mistakes it for me walking out on him. The bathroom door in his room flies open and quick feet speed past the bathroom I'm in. With a crash, he wrenches the front door open, yelling my name. *"Trin!"*

Desperation and fear etch into his voice like a shard of broken glass. I grip the edges of the sink, sighing with relief. It's not that I enjoy hearing his pain—I don't in the least. But I can't say his reaction doesn't reinforce what I believe. Without intending to, and through his actions, Callahan just proved I mean more to him than he's ever claimed.

Again, I wipe my tears, and call out when he yells my name again. "I'm in the bathroom."

There's a brief pause before his bare feet pad against the hardwood floor and stop outside my door. "You all right?" he asks on the other side.

I wrestle with how to answer, not wanting to lie. I'm not all right. I can't be knowing he hurts as much as he does. "I'll be out in a minute," I manage.

I find a spare toothbrush and comb, and freshen up. The comb is one of those tiny ones from a man's grooming kit so it takes me some time to run through my thick hair. When I step out, he's leaning on the opposite wall with his arms crossed, wearing nothing but an old pair of sweats cut into shorts.

He lifts his head. "I thought you left."

In two strides I'm in his arms. He kisses the top of my head, curling his body around me. I almost tell him I would never leave him, but that's a lie. My time in the Corps is coming up fast. It's already August 1st, and I'm scheduled to fly out the second week in September. I've asked for extension in writing, knowing I can't simply walk out on Callahan—not this soon—not after everything we've been through.

My struggle is, I may just have to.

I've committed every part of my being to Callahan. But I've also committed the next two years and three months of my life to the Corps. I'm trying desperately to push it off as long as I can, but even that feels wrong.

The director emailed me back a few a days ago. She said she'll see what she can do. But she made it clear how few volunteers are being recruited, and how desperate they are for people with medical training. She reminded me how many kids they're losing who could've been saved through vaccinations. Children are dying, and here I am making excuses so I can be with my boyfriend.

All logic and common sense compel me to be honest with Callahan. I *have* to tell him. I know this. But I just told him I love him, and he reacted so badly when he thought I took off on him.

I bury my face against his chest. Things are screwed up, and there's no simple solution. He won't follow me across the world. No matter what he feels for me. He made it clear the other week when I asked him if he'd ever leave the country. I intended to tell him about the Corps then, and ask him to consider coming with me. But his decision to never to leave the states was absolute. I can't blame him, not after being gone for so long and everything he's endured.

But I can blame myself for placing me *and* him in this

position.

"You know what you said," he asks, his voice deepening as his hands trail to my hips. "What I told you to take back?"

I almost repeat it, but I don't think he needs to hear those words just then. "Yes."

"I'm going to tell you a few things about me—facts very few people know. After I'm done, you can decide for yourself if you want to keep feeling what you think you do. But if you don't, I'll—" He stops, and for a few seconds it's like he ceases breathe. It's not until I hear him swallow that he continues. "Just know you can take it back," he adds quietly.

He pushes off the wall and leads me to the couch, turning down the air conditioning and draping a small throw against my legs when he realizes how frigid the room is. I won't lie, the odd stab to his voice scares me. So when I adjust the throw around me, I can't help but bunch the edge in my hands and clutch it against my chest.

He sits beside me, leaning forward so his big feet are planted firmly on the floor and his forearms rest above his knees. He regards me, the pain in his expression as obvious as the chill spreading along my exposed toes. I tuck them beneath me, trying to stay warm and protect myself from what's to come.

It's only when he turns his head away from me that finally speaks. "I've killed a lot people, Trin," he says, taking a few breaths to force out the rest. "They weren't all adults, and they weren't all men."

I know war doesn't discriminate. But I'll admit, it's not easy to hear those words come from a man who holds me so tenderly.

"I've killed women, and young boys too young to grow their first beards." His hands ball into fists. "But one of my last kills was a little girl who couldn't have been more than five."

This time, I'm the one who falls perfectly still, the first draw of air I manage strangely shallow. "Did . . . did she get in the way?" I stammer. "I mean, was it accident?" In my trembling voice, I'm begging him to tell me yes.

He meets me with ghostly blue eyes. "No. Every kill I made was intentional."

"And she was five?" I don't mean to speak out loud. But I do.

He doesn't answer, returning his attention to the unlit fireplace directly in front of him. "Tell me what happened," I say.

He shakes his head and rams his eyes shut when I sniff. He knows I'm crying, and I hate myself for it. But what he's saying is important, and needs to be said. Not just for him, but for us.

I let my feet slip to floor and drag my heavy body closer so my hip rests against his. My hand slides along his back. "Please tell me."

For a long time, I don't think he will. But when he finally opens his eyes, he does, spilling his soul painfully slow. "It happened three days before my discharge from the Army. Our intelligence discovered insurgents plotting an attack and moving weapons into an area we thought we'd secured the previous month. But the war being what it is, regardless of how hard we fight it, nothing guarantees anything will stay secure for long. In just a matter of days, our so-called clear zone had quickly become hostile territory again."

His eyes briefly dart my way. He wants to know if I'm listening. And I am. Right now, I'm hanging on his every word like it will somehow keep him from slipping away.

"I was one of several snipers positioned on rooftops throughout the city. Given my record, and skill, I was placed deep into enemy territory. Convoys of Rangers were moving in, most of them among my best friends. Like me, they were good at what they did. So they were sent in first to sweep, and locate those weapons before they were used against us.

"I'd been in position for several hours, watching, and waiting without needing to fire a single shot. That's when I saw a mother and her little girl moving closer to my boys. The woman had a detonator in her hand. I shot her in the head—"

My hitching breath cuts him off.

Callahan bows his head. "I don't mean to upset you, Trin. And I can't take back what I did—any of it. But if you want to know the real me, then you should know I didn't hesitate to shoot. Her job was to kill. Just as mine was to protect my men sweeping the streets. So I pulled my trigger . . . and killed her in front of her child."

I press my lips tight, trying to beat back my tears that fall. It's one thing to hear these awful stories on the news, or read about them online, it's another thing to hear the man you love tell you firsthand what he's done, and feel what it's done to him in return.

My body settles against his side as my arms wind around his waist. "I'm sorry you had to do that to her, and her daughter," I tell him. "But you had to save your friends."

He releases his breath in a shudder. "Trin . . . I didn't save my friends."

The blood drains from my cheeks and down to my gut.

Callahan's face is buried in his hands. It's then I know I'm not crying alone. "I didn't hesitate to shoot that woman," he says. "But I hesitated to shoot her little girl. My men trusted me, so when they saw the woman go down, they moved forward, thinking they were safe—believing I'd saved them. But unlike the detonator the woman had—the kind you have to push, her child had one that fires when pressure eases off the switch. So when I killed that child, I killed my friends, too."

"*No.*" My voice is harsh, angry and *vicious*. "Those people—those *cowards*—who strapped that little girl with explosives, and shoved her out the door to die—they're the ones who did that to your friends, *and* her, *and* her momma. You didn't do this, Callahan. That wasn't you!"

I'm on my feet now, but I don't even remember standing.

Callahan rises, his chest heaving in and out faster than

seems possible. "I know what the enemy does, Trin. I lived and breathed it, and saw it every time I was there! I shouldn't have hesitated. Knowing what I know, I should've fired because that's what I was trained to do—it was the right thing to do by those men. But I *didn't*. Instead I watched my friends get blown to pieces!"

I cover my eyes. It's all I can do, unable to fathom what he went through that day alone. It would be like me seeing Hale, Sean, Mason—*my friends* dead. But they weren't. They were Callahan's.

He takes another moment, and another after that, before pressing on. "I wish I can tell you I grieved, that I went down to collect what was left of my friends. But I never had the chance. We came in too close to where the weapons were stored. The mother and daughter were more than just a way to take us down, they were a distraction in order for our enemies to move their shit out. So instead of mourning, instead of going into shock like my body was fighting to do, I added to my list of kills. And this time, I didn't hesitate."

I stand numbly in place for what seems like too long, yet not long enough. "You want to know why I have long hair and a beard?" he asks. His statement catches me off guard, but it's the agony behind his words and those that follow that clench my heart like a vice. "Because after that day, after I let my men down, I couldn't stand to look at myself in the mirror. I can't stand that man I see. He should've died along with his friends. Instead he was given a medal he didn't deserve, and a chance at life they'll never have."

"You're forgetting about me," I choke out.

His head whips my way.

"You're forgetting what that man means to me." I step forward and take his hands in mine. "You had a human moment, in a very inhuman situation. Not every soldier hangs onto his soul during combat, because they *can't*, it's too hard given what you have to do. You hung onto yours, Callahan. You hung on tight all the while shielding your heart. I'm sorry you lost your friends—I'm so sorry you watched so many die." I'm crying so hard, I'm not sure he can hear me, but I continue, doing my best to be clear. "But I'm not sorry you lived. You came into my life when I needed you. And I thank God for that. You may not like the man you see, but I do. He's the best man I know and I don't know what I would do without him."

Callahan tightens his jaw, and for a moment all he does is stare. My chest collapses inward when he slips his hands from mine. "I wish I could believe you. But I can't."

He withdraws from me, not just physically, but in the way his essence tears away from mine.

Time passes like melting snow along a rooftop. My head is pounding. I need to eat, to drink—I know I do. But as Callahan's exhausted form sinks into the couch, I know there's something else I need more.

And maybe he does, too.

His stare travels to the ceiling as I inch forward. "If you want to go, I'll take you home," he says. He closes his eyes briefly and breathes. "And if you don't come back, I'll understand."

I answer him the only way I can, placing my knees on either side of hips and lowering myself to his lap. "You know how you said I can take my words back?" He meets my eyes as another tear spills down my cheek. "I can't," I admit. "Because they're true."

"Trin . . ." he says.

I don't wait for him to say more. "I love you, Callahan." I bend to kiss his lips. "I love you." My lips move to his neck. "I love you so much."

I remove my shirt. The rest my clothes follow between my kisses and whispers of love.

My lover has known too much pain.

From this moment on, I only want him to know pleasure.

Chapter Twenty-Four

Callahan

"Hi." Trinity draws out the word as she greets me with a bright smile, and lifts up on her toes expecting a kiss.

She laughs when I shove the flowers in my right hand in front of her. I don't keep my hands to myself when we're alone, but here at her parents' home is a different story, at least for me. She doesn't share my traditional thoughts, and now following several suppers with her folks, she's even more affectionate around them.

"Now, how am I supposed to have my way with you with these pretty little things rammed between us?" she teases.

"You're not," I say, pretending to be annoyed, but unable to hide my grin. "Besides, these are for your momma."

"Oh, that's so sweet."

I bring my other arm around. "These are for you."

She beams when she sees the yellow roses I hand her. I don't tell her I picked them because they remind me of sunshine and make me think of her. Men don't say shit like that. At least not men from Texas.

"They're beautiful. Thank you."

She flings her arms around me. I allow her kiss, but I don't let it linger. She giggles when I turn my head, to keep her tongue far from mine.

"You sure you aren't a virgin?" she purrs against my ear.

"I promise not to tell anyone if you are, cross my heart."

I groan. "If I was, I think you took care of business a long time ago."

"Hey, Daddy," Landon calls when he sees us, a big grin planted on his face. "Callahan's in the foyer fondling your little girl. Want me to get the shotgun?"

"Already have it," Owen barks from the back.

Trin neither blinks nor loosens her hold around me, even when I try to pull away, choosing instead to rise to my defense. "He's not fondling me. I'm fondling him!" she hollers back. "But Landon's being rude and interrupting. Momma, shouldn't you send him to his room or something?"

"Christ," I mutter.

The last few nights we've had supper, Owen has been exceptionally quiet, and so have I. I suppose our talk on the first night we met, and then my long talk with Trin the next day, took us to a place neither of us enjoyed revisiting. If it weren't for Miss Silvie's quiet interjections and Trin and Landon going at it nonstop, supper would be more silent than church on Monday.

Trin pouts when I ease away. "Fine," she pouts. "But you'd better make it up to me tonight."

I give her a knowing wink, letting her know that's exactly what I plan to do. She pauses, to give me one of her more nymph-like stares before leading me through the foyer and across the house.

We step onto the terrace where her father's sitting at the table . . . cleaning his shotgun.

For the first time, he smiles when he sees me. "Hello there, son," he says. "How you doing this evening?"

"Fine, sir." *And please don't shoot me in front of your daughter.*

Landon comes up behind me and claps my shoulder. "Look a little nervous there, cowboy. You all right?" He plops down next to his father, a big shit eating grin spreading along his face.

Miss Silvie appears then, placing a basket full of wet sheets at the other end of the patio table. "Hello, Callahan."

"Evening, ma'am. These are for you." I hand her the flowers, not just to get rid of them, but so I can move quicker if I have to make a run for it.

"Oh, isn't that lovely." She steals a glance toward her husband. "Can't remember the last time a handsome man brought me flowers."

She means well, but her comment doesn't earn me any points with her husband.

"Now, Daddy, quit looking at Callahan like you want to kill him and be nice," Trin says, staying true to her cheery disposition. "Here, Momma, let me get your flowers in water before they wilt."

"Oh, sweetie, I can do that. I have to check on the pies anyway," Miss Silvie answers.

"Well, then I'll help," Trin says. "Have a seat," she tells me, patting my ass. "I'll just be a minute."

And yeah, her daddy and brother notice the ass pat.

I lower myself to the chair directly in front of Owen who happily cleans his weapon of choice while he continues to eye me. Landon sits back in his chair and swigs a beer, appearing to have the time of his life. He reaches between him and his father and pulls another beer from the cooler. "Want one, Callahan?"

"Sure, thank you." I don't really want one. I mostly just don't want to piss anyone off. I catch it when he pops off the cap and slides it across the table at me.

It doesn't take long for Miss Silvie to return, but it seems like a long time when there's a protective father with a 16-gauge waiting across from you. She lifts one of the pillow cases from the basket and examines it. "Trin's just adding more marinade to the steaks. You like steaks, don't you, dear?" She asks me.

"Yes, ma'am. Thank you, ma'am."

Owen continues to regard me, but doesn't say anything.

Meanwhile, back at the ranch, Landon's having a good old time watching me squirm.

"I don't know if I like this new bleach," Miss Silvie says like her husband isn't seconds from shooting me between the eyes. "These sheets look dull. Don't you think, Owen?"

"They're fine, sugar," he says to her, keepings his stare trained on me.

I take in the pile of wet sheets in her basket. "If your dryer's broke I can take a look at it for you, ma'am," I offer. Hell, anything to escape right now. "I'm pretty good with my hands."

"I kind of figured, seeing how you can't seem to keep them off my little sister," Landon says. He's laughing. I'm not. And neither is his daddy.

"Leave him alone," Miss Silvie tells him. She pats my shoulder. "Thank you for the offer. The dryer's fine. In the summer, I always hang my sheets and iron them afterward. There's nothing like sleeping on sheets dried in sun," she says.

"In bed," Landon adds. "With her husband. Because you know, *they're* married."

Landon wasn't warm the first time we met. And the past few times I've visited, he hasn't said much to me, quieting and watching every interaction between me and Trin closely. He probably doesn't know what to think of me yet. But I have to admit, something changed between us when he learned of my past.

I'm not sure if I've earned his respect. Nor am I certain if he's busting my balls because he likes me, or because he can. The one thing I'm sure of is his daddy doesn't find his son as funny as his son thinks he is.

While I'm not thrilled with the attention, and my preference is time alone with my girl, I know it's important to Trin that I'm here. So I take a sip of my beer and do my best to relax, smiling softly when she sweeps back onto the terrace.

"You doing all right?" she asks.

"I'm good. Thanks," I tell her.

Landon offers me a wry smile. Apparently, he's not on board with my plan to fit in and not die. "So what's it like living in sin with my sister?" he asks. "You think you might go to hell for that?"

Trin, because she likes to help, flops on my lap and wraps her arms around me, snuggling close. "Momma, Landon's giving Callahan and me a hard time for having consensual adult relations . . ."

I squeeze the bottle in my hand tighter. *Jesus Christ, no.*

"Are you going to let him embarrass our guest like that?" she continues.

"I'm just watching out for you, Trin." He winks at me. "Making sure things stay right and proper, just like Daddy always was with Momma."

Miss Silvie exams another pillow case. "You mean before or after he deflowered me in the middle of the Amazon rainforest?"

I choke on my beer at the same time Landon spits his out.

Trin lifts the beer out of my hand and takes a sip, an evil grin unlike I've ever seen aimed at her brother. "Aw, Momma, that's so romantic," she gushes. "Why don't you tell us all about it?"

And then she does!

"Oh, it was sweet," Miss Silvie says, fondly. "Owen was fresh out of the Marines and I was finishing my degree in Anthropology when he joined our volunteer group. Well, he didn't know anything about fruit trees, or so he claimed. So one night, after everyone went to bed, he talked me into taking a walk with him in the jungle so I could teach him." She sighs, as if remembering. "But he's the one who taught me."

Lord, help me.

Miss Silvie tosses the pillow case on top of the basket and plays with the long braid in her hair. But she's not done talking. Nope, not Trin's momma. "Turns out this young stud just wanted a taste of my fruit," she says, adding a wink. "If y'all know what I mean."

By now Landon's covering his ears. "Momma, please stop right there," he begs her.

I drag a hand down my face. *Yes. Please stop.*

Trin, being Trin, only encourages her. "Is that how Landon was conceived, Momma? Up against some mango tree?"

"No . . . I think they were plantains—"

"No. *Hell*, no!" Landon says, mercifully cutting her off. He pushes off from the table shuddering. "I could have gone my whole life without hearing that."

Owen in turn keeps cleaning his shotgun, but now he's laughing, and offers his wife a wink of his own. "That was a nice night, wasn't it, sugar?"

Landon chugs the rest of his beer, his face grimacing in pain. This time, it's my turn to laugh at him. He notices and points at Trin who's adjusting my arms so I'll actually hold her. "I was watching out for you," he tells her. "He's a bartender for shit's sake."

"Says the man dating a stripper," she replies simply.

Landon lowers his hand as all eyes fall on him. Silvie steps away from her basket and closer to her son. "You told us Bernadette was a professional dancer," she tells him, slowly.

"Oh, that's her profession, all right," Trin says.

"You're dating a stripper," Owen repeats, appearing equally as thrilled as his wife.

And suddenly, I don't feel so bad about being a bartender. This time, I'm the one smirking as I drink my beer.

Owen starts throwing his cleaning supplies back in his kit, looking ready to lift his gun and smack his son upside the head.

Landon releases a sigh. "She's only dancing to put herself through engineering school," he says.

"That school of hers takes singles?" Trin asks. "Just wondering," she says upon catching Landon's death glare.

"You're dating a stripper," Owen says yet again.

"With a bedazzled vagina," Trin throws in.

"How did you—" Landon cuts himself off and clears his throat.

And now, Trin has everyone's attention. "I went to that gentleman's club in Charleston where she works," she says. "Over Spring break when I was home."

"What were you doing in a place like that?" I ask her, at the same time her father questions the same thing.

"It was no big deal," she tells, stroking my beard with the back of her hand.

"Yes it is," I say, my frown deepening. "I don't want you in a place like that."

The corners of her mouth curl. "I didn't go by myself. Hale, Mason, and Sean were kind enough to go with me."

"Wasn't that nice of them," both her daddy and I mutter.

We exchange glances. While I still don't think he's fully accepted me, I can't shake the feeling that we have more in common than our military careers . . . like not wanting any harm to come to this sweet young woman in my arms.

Landon leans back on his heels. "Why'd you go there?" he asks.

The humor fades from Trin's face. "I didn't get a good feeling from her when you brought her home for Christmas." She waits as if unsure if she should say more. But she does only because I think she needs to. "She's not a good person, Landon. And I'm not just saying that because of what she does for a living. There're plenty of nice girls out there who dance at those places. But she's not what of them."

He squares his jaw. "I'm sorry you feel that way because I asked Bernadette to marry me. And she said yes."

If a dead body had fallen from the sky and landed on the table, I don't think the impact would have been any different. For a long moment, no one speaks.

I thought Trin would say something first, but it ends up being Owen. "We've been planning this week for a while now, boy. To surprise Trin, and for us to have time with her and her fella'."

"Yes, sir," Landon says.

"Then why isn't Bernadette here? If you're bringing her into this family, why isn't she here with us now? This here time's important."

I frown, wondering what he means exactly. But as I realize how serious Trin and I have become, I dismiss it as an important next step in our relationship. My attention returns to her brother, recognizing the hurt behind Owen's anger.

Landon pauses, anger flickering beneath his stance. Somehow though, I don't think it's directed at his father. "Bernadette's busy with school and can't get off work, sir."

"It's *summer*," Owen says. "How heavy can her course load be? And if she's latched onto you, she knows you can take care of her so she doesn't have to work—especially where she's working."

Landon doesn't have a response for that. Silvie who's been quiet lifts her basket. "Trinity," she says. "Be a dear and help me with the potato salad. They should be cooled off by now."

Trin eases off my lap. "Yes, ma'am," she says. She walks into the house, but not before sparing me a worried glance over her shoulder.

"Momma," Landon begins.

Miss Silvie shakes her head. "Not now, son."

We watch her disappear down the steps. No one says anything for a long time. After a moment, Landon returns to his seat beside his father. I don't remember any quiet father and son moments myself. Those few times my daddy bothered to make an appearance, our interactions were loud and fired with resentment. This isn't what's happening here. Yet it doesn't make the moment any less tense.

"I'll let you two talk," I say.

I push my seat away from the table. But before I can rise Owen shakes his head. "No. Stay. There's nothing to talk about." He looks at Landon. "He's a man. He can do whatever he wants."

"Thank you, sir," Landon says quietly.

"Don't thank me for this, son," Owen says. "Not even a little bit. But if you want to stay a part of this family, you'll have a pre-nup drafted and signed before you slip a ring on her finger."

Landon doesn't look at him when he answers. "Yes, sir."

Owen loads his shotgun, the aggression in his movements reminding me that just because he's mad at his son, doesn't mean he's forgotten that I'm the man sleeping with his little girl.

"You going hunting?" I ask him.

"No. I keep it loaded for intruders." He lays the shotgun in front of him and levels his stare on me. "And for anyone who tries to hurt my family," he adds.

This time, I'm the one to meet him square in the eye. "I would never hurt anyone in your family, sir," I tell him truthfully. "Especially Trinity."

He leans back in his chair and considers me. When he speaks, I'm caught off guard by what he asks. "Do you hunt?"

I frown, wondering where he's headed with this, but manage to shake my head. "I used to," I respond. "But not anymore." I don't add that once you hunt people, you don't look at hunting the same, even though it's true.

He picks up on what I left unsaid. "I haven't hunted either . . . not since Somalia."

I tilt my head slightly so he knows that I understand. Yeah, me and Trin's daddy have plenty in common.

"Have you picked up a gun since Iraq?"

"Just a rifle I own," I admit. "But only to move it here. Like you, I keep it around for intruders even though it's unlikely I'll encounter one on Kiawah."

"How are you with gunfire?" he asks. "Blasts, explosions. That sort of thing."

"Not good," I answer.

He nods. "It was bad for me, too, and I didn't go through

what you did."

"Did you ever get over it?"

"Not completely. I can function to a point, pretend like I'm not reliving some of that shit I went through. But no matter how good things are for me, and how much good I've had since, some memories stay with you forever."

"Yes, sir, they do," I agree.

Trin returns then with a bowl of potato salad and some chips and salsa. She kisses my cheek when I stand and lift them out of her hands.

"Thank you," she says. "Y'all ready to start grilling?"

"I'll do it," Landon says. He pushes away from the table and heads for the grill, keeping quiet.

"I'll bring out the steaks and corn," she says, eyeing him closely.

I watch Trin leave again, my need to always know where she is catching Owen's interest. "You watch her a lot. Don't you, boy?"

"Sir?" I question.

Owen laughs, with what I don't think is actual humor until I see the corners of his eyes crinkling. "Trinity," he explains. "You watch where she goes to make sure she's safe. I've seen you."

"Yes, sir. I do." I pause, debating whether to tell him how I feel. Ultimately I do, because we are talking about his daughter and I mean what I say. "She's the best thing in my life," I admit. "I don't want anything to ever happen to her."

He quiets, examining me closely. I'm not sure he's happy to hear how I feel or how serious I am when it comes to Trin. But then I realize he's been waiting to hear what I have to say.

"I was the same way with Silvie when we first met," he tells me. "It's like I had to keep her safe, and whole, and *alive*. In a lot of ways I still fret. Still worry something will happen to her if I'm not there beside her."

"I think I know what you mean," I say, although that's putting it mildly. I don't admit how crazy I get if something keeps Trin longer than she expects, or how I can't stop thinking about her when she's gone—wondering if she's okay and if anyone is bothering her. But I think he knows, and for that I'm grateful.

Owen stares past me, smiling when Miss Silvie returns to the terrace from hanging her sheets. She winks at him, and nods my way before walking off to help Trin in the kitchen.

As he watches her bustling around preparing supper, he seems to drift off and lose himself in his thoughts. It's only when I catch his eyes run the length of the shotgun that I realize he's back in the moment.

He motions to the barrel with a tilt of his chin. "Feels good not to have to use it anymore, doesn't it, boy?"

I release a breath, remembering what it took to need something so powerful. "Yes, sir. It does," I say, realizing something else had taken its place.

Chapter Twenty-Five

Trinity

Hale's head pops up as he finishes climbing up the chair. He takes his seat beside me as I adjust my binoculars to check on that couple one fondle away from having sex in the water. "How did it go?" I ask.

He huffs. "Kicked that asshole and his whole family off the beach. Called the others and told them they weren't allowed back and texted a picture of their faces and the idiot's license plate."

"Good. He sounded like an idiot. I appreciate you taking care of it." The couple starts to move closer to the shore, but now the woman appears annoyed which in a way gives me a sense of relief. There's nothing worse than having to blow your whistle because someone is getting his blown. I lower the binoculars and replace them with my sunglasses.

"How did Mason take everything? I really hate he had to deal with that garbage." I'm trying to keep my voice casual so I don't fire up Hale more than he is. But it's hard.

"He was mad," Hale says. "He knows that dick wasn't listening to anything he had to say just because he's black." He shakes his head. "Gotta give Mace credit. He handled it like a pro and as calm as ever. I was more pissed for him. Took all I had not to knock that fucker out."

"Well, thank you for not punching him. Although, it might have been worth the paperwork." I check on the kids splashing near the water, counting each one to make sure they're still there. It's not until the little girl bounces up to the surface from holding her breath that I'm assured they're all present and accounted for.

I glance at Hale. He's quiet. But since I know him as well as I do, I know it's not because he's calming down. When Hale's upset he withdraws and that's exactly what he's doing now. "You okay?"

He shakes his head. "Not really. You know, the south gets a bad rep because of shit like this these hillbilly rednecks pull. It's not right. Here's Mace, an educated man headed for law school and a genuinely good guy. But that prick couldn't see past the color of his skin. What got me more though was his kids were watching and learning from him, you know? He was teaching them that anyone who's different doesn't deserve to be treated with respect."

I sigh. "With luck, maybe they'll learn better when they're out on their own. Take Emery Madison. For all he claimed he wasn't racist, he was, terribly so. That boy hated anyone who wasn't white. But after a year at Columbia, his eyes opened real wide, and he changed for the better."

"Yeah?"

I nod and lift my binoculars to do another sweep again. "His sister told me he's marrying a sweet Asian woman next fall and that his best man is a Latino guy he roomed with for four years."

He shifts, adjusting his weight. "Well, shit. Maybe there's hope yet."

I smile as I adjust my binoculars again. "There's always hope, Hale. You just have to believe."

We sit in silence for a beat. But it's okay since I'm comfortable around him, and because I know this silence isn't due to his anger. All the negative emotions he returned with are fading, just like those flock of gulls heading into the ocean.

"How's it going with Callahan?" he asks.

There's that smile of mine. And to think all it took was a name. "Good. Real good. He and my daddy are out deep sea fishing today." I reach for my bottle of water, but wait before taking a sip. "They're bonding in ways I can't with him and I think it's been great for both of them. Just last week Daddy took him to that veterans group he belongs to while I was at work."

"How did Callahan feel about that?"

I think back to how he quieted when Daddy first approached him, and how it took some time to convince him. Daddy was really good about it, trying to be supportive and encouraging. I was almost surprised Callahan agreed, seeing how private he is. But ultimately, I think he went because of me. Which is one more reason to love him.

"He didn't want to go at first," I admit. "When he first came back from war, he was encouraged to be part of a veteran's association, but he was still raw from the experience." I shrug, not wanting to say too much. "It wasn't a good time for him to connect with strangers even though they were already connected by war."

"I can understand that," Hale says. He reaches for a bottle of sunscreen to add another coat to his legs. "Did you tell him you're leaving in September?" My fading smile is enough of an answer. He tosses the can back into the bag. "Shit, Trin. Why haven't you told him?"

"It's never been a good time."

"What the hell do you mean by that? Y'all have been inseparable."

I reach for a towel to wipe the binocular lenses, giving me a moment to form my words so they don't sound like the pitiable excuses they are in my head. "At first, I was just working on getting to know him. He had such a wall up, I was worried if I told him I was leaving soon, he wouldn't give me a chance to know him."

"And now?"

"Now, it's almost worse," I confess. "He talks to me a lot, Hale. Tells me things he's gone through that I don't think he's ever shared with anyone else."

"You mean about his time in Iraq?"

"Among other things," I answer quietly. "He's had a hard life. When he talks about his past . . . I don't know. It's like it leaves him worn. It's therapeutic, I'm sure. But it's no less exhausting emotionally. I don't want him to shut down—not when he doesn't seem to have anyone else to share these memories and feelings with. That's why I'm so glad, he's connecting with my Daddy, and some of those vets he's met, too."

"But they're not you," he points out. "Have y'all even known a night apart yet since your first?"

I shake my head.

"Damn, Trin," he says quietly. "You need to tell him."

"I know, and I've wanted to—believe me I have. But it's like every time I see him, he's so happy to be with me, like I am with him. I wait, promising myself I'll tell him once we're settled. But then we're talking or well, doing other things, and the moment never comes." I pull out my ponytail and shake out my hair, more to relieve some of the tension I'm feeling. I try to gather it again, only for my hands to fall to my sides, my frustration growing under Hale's scrutiny. "How do you tell someone who's become everything to you that you're leaving soon and won't be back for two years?"

"I don't know, Trin. But you have to find a way." He leans over the rail. "Excuse me, sir?" he calls down. "Would you mind setting the blanket a little farther from our station? Thank you, sir. Much obliged."

He resumes his pose next to me, but it's that stiff one that demonstrates he's disappointed in me and all I have to say. I can't say he's alone.

"I'm not going to pretend that what you have to do is easy," he continues. "And I'm not going to tell you things will be fine because I don't know if they will be. But regardless of the outcome, you owe Callahan the truth, and you owe it to him soon. How good he treats you? That man is head over heels for you."

My lids close briefly. Hale doesn't realize how in love I am with Callahan. For the life of me, I don't know how I'm going to survive without him. But when I say I'm stuck, I mean it. He's never leaving the U.S. again, not after the trauma he experienced during his time in the service. He's finally home. How can I ask him to leave the security and peace he finally has to follow me to an impoverished country somewhere across the globe?

"I have to tell you, even though your situation is far from perfect and less than ideal. It's good to see you with someone," Hale says, interrupting my thoughts. "'Bout time you picked a decent one from the bunch."

"Excuse me?" I ask, my brows lifting over top of my sunglasses. "What do you mean from the bunch? There was no 'bunch'. There was one. Unless you count seizure boy and eraser dick."

He laughs, I assume because he nicknamed the latter. "You don't get it, Trin," he says, shaking his head like I'm the crazy one here. "You never have."

I stand and blow my whistle. "Sir, back away from the ropes. *The ropes*! Thank you!" I say when he releases the buoy. I sit back down. "Okay. What exactly don't I get?" I ask Hale.

He considers me and chuckles. "That you could've had any guy you wanted. You just never took any of us up on our offers."

The whistle falls away from my hand, smacking me in the chest. "What are you talking about?"

"Me, Sean, Mason—hell, anyone of the boys you grew up with. Not a single one of us hasn't crushed on you at least one time since we've known you."

My mouth is so wide open, it's a wonder a bee hasn't

flown in. "*What*? Wait. You liked me? As in *liked* me?"

Hale just laughs. "Like I said, me along with many others."

I think he's blowing smoke, because none of what he's saying makes sense. "If that's true, how come none of you ever acted on it?"

"We all did. Every last one of us," he says. "Remember that time Sean took you to your first keg party?"

This time, I'm the one laughing. "Oh, you mean the one in that field? The one where the cops showed up and we had to climb that tree and hide—the one where he was so wasted he threw up in my hair when we were trying to find our way back to your car? You're right. I should have realized that boy wanted me bad."

Hale cracks up. "I forgot about that part, seeing how Mason and Becca were dragging my ass following my first beer bong. But yeah. To this day Sean considers it your first date."

"Are you serious?" I ask, throwing back my head and laughing.

"And don't forget Mason. When you and he went to Becca's sweet sixteen together. He really like you. Talked about you all the time."

I take a sip of my water as the breeze dies down. "If that's so, how come I caught him making out with Becca's cousin at the same party? I even ended up driving the two of them home so they could finish making out in the back seat."

He smirks. "Because along with being smart, funny, and pretty, one of your super powers includes the ability to kill a boner in a single bound."

I gasp. "Mind explaining yourself, sir?"

"Sean threw up on you that night because he drank himself stupid, all upset because his folks were splitting up. You told him not to worry. That he was your dear friend and always would be. Trin, just so you know, no horny teen hot for a girl, wants her to call him a 'dear friend'. 'Dear friends' don't get to feel up the girl they're hot for much less get laid."

"He was upset," I remind him. "I was trying to make him feel better."

"Like you were trying to make Mason feel better?" he asks, smiling. "He liked you, and you shoved him into another girl's arms."

"Only because Becca's cousin couldn't pry her eyes off him," I point out. "He should have said something."

"What did you expect him to say, Trin? You took his hand, brought him over to her so they could dance together. Which is why he ended up kissing her at the end of the night, and not you."

I'll admit, as flattered as I am, this conversation is also freaking me out. I never knew any of this. *Never.* "I thought he liked her."

"He did," Hale admits. "But he liked you more. Just like I did."

I don't think he can see my stare soften, not with how dark my sunglasses are. If he could, he'd sense my heart, and how it warms then. He, Mason, and Sean. What can I say? They've always been my family.

"Remember how we went to prom together?"

"Of course I do," I answer, quietly.

"Remember how we danced all night, laughed, raised hell, had a good time?" Again I nod. "I'm thinking it looks good for me, and that I'm finally going to get to kiss you—and hey, it's prom night, so maybe a little more than that."

I gasp. "*Hale!*"

He keeps his grin despite my dumbfounded response. "But then what do you do the moment we get back in the limo? You throw your arms around me and tell me that you love me like a brother. Now, nothing kills a boner like hearing that girl you adore thinks of you as her brother."

"I'm sorry," I say, barely able to speak. "I honestly never knew."

"It's because you never gave yourself enough credit.

You're a great girl, Trin. I'm proud to know you and call you my friend." He angles his chin. "Now, don't go lookin' like your favorite episode of *Teen Wolf* got deleted. It wasn't love—not *that* kind anyway. Besides, I realized long ago it was for the best. The group of us—with all the shit I've been through with my family?—I don't know how I would have survived without your friendship. I could have ruined it with that kiss." He thinks about it. "Or if I'd taken your panties off like I'd planned."

We both laugh because we can and because we're just that close. The best part is that when we quiet, I hold onto my smile and so does he. "Thanks, Hale."

He slings his arm around me and kisses the top of my head. "Always, sugar," he says.

I lean into him. Maybe Hale and I could have been great given we were always great friends. But I can't imagine feeling what I feel for Callahan with anyone else. And like Hale said, it may have interfered with our friendship, or God forbid, ruined it. Then where would I be without my boys?

In looking back, it was hard spending all those nights being the odd duck out. Being the one without someone to cuddle and kiss. But as I adjust my position against my friend, I would have relived those lonely nights a thousand times over, knowing that even though I didn't have a date, I was still loved. Just like I loved them in return.

"What about Becca?" I ask him after a moment.

"That girl's always looked good in dem jeans."

"You know what I mean," I tell him softly.

He lets out a harsh breath. "There's almost no point. Becca's going to marry another silver spoon with plenty of money and a lot more attitude."

The words I have to say I choose carefully despite how I would love these two to fall hard for each other and never look back. Becca's my friend. But for as long can remember, her family's always had a plan for her. And despite that she's never agreed with that plan, Hale's not too far off with his prediction. "Your family comes from money, too," I remind him.

"Not like hers," he says. "Hers has a shit ton and the pedigree to go with it. Like too many folks around here, they think me and mine are nothing more than a bunch of mongrels who got lucky."

I run my gaze over where the kids continue to splash and do a quick count as I speak. "Well, then they don't know what they're missing. You're a good person, Hale. One of the best I know, and someone who deserves that equal best in his life. Anyone would be lucky to count you as part of their family."

"Doesn't matter as far as her family's concerned." He squeezes my shoulder. "Did she tell you we finally went out the other week?"

"She did. She said she had a nice time," I say, more than putting it mildly.

His finger taps against my skin. "Did she tell you she had to meet me at the restaurant?"

Yes. Making it clear her daddy didn't want Hale near his land or his daughter. I wish I could tell him that Becca called me after she left him, crying about what could have and would've been with him. I want him to know that she finally admitted what he means to her, and how she regrets denying her feelings and keeping him at a friendly distance. But I can't. I won't hurt either of them this way. That doesn't mean I don't pray that somehow, they'll find their way to each other.

He gives my shoulder another squeeze. "I don't have a shot in hell with Becca, no matter how bad I want to. But, Trin, you have something special with Callahan—something not every person is blessed to find. Don't ruin it by not coming clean with him. As good as he is to you, you owe him that same respect back."

Chapter Twenty-Six

Callahan

The front door opens. "Batman?"

I laugh as easy as that, because Trin makes it easy. "In here," I call.

I dip my paintbrush into the open can of light blue paint she talked me into buying. "Carolina Sky Blue" it's called. Although I'd planned to paint this room white, the color's not as bad as I thought. I look up in time to see her step onto the paint tarp wearing a grin and nothing else.

Holy shit.

She strolls around leisurely, examining my work while allowing me to take a very long and much appreciated glance at that body I can't stop touching.

"Hmm. Looks good." She smiles playfully over her shoulder. "See, not so bad is it?"

Considering everything down south is harder than a steel rod, it's not so bad at all.

"What are you doing?" I say, because I know she's dying for me to ask.

She shrugs innocently and wanders over with enough skip in her step to flick her ponytail and bounce her breasts. "I didn't want to get paint all over my clothes." She offers me a brief kiss, her fingers trailing down my shirt. "You don't mind me naked, do you?" Her hands go further down, outlining my now painful erection. "No," she purrs. "You don't mind at all."

She falls to her knees, pulling the waistband of my old board shorts with her, and me right into her mouth. I drop my brush with a grunt while my other hand slaps the wall I just painted. Like so many times before, my hips begin to pump as she lures me further in. I watch her take me, swearing when I sense the back of her throat.

My hand curls around her head. I don't think about everything still left to do before I call it a day, or how my clothes are coated with paint. I only think about how good she's working me and how she digs her short nails into my hips to keep me going.

My vision fogs as I'm overcome with lust, my groin clenching and those familiar spasms overtaking me.

"I'm going to come," I warn between hard draws of air. I curse again when she increases her speed and goes deeper. "*Baby* . . ."

It's all I manage cause in truth I don't want her to stop, I want her to finish me this way.

And she does.

My legs shake and my body coils forward. I release her, splaying my fingers against the wall to keep me steady. Sweat trickles down my back. I groan loud enough for anyone passing to hear. But I don't care, and neither does she.

She doesn't stop, taking everything and keeping her pace long after I'm done. "Trin," I gasp. "*Fuck*, baby."

She moans around me, appearing to smile as she continues. In looking at her, she appears satisfied, but I know she's not. At least not yet.

I'm already hard again, and this time, it's my turn to please her.

I pop out of her mouth and wrench her upward, spinning her so she's facing the wall. My teeth trail along the soft curve of her neck. "Open your legs for me," I whisper against her ear.

With a small sigh and a shudder she complies, knowing

what's coming. I reach around her belly and slide the fingers of my clean hand down. Her breath hitches when I find that spot. She's already slick, but that's not good enough. I want her begging me for it. So I begin my massage, slowly at first, increasing my flicks and passes until she's shaking with need and rubbing against me.

I tug on her ear with my teeth and pass my other hand along her breasts, pinching and pulling her nipples, making her whimper with need. "I'm going to make you feel good," I promise, slipping two fingers inside.

Her head flies back and strikes against my shoulder. "*Callahan*," she says, smacking her hands against the walls.

My fingers quicken their pace, working to incite her. She clenches her knees together, spasming hard. One orgasm down, then another, until she's grinding against me, pleading with me to push inside her.

I ease my way in, trying to be gentle. But once I'm in all the way, I can't hold back. I clasp her hips, pumping hard, my swears and grunts drowning out hers.

It feels like heaven when I'm inside her, gripped by her possessive hold, surrounded by her heat and want. It's only because it's our second time that I last as long as I do. I slow my thrusts, my chest trickling with sweat when I finish once more.

Trin's body trembles as I press a kiss on her shoulder, and another one behind her ear, wishing I never had to let her go.

"I'm going to pull out? All right?" I ask as her quivers subside and her body begins to cool.

She nods, her head dipped low as if too heavy. My arms wrap around her waist, catching her when we separate. I'm worried I hurt her until she laughs.

"Hmm," she says. "Maybe I should walk in naked all the time."

"Maybe you should," I say. "You won't hear me complain."

I don't release her until I'm sure she won't fall. As I step back to look at this beautiful thing I call mine, my heart aches a little. As easily as she draws my grin, my laugh, my passion, sometimes it hurts so damn bad to look at her. But I don't tell her. She won't understand that this is the best kind of pain I've ever felt.

She turns around, smiling as she extends her arms. Splotches of light blue cover her breasts, stomach, and left hip. "See?" she says. "If I hadn't gotten naked, all this paint would be splattered on my cute clothes.

She struts to me, smiling as I gather her in my arms. She tilts her head when she realizes I'm not smiling back.

"Why?" I ask her.

She knows I'm no longer talking about the paint or anything we did.

"Why what, hon?"

I take in her face and how easily our bodies conform against each other. "Why did I have to wait so long for God to bring you into my life?"

Her brown eyes brim with tears. I cup her cheek, stroking the first tear that trickles down her face. "I love you, Trinity," I tell her, because it's true, and I've already waited long enough.

She covers her mouth, trying to stifle a cry before throwing her arms around me.

These are good tears I tell myself as I stroke her hair and kiss her cheek. She's the one who's been missing, the perfect person to come in my life and save me.

So I let her cry, and I hold her close, keeping her warm as the air conditioning unit blasts cold air and the sunlight crawls along the room.

Chapter Twenty-Seven

Callahan

Labor Day comes too soon for Trin and her friends, and maybe too soon for me, too. Tonight we're all gathered outside my house around the fire pit I put together from the flat stones Trin and I gathered around the island. I'm holding her as she and I lay across the lounge chair. This time when Sean picks up my guitar, there's no laughter, no jokes, only quiet, a rare occurrence around this tight crew.

Mason's leaving in the morning for D.C.. Unlike the others who are headed straight into the work force, he's starting law school at Georgetown. There's no doubt in my mind, he'll do well in life. Trin's friends, or should I say, "our" friends will all do well. They work hard, and ball-busting aside, they have good hearts.

Sean's leaving later this month for a pharmaceutical job he has lined up in Philly. Hale's supposed to drop him off on the way to New York where he's secured a job in as a financial advisor on Wall Street.

Trin hasn't interviewed for any teaching jobs, despite that school's already started. I don't ask, and I definitely won't push, knowing once she starts, I won't see her as frequently. Besides, she'll have no problem finding work once she decides it's time.

I have the feeling she's waiting for Becca to leave and start that public relations job in Charlotte. Becca will be the last to pack up and go. I thought her leaving would be the hardest on Trin. But seeing how quiet she is, saying goodbye to Mason won't be that much easier.

Sean lowers his head, his long arms swung over the guitar, but not really holding it like someone who enjoys playing as much as he does. With a sigh, he lifts his head and forces a smile. "Last song. What'll it be?"

Mason chuckles when we all turn his way. He doesn't look up, but does stop running his hand down his date's back. He's already feeling their goodbye, despite that smile he's doing his best to hang on to.

"You pick," he says.

"I'll sing if y'all sing with me," Sean responds. "But I'm not picking the damn song."

At first, no one says anything. We all know once the song finishes, it'll be time to say goodbye. Hale and Becca are sitting together, close enough that their legs are touching, but not close enough to make me think he's acted on his feelings for her.

She tugs down the sleeves of her jacket when the breeze picks up and smiles. "How about some Springsteen?" Her eyes scan the area, stopping on each of her friends, including me. "Maybe *No Retreat, No Surrender?*"

I couldn't have picked a better song for this bunch, even though I know it'll be hard for them to get through. Sean starts playing. Everyone joins in, even me.

"Well, we busted out of class, had to get away from those fools. We learned more from a three-minute record, baby, than we ever learned in school . . ."

At first, the five friends all smile through their sadness. But the moment they hit the chorus, Trin and Becca start crying. Tears stream down their faces as they try and push on. Becca clutches Hale's shirt when he tucks her against him, giving up halfway through the song to cry softly against his chest.

I gather Trin close when she covers her face and can't continue. By the time the song ends, Sean's the only one singing. He finishes, all the way until the last string is plucked. He then places my guitar on the empty chair beside him and wipes his nose with the back of his hand.

"Y'all suck," he says, glancing away.

Everyone laughs except for Trin. Although she's stopped crying, she looks sick with grief.

"What's wrong?" I ask, because I know something is, and that it has more to do than with Mason's departure.

She shakes her head, her face pale.

"Trin, what is it?" I press, keeping my voice low.

"I need to talk to you later," she says. "It's important."

Something in her solemn tone worries me. I've never heard her sound so . . . *hopeless*. Whatever she has to tell me isn't good news.

My eyes widen briefly. Shit, is she pregnant? I'm trying to remember the last time she had her cycle, but at that moment panic fills me and I can't. She's on the pill, but . . .

She wipes her eyes and stands when Mason begins his goodbyes. He and Sean are first, speaking quietly, and talking about meeting up in D.C. with Hale as soon as they can work out a weekend. They hug like brothers with Mason thanking him for always having his back.

Sean releases him and slaps his arm. "Fire needs more wood," he says, abruptly taking off and down the path.

Hale and I exchange glances and watch him disappear. It bothers me that Sean's taking it so hard. But what's worrying me more is Trin. If she's pregnant . . .

Mason steps in front of me and offers me his hand. "Callahan, it's been a pleasure."

I clasp his hand and shake it strong. "You're a good man, Mason. And you'll make a damn fine lawyer."

"Thank you," he says, knowing I mean it. He turns to Trin and Becca when they walk toward him, lifting them both in his strong arms. "My girls," he tells them quietly.

Hale glances down the path, but there's no sign of Sean. I'm scared shitless right now. I know I'm not ready to be a daddy. But I also know I love Trin, and that I'll do right by her . . . and anyone else who comes along. Except I can't talk to her about it until everyone leaves. So I step back and allow her a moment to say goodbye to her friend.

"I'll go look for Sean," I tell Hale.

"Thanks," he says.

I take off in a steady jog, but as I reach the end of my property, there's Sean, rummaging for pieces of wood.

He glances up. "Hey," he says.

"Hey," I say back.

I'm not a girl, and neither is Sean. I'm not asking him to pour his heart out or "share". I'm going to gather some wood with him because that's what men do. We wait in silence until someone speaks. Or we don't speak at all.

I've already gathered an armful of twigs before he says his first word. "Mason was the first friend I ever made. Trin might have been my second if you don't count Eddie Gufferson who spent recess picking his nose. I think he's running for office in the fall, hopefully he's a lot smarter now than he was then."

"Hmm," I say.

"Did you know me and Mason were roommates in college?"

"Yeah, Trin told me."

"Everyone warned us it would be the end of our friendship. Too much of a good thing, they said." He adds another stick to his pile. "But they were wrong. We were buddies through school. But in college, shit, we became family."

"You'll see him again, Sean. When people are that tight, they find a way to stay close."

He sighs. "I don't know. Mason's going places. He won't just have a job; he'll have a career—maybe even change the world for the better while I spend my life saving men like Old Man Perrington from erectile dysfunction."

"Someone has to, Sean," I say, meeting him with a grin.

But he doesn't smile back. If anything, he seems worse. "How are you doing it?" he asks. "I mean, *damn*, I can barely accept my best friend being a state away, but how are *you* doing it?"

I straighten, unsure what he's talking about. "Doing what?"

He shakes his head. "I know you and Trin haven't been together long, but I can see what she means to you. How the hell are you going to let her go? Especially to some shithole country the Peace Corps will stick her in—"

"*What?*"

He freezes. "What?" he repeats.

Steps close in behind me. I glance to my left to see Hale, but he doesn't keep my attention.

I toss my stack of wood aside and march toward Sean. "Tell me what you said." He shakes his head, like he's ready to bolt, but doesn't answer. "*Sean,*" I say again. "What did you say about Trin?"

"Shit, I . . ." He looks to Hale for help. Hale's eyes are wide, but not because he's shocked by what Sean said. He's shocked by what he *did*. He told me something I wasn't supposed to know—something apparently everyone else knew but me.

"Trin's going into the *Peace Corps*?"

Hale shoves his hands in his pockets and moves to stand by Sean. "Callahan," he says. "You really need to talk to her about this."

Yeah. I do. I storm down the path. Mason and his date are gone. Trin and Becca are sitting by the fire speaking quietly. They stop talking when they see me.

Trin stands, reaching for me. "What's wrong, hon?"

I step out of her reach. "Please tell me you're pregnant," I tell her, my voice harsh. "Please tell me that's what you want to talk to me about."

She frowns, appearing confused. "I'm not pregnant. I had my cycle two weeks ago. Why would you . . ."

Her voice trails when Sean and Hale appear. "Sorry, Trin," Sean says. He meets her eyes briefly as he passes her and walks toward the front of the house.

Hale pulls Becca up from her seat. "Come on. We have to

go. They need to talk."

"What . . . oh, *shit*," she says, as they pass us.

Everyone knew. Everyone, but me.

Trin's breaths appear tortured and she's focusing hard on the ground. But right now, she needs to focus me. "You're going into the Peace Corps," I say. "You're going to be gone what? Two years? And you never thought to tell me?"

A tear escapes her eyes. "It never seemed to be a good time," she says.

"You have to be *fucking* kidding me."

"Cal—"

I hold out my finger. "No. *No*. We've been practically inseparable. Don't stand here and tell me you never had a chance to talk to me about this."

"Callahan, you've been through a lot—"

"No *shit*," I snap.

"Please, hear me out." She tries to reach for me again. Again, I deny her. Her hands fall at her sides. "Baby," she says. "When we're alone, we're *always* intimate. You tell me about the horrible things you've lived through, and I do my best to help you through them. I didn't want interrupt you when you talked about your past—knowing how hard it is for you to open up. Nor did I want to ruin an opportunity to grow closer to you. So I kept my mouth shut, and waited for a good time that never seemed to come."

I scowl. "You're telling me that we've never gone out, or sat around talking about life? That all I've done is bitch about the shit I've been through, or dragged you to bed—is that what you're saying? No opportunities for anything else like, I don't know, the *truth*? Just bitchin' and fucking, right?"

"Don't say it like that!" she bites out. "Don't belittle what we have—"

"We've got *nothing*, Trin!"

Her head snaps back like I slapped her. But as angry as I am, as much as could tear this whole place apart, I would never put my hands on her in anger. *Never*.

But I can't say she's not killing me.

"Please don't tell me that." Tears pool in her eyes. "*Please*."

"What would you like me to say, Trin? At least I'm being honest." I hate the tears dripping from her face, and I hate that I'm the one causing them. But Jesus, the pain ripping through me is more than I can take. She's leaving. She's fucking *leaving* me.

"The intimacy I'm talking about extends past our time in bed," she says, placing her hand on her chest. "Every time we're alone, I can feel us growing closer. The last thing I wanted was for something to wedge us apart."

"Like you leaving for two years?" I cover my face when she starts crying. "God damn it, Trin. You should have told me . . . You shouldn't have kept something like this from me."

I settle myself in a chair, concentrating hard on the flames dying in the pit. Trin takes a seat next to me, but keeps her distance. When all that remains are nothing more than glowing embers, she edges closer and takes my hand in hers. When she squeezes it, I don't squeeze back. My hand simply lies between hers.

"What has all this been?" I ask her quietly. "You introducing to me to your friends. Those suppers with your folks. All the times you fell asleep in my arms." I look at her. "What did it mean to you? Was I just something to do to pass the time until you left?"

"Of *course* not." Her voice shakes, her eyes so red, I know she hasn't stopped crying. "This time with you has meant everything to me. I love you, Callahan—"

I pull away from her. "Don't," I tell her, my voice splintering. "Don't say that to me."

I bury my face in my hands. This can't be happening. No way can she betray me like this. Not her.

It takes me a long moment, but eventually I drop my hands away and force myself to speak. "When do you leave?"

She stiffens beside me. "I was supposed to leave in two weeks. But I've been granted a short extension—"

I don't hear her last words. My blood is boiling and scorching through my veins like acid. I stand, anger shaking me down to my core as I stomp toward the house.

"Callahan, *please*."

I whip around. "Please *what*? When I told you I loved you, it was one of the hardest things I've ever had to say because I was saying forever, and wanting it, and meaning it—even though I didn't think I deserved it. But you made me think I could. You made me mean it just for you!"

She stands inching toward me with her palms out. "I mean it, too."

"No." I pitch her with a cold stare. "Your idea of forever stops in two weeks. Then you move on to the next person you have to save. Your next charity case."

Tears flow in streams down her face. "That's not what you are to me."

"Aren't I? Come on, Trin. It's the reason you were drawn to me in the first place. You saw someone you thought needed saving. So you swooped right in didn't you?"

"Callahan, don't do this," she chokes out.

"Don't do what? Tell you the truth? One of has to." My stomach is in knots. I should be curled over in agony. But my voice stays even and cold. "You were put on this planet to help others. You've said so yourself. And you have. You helped me. But your work here's done and you can go."

"I don't want to leave you," her face is blotchy, and swelling with how hard she's crying. I should hug her because I love her. But I can't because no matter what she thinks she feels, she never meant it to last.

"You don't want to go," I say. "But you will. Just don't look back because I won't be here."

I storm off into the house and slam the door, my head pounding so hard I can barely think straight. Somehow, I manage to grab my car keys and remember my wallet.

This isn't love, I tell myself. Love's supposed to be forever, good, and gentle. It's not supposed to drive a stake through my Goddamn chest. It's not supposed to feel like my soul is breaking away in pieces.

I rush out the door and into my truck, cranking the engine, not bothering with a seatbelt.

My foot stomps on the gas as I peel away. The last image I catch in my rearview mirror is of my house . . . and Trin leaning over the railing, sobbing.

Chapter Twenty-Eight

Callahan

"What's her name?"

I look up from drinking my coffee.

My mother rolls her eyes and takes another drag from her cigarette, while my sister's son sucks his thumb on her lap. "Come on, Callahan," she says, blowing the smoke over her shoulder, and thankfully away from the kid. "I haven't seen you in two Goddamn years. You show up here, looking like shit, working at a job you can't stand. If this ain't about a girl, I don't know what is."

I don't remind her that the reason she hasn't seen me before now is because two years ago, when I beat up her boyfriend for beating *her* up, she told me not to come back. Her new boyfriend, Perry, sits in front of the TV drinking a beer. He doesn't say much, mostly because he knows I help pay the bills, and because he's probably already drunk. To his credit, he's not a mean drunk, not like the last few men in my mother's life.

"Her name's Trinity," I answer.

"That's a pretty name," my niece Cassie says. She's all of fourteen, dressing like she's twenty, and typing away on a smart phone she shouldn't be able to afford. Like her mother, and my mother, she'll probably be pregnant by the time she's fifteen. She looks up. "What's her last name?"

"Summers," I mumble.

"Is she pregnant?" Momma asks, taking another drag.

"No." The question shouldn't upset me because Trinity isn't pregnant, but it bothers me because in a way, I wish she was.

I wasn't ready to be a father. That doesn't mean I wouldn't have stepped up and married her. Not just because she was pregnant, but because I really love her, and it would have been my excuse to love her forever.

Instead, I find out her idea of love and commitment didn't extend past the summer.

I left Kiawah and drove all the way back to Linden, Texas, stopping only for gas and the occasional bite of food. I think I was almost to Arkansas when I realized I didn't have my phone. But it was too late to turn around, and by then, I didn't see the need. Who the hell am I going to call anyway?

So now I'm here, working as a bouncer because there's not much else, and living at a motel because it's better than living with the only blood I know.

I lean back in the chair and look around the shabby double wide trailer. With the exception of the warped peel and stick tiles, this is almost the exact replica of the house I grew up in, and the one I lived in during high school. Nothing's really changed for Momma. But for change to happen, you have to want it.

My thumb skims over the handle of the chipped ceramic mug Momma mixed me some Sanka in. I'm not sure why I'm here. I guess I simply needed to leave, to feel like I still had someplace where I belonged. But who am I kidding? I've never felt like I belonged with my mother, my family, or anyone else.

Except maybe with Trin.

Cassie perks up, her attention fixed on the screen of her phone. "Is this her? Oh, my God, Uncle Callahan, is that *you*?"

I glance at the screen when she shows it to me. It's a

picture of me and Trin at a veteran fundraiser her daddy asked me to attend. I didn't want to go. But I knew he wanted me there and that it was important to Trin. So I went, and spent more time with her daddy than I did with her.

Owen is a good man. We made the rounds with him introducing me to men who had served in Vietnam, Dessert Storm, and Iraq. Yet the one thing that he did what really struck me was what he did the morning of the fundraiser.

He took me to a barbershop that belonged to a man whose father had served in the Korean War. Understanding that some men will always see their sins staring back at them in their reflections, he purposely didn't hang mirrors in his shop, and only offers small handheld ones when asked.

I had my first haircut in a long while, and my first shave with a straight razor. I also had my first real look in the mirror in what seemed like forever. I couldn't recognize the young man staring back at me, and neither could Trin.

She answered the door when I knocked, smiling politely. She started to say, hello, until I winked at her and she realized it was me beneath that clean-cut face and Army blues. Her eyes flew open, half a second before she launched herself into my arms.

"*Damn,* baby," she'd squealed.

I was thinking the same thing when I saw her in that dark purple dress and her hair all done up. She laughed when I couldn't stop staring at her. "Didn't know I could clean up so well, did you?" she had teased.

No, I did. But like always, I couldn't take my eyes off her.

Her father was being honored for his work with U.S. vets. But somehow, Trin and I ended up with our picture in the paper. It was the same photo Cassie's showing me now, the one the photographer took of us while we were dancing. Trin's smiling in my arms and resting her head against my chest as I hold her close.

"Yeah. That's her," I answer.

Cassie clears her throat and reads the caption out loud. "Socialite Trinity Summers dancing at the Charleston County

Veteran's fundraiser with Iraq war hero, Callahan Sawyer—"

"*Socialite?*" Momma mashes out her cigarette and snatches the phone from Cassie's hand. She scowls as she takes in the picture. "You went out with a rich girl?"

The way she asks is more of an accusation than a question. Her scowl deepens when I don't answer. "Shit, Callahan. You could've been set for life. Instead you're here, taking up space in my kitchen."

"I wasn't with her because she comes from money," I snap.

She raises her eyebrows. "So then what was it? Love?" She huffs. "Love doesn't pay the bills, Callahan. It just leaves you knocked up with a bunch of kids you can't afford."

Yeah, like me and my sisters were to her.

She shakes her head, her eyes narrowing. "Maybe you should've knocked her up. Then you'd be in a big fancy house, with big fancy servants, and not with those so *far* beneath you."

I push away from the table, taking my cup with me and dumping it out in the sink. At my house, or Trin's, I would've washed it by hand, or set it in the dishwasher. Here, I just add it to the pile between the baby bottles and plates caked with leftover SpaghettiOs.

My mother's words hit me hard. It's not that I think I'm better than her or anyone in my family. It's more like I know I don't belong with them.

I reach in my wallet and drop a few hundred dollars in front of her.

"You're leaving?" she asks, her eyes fixed ahead where Perry's begun to snore.

"Yeah, I am," I answer.

She reaches for another cigarette and pops it in her mouth. "You're not coming back. Are you?"

"No, ma'am. I'm not."

She huffs again. "Maybe that's a good thing," she says, lighting the cigarette and taking a long drag.

Regardless of what she says, and the way that she says it, I think she knows I'm better off without them and away from this life they've carved out for themselves. But my mother and I have never been close enough for me to ask. So I'll do what I've always done: send her money, and keep my distance. Like I said, for change to happen, you have to want it. And looking at her, and my sisters, I know I don't want this.

What I want, I'm no longer sure I can have.

I bend and kiss her head. For all that she is or isn't, she's still my momma.

Cassie follows me out to my truck. "Can I have twenty dollars?" she asks.

I turn around and take in her face that's too made up, and the clothes she shouldn't be wearing. I want to yell at her to snap out of it, to not be her mother, or her grandmother, or hell, anyone of my sisters. Instead, I reach in my wallet again and hand her a few bills, knowing that for now, this is all I can do for her.

"Thanks," she says.

"You know it doesn't have to be like this," I tell her. I don't have to explain myself, she knows what I mean.

She shrugs. "This isn't so bad. It just is what it is." She takes the bills and runs them between her fingers to smooth them out.

I take another good look at her. Christ, she's just a kid. But already she's probably been through too much. "You've got my number in there?" I ask her, motioning to her phone. She nods. "Make sure you keep it. If I can ever help you, I will, okay?"

She nods briefly and glances down. "Can I ask you a personal question?" she asks. She doesn't wait for me to answer. "Was it love? What you felt for that rich girl?"

"It still is," I answer truthfully.

She smiles softly, it's only then I see that little girl lying beneath all that makeup. I think she wants to know more, but when she doesn't ask, I slip into my truck and drive away.

In less than an hour, I'm headed back to Kiawah, knowing

my house won't be my first stop.

Chapter Twenty-Nine

Trinity

Today should have been a good day. I immunized the last few children from the neighboring village, then helped the team finish the new water system this village so desperately needs.

There are cheers when the first trickles of water shoot from the spout. The children rush forward, cupping their hands to have a taste. And while their smiles warm me, the joy I feel is minimal and fleeting. I don't feel emotions the same anymore. At least, not the good kind.

Feelings that evoke sadness or pain, those I feel to the extreme. I walk away as more people gather and in the direction of the small cinderblock house where I'm staying.

"Trinity," Marty calls. He jogs up to me, leaving the crowd of squealing children happily splashing themselves. "Hey," he says stopping in front of me. "Pablo says they'll be playing their guitars tonight. Do you want to come listen with me?"

I shake my head. "I'm tired. Long day, you know?"

I don't dare tell him I'll go another time. I think he likes me and I don't want to encourage him. If I think about it, I suppose Marty's a fine looking man. This is his second tour with the Corps, and he'll probably be a "lifer" if his U.N. aspirations fall through.

He says he's passionate about helping others, and believes he was put on this earth to serve. I guess he's being honest.

He seems like that type of man. Once upon a time, he probably would have been someone I could connect with. But I don't connect with anyone. Not anymore.

"Goodnight," I tell him.

I trek up the steep cobblestone road, waving to the children running past me eager to get their turn at the spout. I pause as I reach the bright orange-colored house, the one where the little old lady who thinks I'm cursed lives with her daughter.

"Only darkness could fade a girl's smile like Trinity's," she told Pablo.

No, ma'am, I wanted to say. Heartbreak can do it, too.

I stayed at Callahan's house over a week, waiting for him to return. He'd left his cell phone charging on the kitchen counter. Whether it was intentional, or unintentional, I'll never know. All I know is that September became October and he never came home.

The only person who had heard from him was the owner of Your Mother's. He called to tell her he'd quit and to thank her for the opportunity. So when October 15th came, I said goodbye to everyone I loved and stepped on a plane bound for South America . . . well, almost everyone I loved.

The sun begins to set as I reach the top of the hill. Chickens skitter past me in their haste to find their nests. I sigh and rub my shoulders, feeling unbearably tired.

The house where I live is just ahead and to my left. I should go right to bed given how I'm feeling. But sleep is something of a lost luxury, one I don't foresee reclaiming any time soon.

I open the front gate, forcing a smile when my sweet landlady waves from where she's sewing on a rocking chair beneath a large mango tree.

"*Buenas noches*," I yell. She's almost deaf and I doubt she hears me, but I don't want to be impolite.

I cross the small courtyard that separates my room from the rest of her house. There's not much to my tiny dwelling, more like a cinderblock room big enough for a bed, desk, and wardrobe.

Metal bars line the windows and doors. I use my key and lock the door behind, leaving the privacy panel open so the evening breeze can sweep in and hopefully spare me from some of the thick humidity.

I pour myself a glass of water. After a few sips of the tepid liquid, I sit and write another letter to Becca.

Dearest Becca,

I'm sorry to hear about Hale's daddy, and everything that surrounded his passing. I've written him a few letters, but I haven't heard back. When you talk to him again please let him know I'm thinking of him and sending him my love.

I miss you and wish I could see you. You asked me in your last letter how I'm doing? In truth, I'm not doing so great.

Tears blur my vision. The first falls and drips onto my paper, causing the ink to run. But I continue, because only to Becca can I say what I say.

I'll never forgive myself for what I did to Callahan. I screwed things up so bad. There never seemed to be a good time to tell him I was leaving. But I should have found one. Even if he left me sooner, I owed him the truth.

I wipe my eyes, remembering the look of devastation and anger on his face. I hate myself for hurting him, and pen these same thoughts to my letter.

I know you're convinced he'll wait for me. But I think you're wrong. It's already been eight weeks since I last saw him.

The reality of my words won't allow me to continue. I drop my pen and cry into my hands.

My momma used to tell me time heals all wounds. I once believed her, but I don't anymore. For as much time that's passed, the pain I feel surrounding my break up with Callahan remains raw and constant.

Not that I don't think I deserve it.

Or believe it wasn't my fault.

My fear is he'll move on—find another girl, and maybe even be married and have a child by the time I return. But what scares me more is that he won't—that he'll regress and become that recluse I first met, the one drowning in his own pain.

I don't want him to be with anyone else. To touch anyone else. Or love anyone else. But if it means his happiness, I pray to God that love with another is what he finds.

My eyes sting at the thought, but I mean what I say. If there was ever a man who earned his happiness and peace, it was Callahan.

"*Aqui*," someone squeals.

I straighten. *Here*?

The voice is familiar. I recognize it as Elbia's, the little girl with the long hair who looks for me after school so I can check her blood sugar, and braid her hair.

"*No. No. Aqui.*" She giggles. "*Aqui.*"

I wipe my eyes, not sure what she's up to. When I hear her laugh again, I shove the chair away and rise, thinking I better take her home when a more familiar, and *very* deep voice says, "Here? Trinity's here?"

My heart stalls along with my breath when Callahan's large body steps in front of the metal bars that make up my door. His stare latches onto mine when he sees me standing there. Like me, he's simply cemented in place. I clasp my hands over my mouth, to stifle my sob, barely believing he's here.

Callahan reaches for the door, rattling the bars when it won't open. I hurry forward, my hands trembling as I unlock it with my key and step aside to let him in. He rushes in, tossing his heavy pack and hauling me to him.

The door clangs shut as I fall against his chest, gripping him so hard I'm sure I'm crushing him.

"I'm sorry," I choke out. "God, I'm so sorry."

He strokes my hair, letting me cry. "Shhh. It's okay. I'm here now, baby. I'm here." His lips sweep kisses all over my face. But when his mouth nears mine and I turn, those sweet kisses become something more.

It's like we were never apart, and we never stopped loving, our bodies pressing tighter and our mouths claiming each other. Callahan scoops me in his arms and carries me to my bed, lowering me so I lay across his lap. Slowly, he edges away, taking me in as if I might somehow vanish.

My hands stroke his beard, relishing the familiar tickle of his whiskers. "I can't believe you're here," I stammer, crying all over again.

He smiles softly, lifting my hand to kiss and prove he's with me. "I was worried you wouldn't see me and turn me away."

"Why would you think that?" I try to take a few breaths and calm, but my words release in shaky spurts. "I've been lost without you."

His hold on me tightens as he clutches me to him. "And I've been *nothing* without you," he admits, his voice rough. "Nothing mattered anymore when I left. . . I love you, Trin. God, I love you so much."

"I love you, too," I whisper . . .

An hour later, he's gathering a sheet around our naked bodies and tucking me against him. My hand skims across his chest to rest over his heart.

"I'm sorry I hurt you," I tell him, my voice just above a breath along the dimly lit room. "I thought if you knew I was leaving, you would never give me and us a chance. I liked you from the beginning. But then we grew close, and telling you became that much harder."

His hand trails down my arm. "I didn't like what you did, but I can't be sure you were wrong in what you thought. I came to Kiawah to be alone, and that's how I might have stayed if you didn't find a way to get through to me."

"I still shouldn't have done it."

"Maybe," he admits. "But I've thought about that day I left too many times. It's in the past, baby. Let's leave it there where it belongs."

"Okay," I say quietly, even though I'll never stop feeling bad for what I did, and how I made him feel.

I press a kiss to his chest and push up on my elbow so I can see him. He traces his finger along my jaw, staring at me with those blue eyes that have haunted my dreams, and stirring a tickle with his touch that makes me smile.

"God, I've missed this face," he says.

My grin widens, despite the lingering sadness I've carried for so long. "How in the world did you find me?"

"Your daddy helped," he explains. "I went to see him to talk over a few things." His hand smooths through my hair. "I flew all night and travelled on bus most of the day. The bus got me as far as the neighboring village and I walked from there. But once I arrived, I didn't know where to look.

"There was a guy near a fountain of sorts. I approached him, knowing he was American and introduced myself, told him who I was and that I needed to find you." His voice lowers. "I knew he knew you, but he refused to tell me where you were. I wasn't in a good mood. It took a shit ton of time to get here so I told him if he didn't tell me, I'd knock the peace right out of his corps."

I cover my face, but then drop it away. "I think you mean Marty. He's not a bad guy. He probably just wanted to make sure I was safe."

"No. It's more like my arrival ruined whatever the hell he had planned for you. If it wasn't for that little girl tugging on my arm and pointing up the hill when she heard me say your name, *Marty* would be on the ground bleeding."

I lean closer and kiss his cheek. "The little girl's name is Elbia. She's my buddy."

I snag a small frame from the top of my desk and hand it to him. "I showed her your picture and told her all about you."

He scans the photo Becca took of us the night he sang to me at my house. "That's the first night I kissed you," he says quietly.

"I know," I answer, sadness finding its way into my voice. I don't want to ask what I do next, but I have to, knowing I can't leave. "How long can you stay?"

He pauses. "How long do you want me?"

Tears fill my eyes and my voice cracks. "Forever?"

He hands me the picture and scoots out of bed, reaching

for his boxers and jeans. I place the frame back on the desk and scramble to the edge of the bed, gathering the sheet around my breasts. "Callahan, where are you going?"

He sighs and yanks on his clothes. Except for his shirt and socks, he's now fully dressed. "These past few weeks have been hell," he tells me.

I wipe my eyes, trying not to full-out cry. *Please don't leave me.*

"I never want to feel like that again," he continues, his beautiful eyes welling as they meet mine. "If you agree to be my wife, I won't have to, and neither of us will ever know another night apart."

He drops to the floor on one knee and pulls a ring from his pocket, taking my hand as tears of joy and shock run down my face. "Trinity Summers . . . will you marry me?"

Epilogue

Callahan

Three minutes.

That's all we have left.

Three minutes more and this ends.

But as I stare into the eyes of my son, and see him laughing as he rocks on his belly, three minutes more of tummy time doesn't seem like long at all. "You're a lot tougher than that book says. Aren't you, soldier?"

He squeals when I tickle his chin. People say Cal junior has my eyes. Maybe. But the sparkle of mischief within them, and that wide contagious grin, that's all his momma.

I adjust my hips against the sand, thankful that for once the agonizing ache is a thing of the past, and so is the numbness I once searched for like a friend.

My eyes tear when the breeze picks up and shoots a bit of sand in them. The sneeze it stirs makes Cal giggle so I don't mind. A laugh from my son is well worth a little sand, and a lot more.

I pick him up and kiss his chubby cheeks in time to hear a car pull up the driveway. It's not long after that that those familiar footsteps bounce through the house.

"Batman? You out back with Robin?"

I chuckle. "Yeah. We're out here, baby."

"Robin" starts flapping his little arms excitedly the moment he sees Trin walk through the back door. Can't say I blame him. She's only been gone a couple hours, but like him, I missed her the whole damn time.

She smiles brightly and reaches for him. "Hi," she says, drawing out the word. "Here's my little super hero." She cuddles him against her, but greets me with a kiss packed with one hell of a sizzle.

She tugs on my bottom lip as she pulls away. I grin against her mouth. "I wouldn't start anything you can't finish," I tell her.

"Now, baby. When have I ever not finished?" She tosses me a sly look over her shoulder as she carries our boy back into the house. "Besides, you need to give me something to do once our little bird goes down for his nap."

I rub my jaw and chuckle. For all I suffered, I'm convinced she and our baby must be my reward. It almost seems wrong for a man like me to be given such love, to have his heart so filled with joy, but I'll take it. And like I promised Trin on our wedding day, I'll never let us go.

I find them lying on our bed as she feeds him. It's cold in here from the air blasting through the A.C.. I grab the blanket at the foot of the bed and gather it around us as I lie beside them, positioning my body so I can see my pretty wife's face. She smiles when I stroke her cheek.

"Did you get to see Hale?" she asks.

"Yeah. For bit."

Her face shadows with concern. "How's he doing?"

"He's all right. These past few years have been rough, dealing with what he's had to deal with, and being so far away. We're supposed to get together later for a beer and talk."

"That'll be good for him." She adjusts the blanket around Cal's shoulders and asks, "Did you ask him about dinner Friday?"

I try to keep my face neutral, but it's hard since I know what she's really asking. "Yeah. He said he'll be here."

She raises her brows, hope sparking that gleam in her eyes. "Did you tell him Becca will be here?"

"I did."

"*And*?" she presses.

"And what?" I ask, doing a shitty job at playing dumb.

"*Callahan* . . ."

I chuckle. "Well, for a man you claim had lost his grin. He sure found it when I told him she was coming."

Knowing Trin's all but planning Hale and Becca's wedding, I quick change the subject. "How was lunch with your momma?" I ask her.

She gives me "the look" the one that tells me she knows I'm trying to distract her. But even so, she answers. "It was good. Landon sold his robotics technology for a cool fifteen million." She shakes her head. "Everybody used to tell me I was the smart one. Little did they know Landon would graduate from M.I.T and develop something so high-tech it would change the world."

"Yeah. Your daddy told me all about it when he was over earlier. Also said Landon donated ten of those millions to his charity."

"Landon's always had a good heart." She loses her smile. "Too bad he had to go and marry that stripper who broke it. Good heavens, she and her bedazzled vagina were awful."

I laugh. I don't tell her Landon probably thought he'd scored big time. Instead I fill her in on my talk with her daddy as my fingers leave her face to smooth over Cal's soft curls. "Owen wants me to help spearhead the charity, oversee construction, and talk to some of the vets. He's hoping between the two of us, plus some of the boys from the V.A., we can figure out who's home is in need of repair, or who doesn't have one so we can build it for him—or her."

"How do you feel about that?"

"I told him I would. He mentioned I'd have to travel with him some, but that you and Cal would come with us if any trips required an overnight stay."

"Momma would have to come, too," she says.

"Of course she would. After all our time in the Corps, she misses you."

"I've missed her, too." She adjusts her weight, a hint of something sparkling her eyes. "Although you have to admit, Papua was fun." She dances her eyebrows. "And more romantic than Ecuador, don't you think?"

"It was," I agree. Which is why Trin was already six months pregnant by the time our term in the Peace Corps was up. Yeah, I joined, too. I was already there, and figured this way I could help, too.

"It's good to be home, though," I say, meaning it down to my bones. "I want to set down some roots, and maybe give Cal a brother or sister to play with."

"I'd like that." She sighs, thoughtfully. "This way, both our babies will be walking by the time Hale and Becca get married."

"Trin," I warn.

"Two little ring bearers—Or maybe a ring bearer and a flower girl. Doesn't matter which, really. Either will be cute, don't you think?"

"*Trin,*" I insist. "Hale and Becca haven't seen each other in years."

"Oh, that doesn't matter, hon," she says, dismissively. "When it's meant to be, it's meant to be." She glances down at our little bundle. "Speaking of which, guess who's asleep?"

I shake my head and lift Cal junior carefully, knowing his momma's up to no good, and knowing there's nothing anyone can say to stop her. With a wink her way, I carry our son into his room, taking a moment to kiss his head before I lower him to his crib and cover him with a blanket.

When I return to our room, I'm half-expecting Trin to be on her laptop, online shopping for Becca's wedding dress.

Instead I find my beautiful wife perched on the edge of our bed, leaning back on her hands, her dark hair falling behind her, her legs crossed, and the clothes she was wearing in a pile by her feet.

"Hey," she says, pegging me with a heat-filled gaze that

never dwindles and always proves how bad she wants me. "Ready to report for booty call, soldier?"

"Yes, ma'am." I strip out of my shirt and toss it, kissing her hard as I lower myself on top of her.

It's been three years since Trin swept into my life. Yet she's still as kind and strong as ever, still loving, still gentle. She's everything I desire, and all the woman I'll ever need.

She's my forever. And forever, y'all, has never sounded so sweet.

This book contains excerpts from *Let Me*, *Feel Me* and *Crave Me* the forthcoming books in the O'Brien Family novels by Cecy Robson in addition to *Of Flame and Light*, the next installment in her Weird Girls novels. The excerpts have been set for this edition only and may not reflect the final content of the forthcoming novels

READ ON FOR AN EXCERPT FROM

Let Me

An O'Brien Family Novel

Cecy Robson

Chapter One

Finn

I see the strike coming at me a split second before it connects with my skull. My head snaps back from the force, the crowds' hollers resonating like a muffled cry in the distance. It was a good punch—lightning quick with enough impact to knock most guys on their asses. But I'm not most guys.

You hit me, I'm only going to hit you harder.

My right hand shoots up, blocking and smacking away the kick gunning for my ribs. I pivot out of the way, again, and again, and again, avoiding Easton's arms and legs as they come at me. He's fast, strong, with a six inch reach advantage. But he's too eager to take me out and not pacing himself like he should. Already he's breathing hard and it's just the start of the second round.

I take my time to figure him out, planning each move, searching for that opening I need. Do I take a few bashes because of it? Sure. It's part of the job. But believe it or not, it's part of the job I look forward to.

Those punches and kicks remind me that I still *feel*, that I'm still human. And that for now, I'm still alive.

"Oh!" some drunk behind me yells when my uppercut finds Easton's chin.

He staggers back, swiping the blood oozing from his lip, yet he keeps his grin. He's trying to make like it was a lucky shot. That it won't happen again.

Like me, Easton needs to win this match. And if he does, he'll move up to the top ten, making him a contender for the UFC Lightweight title.

Talent aside, the guy's a raging asshole, and so are the idiots in his training camp. They've been trash-talking since the moment I agreed to this match. I didn't really care and laughed most of it off until they got personal and took it a step too far.

Again he nails me in the head. It's not as hard as it was last time which tells me he's getting tired. Does it hurt? I guess.

But let's say I'm a guy who's used to pain.

Easton grins. He thinks I'm afraid of him. He thinks he has me where he wants me. But fear is an emotion I don't allow myself to entertain. Fear gets you hurt and rips you apart till you think there's nothing left.

I dodge out of reach. He scowls and takes another swing. This one gets close enough to my jaw to create a breeze that whips across my skin.

"Finn," my brother Killian barks from the side. "Take him out *now*."

He's worried about me. So is my family. But now's not the time to think about them. I keep my hands up as I edge away, letting Easton think I'm backing down, that I'm tired and need to catch my breath.

I sidestep when he lunges forward, avoiding his next swing and use the momentum to drop my head and nail him in the temple with a roundhouse kick.

Like I said, Easton's fast.

Too bad for him I'm a little bit faster.

The kick is my signature move, as natural for me as the next breath. He goes down like I planned. But in the Octagon you don't stop just because your opponent collapses like timber. You charge forward. You show him what you're made of. And you prove just how tough you really are.

That muffled screaming, isn't so muffled anymore. The crowd loses their shit as I pounce, my blows nailing Easton in the face until the ref's arms hook beneath mine as he hauls me off. I back away, my fists up because I already know I won.

I should do a back flip or some crazy shit to incite the crowd. This is it. My time has come to own it. But the good things aren't as great as they can be. Not with the memories that haunt me. And not with the anger they stir.

Killian rushes in as the medic wipes down my face. I'm

bleeding from the punch Easton caught me with at the beginning of the round. I didn't think it was that bad, but the way the ringside medic is pressing the towel against my head clues me in the gash isn't closing like it should.

"I'm going to have to stitch you up, Fury," he mumbles.

"I figured," I tell him.

Kill pats my back. "Good job," he says.

Maybe he believes it, but I don't miss the concern in his voice. He thinks I took too many unnecessary hits. I can't really argue, seeing how it's true.

He doesn't understand that I don't feel those strikes the way I should. Hell, I don't think I've felt anything the way I should in a long time. Not like I used to. I try to tell myself that maybe that' a good thing. That numbness is better than pain. But I'm not so convinced anymore, and neither is my family. I try to shrug it off like I'm fine. Except given the way they've been eyeing me, I'm not fooling anyone.

I'm scaring everyone around me. And it sucks. Not only because I don't want them scared, but mostly because I don't know how to stop it.

"The referee has called a stop to this match at two-minutes and forty-nine seconds into the second round," the announcer begins. "The winner by TKO, Finn 'The Fury' O'Brien."

The crowd screams and pumps their fists in the air when my hand is raised. I take the few seconds I need to thank my sponsors, my camp, and my brother, because that's what I'm supposed to do despite the fog clouding my senses. I wish that disconnect had something to do with all the hits I took, but deep down I know that it doesn't.

I'm back in the locker room before I know it getting stitched up, too many people talking at once. God, I barely hear their questions or my responses. But they're there and somehow I make it through.

"I'm worried about you, Finnie," Kill says when everyone piles out.

"Don't. I'm not drinking tonight. I'm headed home," I assure him.

"That's not what I mean," he says. He's sitting in a fold out chair, his arms resting against his muscular legs. "I think you need to talk to someone."

I stretch out my arms. By now they're so tight, they pull against the bones. "I am. I'm talking to you."

I don't have to see him to know he's shaking his head, or that he's looking sad, disappointed, and maybe something else, too. "I'm not who you should be speaking to," he says. "Not for what's going on in your head."

"You're enough," I say, even though I know it's no longer true.

"Finn," he begins.

I don't wait for him to finish, leaving the changing area and heading toward the showers. "Go find Sofia and Wren," I call over my shoulder as I strip out my shirt. "See if they're up for some dinner."

I don't remember peeling the rest of my clothes off. That numbness I've been feeling too much lately claiming me like a mist until it fully engulfs me. Fuck. It's like I've stopped living even though for the most part I think I'm still alive.

I lean against the tile with my arms spread, allowing the water to beat against my back. It's too hot. I should turn it down, but I don't bother. Eventually, like everything else, the sensation fades.

I'm not sure how long I'm in that position. A few seconds? A few minutes? But then Easton and his trainer Yefim are suddenly there. "You got lucky, O'Brien," Yefim calls out, taunting me with his thick eastern European accent.

Shit. Like all the trash talk before the fight wasn't enough.

"Did you hear me, you pussy?" he fires back when I don't answer. "Did you hear me, you goddamn coward?"

Coward? Fuck you. It's what I think, but not what I say, focusing instead on the streams of water that gather along my feet before they swirl into the drain.

It doesn't help. The rage that's building, the one I only manage to barely keep in? It stirs in my gut like a heavy pot filled with hate, sin, and all the curses my Ma would still beat my ass for saying.

"What're you doing?" Yefim asks.

His voice is closer, he's drawing near. It doesn't matter that I'm standing here naked. He wants to be next to me. I shudder, that feeling I keep buried drilling its way up.

"I know about you," Yefim says, not bothering to keep his voice low. "But everyone knows, don't they? Even if you don't want them to."

My body shakes a little more, but it's not from the cooling water. It's from his words and all that anger they trigger. *Don't do it. Don't go there.*

"You like to keep it a secret. Don't you, pussy?"

Yefim laughs when I keep my trap shut. He thinks I'm backing down, just like Easton did before his face met the mat. "He's crying," he calls out to Easton. "What? Not so tough now?"

That's where he's dead wrong. Every muscle I've conditioned serves a purpose—to take down those who fuck with me. And right now, Yefim is seriously fucking with me.

"You like to pretend that it's girls you like, don't you?" he says. "But that's not true, is it? Oh, no, that's not true at all . . ."

I raise my chin, knowing that someone's not leaving without bleeding, and I've bled enough tonight.

Yefim kicks at my calf. "What? Nothing to say? Can't speak without your boyfriend here?"

"Boyfriend?" Easton asks, laughing. "No fucking way."

"Yes. Way," Yefim insists. "Didn't you know this little pussy takes it up the ass—"

I punch him so hard, I feel his teeth crack against my knuckles. For someone with decades of boxing experience he never saw me coming. But I see Easton flying at me out of the corner of my eye. I toss him over my shoulder, slamming him hard onto the ceramic tile floor. Like in the octagon, I throw myself on top of him, my fists colliding against his skin.

Voices rush forward, telling me to stop. A woman screams, but I don't stop fighting off the bodies trying to grab me, breaking through the arms wrenching me back. I need to hit him—I need to feel my fists meeting his face—I need to feel *something*.

God damn it. I need to feel alive.

I don't want the pain.

I don't want the terror.

But once more, it's all I feel.

READ ON FOR AN EXCERPT FROM

Feel Me

An O'Brien Family Novel

Cecy Robson

Chapter One

Melissa

I stare at the nameplate perched on my father's desk: *District Attorney Miles Fenske*. It proclaims his position, allowing those who read it a glimpse of what he's accomplished. Yet it's only a glimpse. It's not a true representation of all he is, or all he means to me. The nameplate is cheap, unlike the generous soul who stares back at me with the same loving expression he's held since the first moment I saw him.

What are you thinking, Melissa? He signs to me, moving his hands in beautifully fluid motions.

We're alone in his office. He doesn't need to sign to keep our conversation private. He could whisper, and I would still be able to read his lips. But he knows I'm more comfortable communicating with my hands, probably because American Sign Language is one of the many things we learned together. As a child I considered it our very own secret language, something he and I could share away from the hearing world.

That you're making a mistake, I sign back.

My comment earns me a smile, but I can see his concern, despite the crinkles around his eyes that deepen when he grins. "You're going to have to trust me," he says aloud.

I let out a breath. He knows I trust him. How could I not?

I was brought to the Lehigh Valley District Attorney's office when I was about six years old, after my biological mother had attempted to sell me in exchange for drugs. My mother probably thought it was a brilliant plan. Being born with profound hearing loss, I couldn't speak, couldn't communicate, and couldn't understand. Which meant, I couldn't tell anyone what was about to take place.

My primal instincts ordered me to run, that I was in danger, so I did—thank God I did. I kicked and fought, dodging the hands trying to grab me, and scurrying out of my window.

To this day, I remember the way the cold metal grating of

the fire escape felt against my bare feet, and the way my mouth struggled to form what I thought were words as I banged on my elderly neighbor's window. Miss Lena, the lady with too many cats and twice as many grandchildren, yanked me into her apartment when she saw me. She called the police, but by the time they arrived, my mother was gone. I never saw her again.

Not that I regret it.

I was placed in foster care, confused and frightened about what was happening and certain I'd eventually return "home". Instead, I was brought before the young Assistant D.A Miles Fenske. He was supposed to handle my case, dispose of it, and move on. He was never supposed to welcome me into his heart. Yet that's exactly what he did.

"Melissa," he says. His words aren't clear—not as clear as they can be, my hearing aids can only do so much, but I hear enough to sense the emotion in the way he speaks my name. "Why are you so sad?"

I raise my chin. "Declan O'Brien will never be the man you are. He's not the right D.A. for this position." I shake my head. "He belongs in the Trial Unit, Arson, Fugitive, anywhere else but where you've placed him."

"I know you don't like him . . ."

I raise my brows.

" . . and that your first encounter wasn't a positive one . . ."

"That's because he was an asshole," I mumble.

He chuckles. "I assure you he deeply regrets what he said. But Declan is smart, quick, and kind."

I don't agree. Not completely. Is Declan intelligent? Brilliantly so, and absurdly astute in court. With short wavy blond hair and a dashing grin that lights his blue eyes, he's also gorgeous, and he knows it. But is he kind? I'm not so sure that he is. "He'll never be the man you are," I repeat.

"I'm not asking him to be. I simply want the best person for the job, someone who will help the victims who need him most."

"That's what you claim. But he doesn't have experience

handling delicate cases where offenders often inflict irreparable trauma.”

“No, but as the head of Victim Services, you do,” he offers with a knowing gleam.

My nails dig into the wooden armrests. “If you’re trying to hook us up, I’m going to be seriously mad at you.”

The edges of his mouth curve. “I’m only asking you to help Declan as he transitions into his new role. This new assignment won’t be easy on him.”

“Because he doesn’t want it. He wants to be the head of Homicide.” I stand with my hands out, pleading. “Daddy, please reassign him. The Sexual Assault and Child Abuse Unit is not where someone who seeks glory belongs.”

My voice trails as I catch a glimmer of his pain. “Daddy?”

At once, his face scrunches, flushing red only to grow alarmingly pale. I race around his desk, clutching his shoulders to keep him upright as he grips his side and beads of sweat gather along his receding hairline.

It’s only because he lifts his bowed head and a healthier shade of pink returns to his cheeks that I’m not screaming for help and dialing 911. “Daddy?”

He offers me a weak smile and pats my arm. “I’m all right,” he says, leaning back in his chair.

“No, you’re not,” I say, my eyes stinging. His light blue dress shirt clings with sweat along his arms and plump midsection. He’s not well. My father is . . . *sick*. “What aren’t you telling me?”

His hand slowly eases away from his side. For a moment his eyes search my face, as they’ve done a thousand times throughout my life. “The doctors discovered new tumors along my colon,” he finally says. “They’re planning to resection my bowel and dispose of the affected area with the hope of avoiding chemo this time around.”

Very carefully, I straighten, despite that my heart has all but stopped beating. My father was diagnosed with colon cancer years ago and barely survived the aggressive treatment. If it’s returned, now that he’s older, and not as healthy . . .

"When were you going to tell me?" I ask, struggling to keep my voice clear as it shakes, my fear likely worsening my speech impediment.

He sighs. "Friday, over dinner."

To give me the weekend to absorb it, no doubt. "And your surgery? When is that?"

"A few weeks." He frowns as if debating what to say. "I'll be out of commission for a while. In my absence, Declan will lead the office as acting District Attorney." He looks at me then. "And I ask that you help him, regardless of your feelings toward him."

Declan

"This isn't where I fucking belong." I'm beyond pissed, and started typing my resignation letter at least six times today only to delete it. Yet for as much as I don't want to head the Sexual Assault and Child Abuse Unit, I'm not a quitter. "Fuck," I mumble, dragging my hand along my face. "*Fuck.*"

My brother Curran crosses his arms over his chest, not caring how it creases the shirt of his Philly PD uniform. But then Curran doesn't care about shit like that. "It's still a promotion, Deck," he says. "You got this D.A. spot straight out of law school and have made more of a name for yourself than most douche-bag attorneys ever will." He holds out a hand. "No offense to the douche-bag attorneys of the world."

"That's my point. After all I've accomplished, I should be the one leading the Homicide unit."

I shove away from my desk and pace. When Miles gave me these new digs, I thought it was just the start of all the good things coming my way. When he assigned me a county car and a personal secretary, it only reinforced that my hard work had paid off. I was on my way ...until I wasn't.

"I spent months dismantling a mafia empire, Curran."

"I know," he says. "I was there."

"I brought down a major crime boss—and his second in

command, and his third."

"Yup. Saw that, too," he agrees.

"I received international attention—the trial of the century, the media called it—and for what? To be shoved someplace I don't belong."

"Why don't you think you belong there?"

Out of all my five brothers, Curran is probably one of the biggest ball busters. But he's not messing with me now. He's being serious.

"Do you want to hear about babies and women being hurt? Day in and day out?" I ask. "These are the cases I'm going to be dealing with."

"Someone has to do it, Deck. It's the right thing."

"I'm not saying it isn't. I'm only saying I may not be the man for the job. This shit's disgusting, what these low-life assholes are capable of."

"Is this about Finnie?" He huffs when I straighten and don't answer. "Christ," he mutters.

As easy as that, my brother nails it on the head. For all he sometimes pisses me off, my brother isn't stupid. "Finnie didn't deserve what happened to him," I say, feeling my anger burn down to my gut.

"Of course he didn't," Curran snaps. "No one does. But as his brother, you owe it to him to put monsters like the guy who hurt him away."

I sit back in my chair and rub my jaw. "I don't know if I can."

Our youngest brother was sexually assaulted by a neighbor when he was ten. It screwed with his mind. What he doesn't realize is we've all suffered, too—not like he has—of course, not like he has. That doesn't mean we don't hurt for him or haven't spent sleepless nights worried about him.

Nothing bad was supposed to happen to Finnie. He was the baby. The one who counted on us. The one we were all supposed to keep safe.

With this new assignment—hearing stories like Finnie's on a regular basis?—God *damn* it. "I don't think I can do this," I say yet again.

"Deck, you have to, man."

A knock on the door interrupts us. I know who it is before I even ask. "Come in," I say, assuming my attorney pose because for now, I have to. For now, I'm a professional. Even though all the Philly boy in me wants to do is rage.

My boss, Miles Fenske walks in, followed by his daughter Melissa. Miles smiles warmly, nodding my way.

Mel? What can I say? She's the one person who's never been taken by my charm. Today's no different. Unlike the other females who work here, from interns to attorneys, she doesn't meet me with a grin, doesn't flash me a little leg, doesn't pretend to flirt. Brown hair, brown eyes, creamy skin, with a steel-hard exterior, she walks in with her hips swinging, her bright red dress hugging her hourglass figure, her full lips pressed into a firm line, and her unyielding stare meeting mine.

She doesn't like me. Not that I blame her. Too bad this is the one woman I can't seem to get out of my damn mind . . .

Crave Me

An O'Brien Family Novel

Cecy Robson

Chapter One

Wren

I drop the keys in Mr. Esposito's hand and smile. He stares at them in his open palm like a precious gift, because to someone like him who's worked hard his entire life, it very much is. "Thank you, Wren," he says, meeting my smile. "I never thought I'd own a new car. Let alone be able to give one to my son as a gift."

"You deserve it, Mr. Esposito," I tell him, shaking his hand. "And so does your son for getting into Drexel. Tell Antonio, hi for me—Oh, and be sure to have someone take his picture when you hand him the keys." I motion to my office behind me. "I want to add it to my memory wall."

"I will." He presses his lips tight as if considering what to say. "Your father would be proud of you," he tells me. His soft brown eyes take in the massive dealership, fixing on the sales board displaying my current rank at number one. "Very proud."

I hold onto my smile as he walks toward the brand new candy apple red F-150 hugging the curb, ignoring the brutal January wind that sweeps in when the doors to the lot zip open. Mr. Esposito pauses when he opens the driver's side door. I had the boys in the back place a bow on dash like I do for all my customers. I think it's a nice touch, and a way to thank them for their business. Apparently, Mr. Esposito agrees. He tosses me a grin over his shoulder, hollering his thanks as he slips inside and pulls away.

The moment he disappears so does my smile. "Your father would be proud of you," he said. He meant it as a compliment. Mr. Esposito has always been nice like that. But instead of filling me with a sense of pride, his comment sparks a twinge of pain. Some things never change. And some people you never forget.

My heels click against the bleached white tile as I cross the showroom. It's been a nasty winter with all the snow we've had, but I can't say it's been bad for business. My eyes narrow when they fix on Oscar looming over Penny. Penny is sweet, smart, and an overall good kid. She hasn't been here long and she's trying. Too bad Oscar is stomping on her success, luring customers away from her every chance he gets.

"You snooze, you lose," he tells her, pegging her with one of his more sleazy grins.

Penny was making headway with the guy who walked in, until Oscar shoved his way between them and baited him away, making Penny look like she didn't know what she was talking about. If I hadn't been busy with my own customer, I would have stepped in. Nothing gets to me more than men who target those weaker than them.

"Wren!" Suze calls, waving from behind the finance counter. "You have a call."

"Okay. Send it through," I yell, hurrying across the floor, but not before I make sure Oscar steps far away from Penny.

The phone rings one, twice, before I slam the door behind me with my foot and reach across my desk. "Erin O'Brien," I say.

There's a brief pause before I hear, "Hi, Wren."

Shit. My stomach twists the way it always does when I hear his voice. "What do you want, Bryant?" I ask, digging out my cell phone from my desk drawer.

"I miss you," he says.

"Do you miss hitting me, too?" I fire back.

I'm talking tough. It's what I do. Too bad I don't feel so tough. Not when it comes to Bryant. That familiar sense of fear sends a chill down my spine, reminding me what happened the last time I pissed him off. I hit the record icon on my cell phone, hoping to catch him saying something I can use against him. But the damn thing beeps and for all Bryant is an asshole he's not stupid.

"Are you recording me, pretty girl?" He laughs when I don't answer. "Now, why would you do a thing like that?"

"Because I don't trust you, because you hit me—oh, and because you're an asshole."

"I don't know what you're talking about," he says, keeping his voice easy. "I'm just returning your call. You keep calling me so—"

"That's a lie," I say, my face heating with anger. Since he knows I'm recording him, he's trying to switch things around. "Don't call me again. I want nothing to do with you."

I hang up the phone then. It's been two months since I last saw him. Two months since he last put his hands on me. I could call the police. The problem is, he is the police . . .

Evan

My Jaguar skids, again, and again, and again, fighting to keep pace with the other drivers insane enough to travel the Blue Route in this weather. Chunks of wet snow pelt my windshield. My wipers squeak against the glass as they race to keep my line of sight clear when yet another vehicle cuts me off, pelting my windshield with more melting ice. My current struggle with life and death does not, of course, discourage Maxine from barking messages over my Blue Tooth. "Yodel called again, they want you to reconsider."

"No," I answer, cutting my steering wheel toward the left when my car veers right. "We're representing Mellon, their biggest competitor. It's a conflict of interests to supply both companies with the same technology."

I mutter a curse, when the minivan in front of me slams on the brakes and I just miss ramming into her bumper. And because we're in Philadelphia, the City of Brotherly love, the woman rolls down the window—allowing snow into her vehicle just to wave an irate middle finger at me. "Rich Bitch loser," she cries out.

I rub my face. Why am I here again? Before I can finish the thought, Maxine reminds me.

"Evan, I don't think your stepfather will agree with your decision. The company needs the revenue."

"Not at the expense of our ethics." The company is at risk, yes, but it's mostly due to poor business practices such as the ones Maxine is suggesting I entertain. I understand she learned these tactics by my predecessor, but he was conniving snake—which is why he's currently serving time for embezzling the company's money and I was recruited from our London branch to save the enterprise from financial collapse.

"What about your eleven a.m. with the V.P. of County General?"

"Have Ann and Clifton begin if I'm not on time. I emailed them the presentation last night—"

"Do you really think they're qualified?" she interrupts.

I open my mouth to argue and insist that they are—and to remind her I'm her superior, not the other way around. But Ann and Clifton are still fairly new. They're not at the level I need them to be. However, they're learning fast under my tutelage and the only ones from the original staff that I currently trust.

"Evan?" she presses.

"Maxine, Ann and Clifton will handle it. That's my final word." I disconnect then, swearing as I take the ramp and practically glide down sideways.

"Get a real car, fucker," another proud Pennsylvanian hollers.

I rub my face again, both because I'm tired and equally frustrated. Three in the morning. That's the hour I arrived home earlier today. It wouldn't have taken me as long had I been driving a vehicle capable of enduring this ridiculous weather.

I glance up, releasing a tense breath when the sign from the Ford dealership I researched this morning comes into view. Saving iCronos will take me time. Time I can't spare driving a Jaguar on roads better maneuvered via dogsled.

My car slows to a stop in front of the massive dealership.

The combination of the vehicle I'm driving along with the expensive suit I'm wearing beneath my long wool coat commands attention. The moment I step inside, a young woman with short dark spiky hair hurries over. "Good morning, sir. Are you interested in acquiring a new vehicle?" she asks.

She seems young, but eager, a respectable attribute. Yet no sooner does she finish speaking than a man about my age steps in front of her, adjusting the jacket of his gray suit. "I got this, P," he tells her. "Get us some coffee, will you?" He holds out his hand. "Hello. I'm Oscar Nelson. Welcome to Ford Nation."

My frown bounces from his hand to the young woman whose face is now bright red with anger, humiliation, and possibly more. "Are you his secretary?" I ask her.

"No," she answers. "I'm a car sales representative for Ford Nation—"

Oscar begins to talk over her, but it's the stomping sound of quickly approaching footsteps that lures my focus. A woman with a pinstripe jacket and matching skirt storms forward, the quick motions of her long toned legs causing the edge of her skirt to brush above her knees and swing her hips seductively. Long hair flutters like a black silk sail behind her, revealing a face better suited for my wildest dreams. Sapphire blue eyes shimmer behind a thick layer of dark lashes, lighting her creamy white skin and full pink lips.

I spent the first two years following my completion of my masters in either a lab or boardroom packed with men in alternating stages of balding, and these last three months working eighteen hour days trying to rebuild an empire. I haven't had the opportunity let alone the time to meet women. But if I knew women like her existed, I would have spared a moment.

Good . . . *Lord*.

I don't realize I'm gaping until she stops directly in front of us and juts out her chin. "Problem?" she asks Oscar.

Oscar stiffens his posture. "No. I was just showing Mr. . . ."

He motions to me. "My apologies, what's your name, sir?"

"Jonah," I say, returning my full attention to the stunning young woman. I offer her my hand. "Evan Jonah."

A smile eases along her face, revealing a set of perfect white and drawing more attention to her delicate features. "I'm Erin O'Brien, but I go by Wren," she says, shaking my hand with a firm grip before releasing me and easing the smaller woman forward. "How can Penny and I help you today, sir?"

"I was looking for either an SUV or a truck than can handle this winter," I answer, doing all I can to keep my eyes from trailing down her body.

"Then you've come to the right place. Penny, will you show Mr. Jonah—"

"Evan," I interrupt, mentally kicking myself for morphing into a fourteen year old boy the moment my eyes locked on this woman.

"Okay, Evan," she says. "Penny, please show Evan our latest members of the Ford family to get an idea what may fit his needs."

"Of course, this way, sir," Penny answers with a smile.

I reluctantly follow behind Penny. Only because it's now obvious I can't rip my eyes away from Wren. But as we reach a black Explorer my attention trails back to her and Oscar. They've moved away from the main showroom and closer to the rear offices. Yet that doesn't stop me from hearing their exchange.

"What the fuck was that?" Oscar snaps.

My spine stiffens. I storm forward, ready to demand he apologize for using such foul language in front of a lady.

"You being a raging asshole," Wren replies.

I'll admit, her response gives me pause. And she doesn't stop there. "Look, I know you have to compensate for your less than average-sized dick. But that doesn't give you the right to mistreat Penny or pounce on every client she approaches. That's bullshit and you know it."

"Um, perhaps a truck will be more to your needs," Penny

says, motioning to the far section of the dealership and away from the heated conversation.

I'm not typically a voyeur. I also don't typically interact with women who speak this way. But it's not just Wren's use of language that captivates me, it's her strength, and her desire to protect her small friend.

"Where the fuck did you hear that?" Oscar responds. "I don't have a small dick."

Of all his possible retorts, *this* is the one he chooses.

"Suze," Wren calls over her shoulder in the direction of the finance counter. "What was it you said about that night you went out with Oscar?"

The woman behind the counter scowls and holds up her pinky. Wren smirks. "Looks to me like you should have called her back." She pats his shoulder. "My condolences to your man parts."

She starts to walk away, pausing when she realizes I witnessed their interaction. She must know I heard her, but instead of making a quick escape or attempting pretend as if I didn't, she marches toward me, keeping her head up. "I apologize, Mr. Jonah—"

"Evan," I clarify as she reaches me. Good heavens, and there's that smile again, stirring one of my own.

"Evan," she repeats. Her eyes skip to her friend. "I see Penny is taking good care of you."

"Actually, I thought perhaps you can take over," Penny says. Her stare bounces between Wren and I, likely recognizing how entranced I am by her.

Wren tilts her head. "I don't want to intrude on your sales pitch," she says.

"You're not," she responds, carefully edging away. "I'll take the next one. Honest."

She watches her walk away, before placing her attention back on me. She considers me a moment, as if trying to figure me out, but then motions back to the Explorer. "This is the latest model in Ford luxury, capable of keeping you safe, meeting your needs, and packed with plenty of toys," she begins.

I follow her as she leads me around the vehicle. The ease in her speech and her relaxed posture reveal a woman who knows her products and her job well. I question her about the vehicle's most basic facts first: mileage, warranty, and safety features, before testing her intelligence further. She doesn't disappoint, explaining the vehicle's functions in great detail down to the engine's construction, adding to my growing attraction to her.

"Would you like to take her for a ride?" she asks. She punches my arm affectionately, drawing my attention briefly away from me face. "This way you can see how smoothly she handles the road and then you can then say, 'Wren, how did I ever survive without a Ford.'"

"I'd like that," I answer, keeping my smile. This woman who appears more elite model than sales rep knows exactly what she's doing. "Very much."

"Good," she says, pointing at me. "You'll wonder how you ever got along without her."

As I watch her walk away, I start to wonder that myself.

Of Flame and Light

A Weird Girls Novel

Cecy Robson

Chapter One

You know it's going to be a bad day when you wake up in the morning and the first word out of your mouth is "fuck."

My right arm—or should I say my *new* arm generated after my real one was chewed off by a psycho werewolf (no, this isn't a joke) —buzzes me awake. That's right, *buzzes*.

I do my best to hide my limb. Not just because it's as white as alabaster. Or because of the fluorescent blue veins that run its length. But because it's doing things I can't control, like, interfering with my magic, glowing like a light saber, and now, making noise.

I lift my head, half-asleep, wondering how a wasp nest found its way beneath my pillow, but too exhausted to run away screaming, *yet*. If you were familiar my life and world, you'd understand pissed off wasps in my bed wouldn't be the craziest, or scariest, thing that's ever happened to me.

My eyes narrow at the quivering pillow as my haze clears. Maybe it's because I'm tired, or maybe it's because I'm bitter as all hell, but I can't help thinking that the arm *and* the pillow are laughing at me. I pull my glowing and buzzing arm from beneath the fluffy white pillow and swear.

"Really? *Really*?" I ask it. "What's next, singing and puppet shows?"

Apparently, my incandescent light saber arm isn't a fan of sarcasm and proceeds to flicker on an off like a twisted strobe light. I shake it hard and smack it against the mattress for all the good it does. "Knock it off," I tell it.

It's not that I think it listens, or that I manage to control it—there's simply no controlling this thing—but somehow the glowing recedes and so does the noise, and my arm resumes its "normal" death-like tone.

It's quiet, no longer casting light. I should be thankful, right? I should be happy, true?

Oh, I wish.

The color is startling, and contrasts horrifically against my deep olive skin. But its eerie tone and its unpredictability aren't the only things that trouble me. There's something wrong with this limb. It doesn't belong on me. And in a way, it doesn't belong in this world.

Maybe like me, it's something that wasn't supposed to be.

I sigh and clutch it against me. It feels like my old arm, the skin soft and smooth. It moves like my old arm—I'm not limited with either fine or gross motor skills. But it's not—I don't know—*human*.

When I lost my real arm, the Squaw Valley Pack Omega, created this new one using ancient werewolf magic. If I were a *were*, I think things would have been fine, peachy-keen, and all that good stuff. But I'm not a *were*, or human, or witch, or vampire, or anything. No, not even a little bit.

My sisters and I may look human, but nothing like us has ever existed on earth. And because of it, earth's ancient magic seemed to really resent helping a weird girl like me.

I used to wield fire and lightning with ease, and catch glimpses of the future. I used to be badass. I'm no longer badass, and the only things I catch now are odd glances cast my way.

"Are you the punishment for my sins?" I ask my arm.

I don't expect it to answer, but it does. Sputtering light and buzzing before abruptly ceasing its response and sinking into the mattress.

To anyone watching, this whole thing might be funny. To me . . . Christ, who am I fooling? Nothing's been funny in a long time.

For a moment, I simply stare at it. There's a part of me that wants to cry, wondering what it will start doing next. But I've already cried too long and too hard for what it has cost me.

Or should I say, *who* it cost me.

I scan the room. Nothing of Gemini remains. Not his clothes, not our pictures together. I even deleted and blocked his number. For all my arm disgusts me, I never expected it to disgust him more. After all, this was the werewolf who claimed me as his mate. The same male who swore he'd love me forever.

I suppose forever only counts so long as I didn't change, so long as I remained perfect in his eyes. But I never claimed to be perfect, even if many believed I'd looked the part.

My arm flickers and *zings*, the electrified charge strong enough to startle me and slap any remnants of sleep away. Shit. No way am I perfect. Not by a long shot, especially with this thing constantly mocking me and reminding me of everything wrong in my life.

A sharp rap to the door has me glancing toward my right. "Taran?" my perky sister Shayna calls. "I heard your alarm clock go off. Want some breakfast?"

I lift the bane of my existence and roll my eyes. Alarm clock? Yeah, I suppose you can call it that.

"T?" Shayna presses.

"I'll be right out," I answer.

She pauses. "Good," she says, sounding relieved. "I made plenty."

It's not that I want to eat. It's that I know how worried my sisters are about me. So I sit with them when I can, and plaster a smile when I need to, but even that's cumbersome which sucks. I don't want my time with my sisters to be something of a chore. I love them. But I've learned some things can't be helped.

My arm fires with its haunting glow. Ah, yeah, case in point.

With a groan, I slip out of bed, pulling on a fresh pair of panties and a bra before heading to my bathroom to freshen up. After a few swipes of mascara and some lipstick, I yank on a form-fitting red dress and shove my feet into a pair of platform pumps, doing my best to strut and not collapse back in bed. Yet even though I'm almost to the door, there's one more thing I need. Most women won't leave their homes without their cell phones. I can't leave my room without my elbow-length gloves. It helps me hide the ugly appendage and the light show that accompanies it.

But now that my arm's buzzing . . .

I pause with my hand on the doorknob. God, what am I going to do about this thing?

I take a breath and wrench open the door, tugging on my gloves as I walk down the hall and into our large kitchen. Shayna abandons the waffle iron when she sees me and skips forward, her ponytail bouncing behind her.

She throws her arms around me like it's been months, not hours since she's seen me. "Morning, Taran," she tells me brightly.

I pat her back, wishing I could hug her for real. But real hugs lead to my very real tears, and I can't keep doing this to my family. "Hey, princess. Wow, everything smells great."

It's the truth, yet my comment sounds phony and forced, even to me.

Her arms fall away slowly. Although she keeps her grin, I sense the worry behind it, as well as her fear. "You look hot," she tells me, punching my good arm affectionately.

No. I look acceptable. I used to spend over an hour styling my dark wavy hair and applying my makeup. Now, I do enough so I don't resign myself to sweats, watching made for TV movies, and stuffing my face with potato chips.

"Thanks," I manage with yet another forced grin. I make a show of taking in all the breakfast foods, including the freshly baked goods. "Yum. Do you need help setting the table or anything?"

"No. It's all good, T."

She says nothing more which is unusual for Shayna. Either she's waiting for me to speak, or she's debating what to say. I can't take another pity party so I lift a pan filled with eggs and plate stacked with waffles and bring them to the table. "Where's your puppy?" I ask. Or in other words, where's her gigantic scary werewolf husband, Koda.

"Oh, he already ate and left. He's doing more at the Den since Celia's been needing more ah, time with Aric."

Okay, now I really grin, and so does she. Time with Aric is a mild way to describe what Celia desires from her husband.

Our youngest sister Emme walks out of the laundry room

blushing, which tells me she's heard us discussing Celia. Shayna's grin quickly turns into a laugh. Emme's shyness has that effect on her.

Emme clears her throat, but not her obvious discomfort. Where Shayna has dark straight hair, Emme has soft blond waves and fair skin that reddens the longer we take her in. "Emme," I offer. "What's the big deal? So what if Celia's banging Aric like the lead drummer at a Fourth of July parade."

Emme holds up her hand. "Taran, let's keep their private life private."

I reach for a glass of fresh squeezed juice. "I would if they weren't so damn loud. I swear, I thought the walls were going to come down around midnight when they—"

"Taran . . ." Emme whimpers, shaking her hands like she can't stand to hear another word.

Emme's always been so sweet and angelic. Me? Not at all. "Hey, do you suppose Celia's more flexible now, given how Aric knocked her up? As in ankles behind the head kind of flexible—"

Emme lifts a muffin with her *force* and sends it zipping my way. I catch it in my hand before it rams me in the mouth. "Eat," she insists. "Just eat."

In other words, for once in your life, shut your inappropriate trap.

Shayna takes a seat beside me, laughing her skinny ass off. Emme sits, too, in time for Celia to stagger down the back steps.

Good God. Celia's long curly hair is tousled from lack of sleep and the insane amount of sex she's had. And her eyes? They're glazed with a hunger that warns me not to get too close. "Is there bacon? Please tell me there's bacon," she growls as if crazed.

Her entire face beams when Emme levitates a plateful of bacon and lowers it front of an empty seat. Like a woman possessed, Celia sits and rams about four pieces in her mouth at once. The rest of us watch her in stunned silence as she chomps them down and reaches for another few slices. She freezes when she realizes we're all gaping at her. "Sorry. Would you like some?"

Her tigress eyes replace her human ones, making it clear she's only trying to be polite. And that only an idiot would get between her and her breakfast.

"No, nope, uh-uh," the three of us answer at once.

This seems to settle her inner beast enough so Celia's human eyes once more blink back at us. I pour her a glass of juice, while Emme and Shayna carefully place plates stacked with food closer to her reach. What can I say, we don't want to be eaten.

"Are you all right?" Emme asks her quietly.

It's only then that Celia slows her frantic munching. "I don't know," she admits, her husky voice trickling with concern. She lifts her T-shirt and shows us her tiny belly. "The baby's not growing."

Yeah. We noticed that, too. Her pregnancy had been unexpected given she was incapable of bearing children. But within two weeks of finding out she and Aric had conceived, her baby bump had appeared and was visible through her wedding gown.

That was two months ago. And now, well, let's say despite how this baby has been prophesized to rid the world of evil, we're all pretty much freaking out that he or she isn't growing.

"But your body's changing," I insist. I don't exactly ooze optimism. In fact, I'm mostly the sky is falling and the earth is swallowing us whole kind of gal. But Celia doesn't need to hear what's wrong. My girl needs hope so that's what I give her. I point to her chest. "If your hooters don't scream you're knocked up, I don't know what does."

She glances at her girls and then back at me, the tension in her shoulders lifting slightly. Yeah. Hope is exactly what she needs.

"They are a lot bigger," she agrees quietly. She gathers her thoughts, appearing to want to say more despite her obvious hesitation. "My body's changing in a lot of ways. Maybe not outwardly, but I can feel the difference inside of me."

"Like in your magic, dude?" Shayna asks.

Celia nods. "The magic that helped me get pregnant seems to compliment mine. But I have to say, my hormones are out of control." Her cheeks flush and she lowers her voice. "Poor Aric. I can't stop having sex with him. It's like every time I see him, I pounce."

It's then Aric bounds down the steps, his eyes glassy from lack of sleep and his five o'clock shadow now a full-out beard thanks to his preference to satisfy Celia's needs instead shave. His face lights up when he sees Celia—kind of like she did at the sight of bacon.

"Yeah, poor bastard," I mutter.

"Hey, beautiful," he says to Celia, bending to kiss her lips.

She smiles against his mouth. "Hey, wolf," she answers, stroking his beard lightly.

Emme inches away when Celia's stare suggests the need for something more than breakfast. Aric, being Aric, returns that look with equal force. I start to laugh, not because of Celia and Aric, but because of Emme's response. She's glancing around at the food like she knows it's going to end up splattered across Celia and Aric's soon-to-be naked bodies.

My laugh lodges in my throat when my right arm jerks as if shocked. Shayna lowers her fork. "You okay, T?" she asks.

I shove my arm under the table. "Fine," I say. I reach for glass of juice with my opposite hand, trying to stay calm. Celia and Emme didn't notice my twitch, and I don't think Aric did either, but something about me lures his attention away from Celia.

He cocks his head, his nose flaring as if his alpha wolf has latched onto something. "Taran, what's wrong?" he asks.

Celia's and Emme's attention drifts my way. Shayna rises, fear crinkling her brow.

"I'm tired," I say dismissively, feeling my pulse start to race. I push my chair out. "I should head back to bed. I didn't sleep much—"

All at once, and without warning, pain burns its way across my affected limb, curling me forward in agony. My arm whips out, sending the table and all its contents soaring with freakish speed. Plates shatter on the floor as the table imbeds with a loud bang *into* the wall—directly where Celia sat seconds before.

I lift my head as the burn recedes, searching for her—panicked I harmed her. Tears of relief and residual pain slide down my face when I see Aric lower her to floor, far away from me. She and our sisters stare back at me stunned. But Aric? Holy shit, he's *pissed*.

"Taran, what are you doing?" he growls.

I shake my head, knowing he's angry I almost hurt Celia. "I'm not doing anything . . ."

The burn returns and so does its torment. This time, I can't bite back my screams. I stumble forward. Aric races to me. I don't see him. I only feel his body and hear the crunch of bone when my arm flails and connects with his jaw.

He crashes against our granite counter with a grunt as my arm jerks wildly and the burn increases tenfold.

My vision fades in and out and my body thrashes, the erratic movements of my limb sending me to smack hard against the wall. I collapse, my arm beating itself against the floor with enough force to splinter and punch through the wood. I'm not thinking. I can't. Everything hurts.

No. Everything *burns*.

"Cut it off!" I scream.

Shayna reaches for a knife, elongating it with her power and manipulating it into a deadly sword. She lifts the blade above my spastic arm, her expression torn. By now I'm sobbing, and all but clawing at my face.

"*Please*, Shayna," I beg. "Cut it off!"

"I can't," Shayna chokes out. "I can't do this."

"Pin it," Celia yells. "Pin it to the floor!"

With a flick of her wrists Shayna changes the sword's position and brings the point down toward my raging hand. I barely feel the prick before the room erupts in a ghostly light and Shayna goes flying.

Emme screams as Shayna collides into the far wall. Aric and Celia are scrambling forward, but all thoughts are lost in my torture. I'm retching with how hard I'm crying and from the anguish crawling from my arm and into my chest.

Just as the burn reaches my heart, and I begin to lose consciousness, a pale yellow light surrounds me. Slowly, very slowly, the heat charring my insides is replaced with a soothing chill I welcome like a draw of fresh air.

My body shudders as the coolness spreads like a cascade of water from a gentle spring. With each sensation of cold, my pain eases and my cries dwindle. It takes a long time for the ache to lessen, and even longer for my vision to clear. But eventually it does.

Not that I like what I see.

Blood cakes the side of Shayna's face. She winces as the bone along her eye socket pops out and her eyebrow knits close. Bile churns my gut. If Koda hadn't passed her his werewolf essence, I would have killed her. There's no doubt based on the amount of blood coating her skin, and what her body had to do to heal her indented skull.

I cover my mouth. "Oh, my God," I gasp.

"It's okay, T," she says, as if I can't see the pain tightening her small pixie face. "It's okay."

No. Not at all, sweetie.

Aric leans forward. Being all *were*, and that of pure blood, his inner beast had healed him faster than Shayna. That didn't mean I hadn't made rubble out of his jaw, or that I hadn't hurt him . . . Or that I won't do it again.

I had no control over my arm. None. Nor do I believe I have it now.

Aric realizes as much. I don't miss how he keeps Celia behind him, appearing to shield her and their child from whatever way I'll lash out next.

"What happened?" he asks, his voice riddled with anger, and maybe something more.

"I don't know," I respond, my voice trembling and my body strangely weak. "I felt pain and it-it just went wild."

"Your arm?" It's a question, but he's not really asking.

I nod as Emme's healing light recedes and her hands withdraw from my shoulders. Her face is unusually pale. She swallows hard, struggling to speak. "It's her fire," she says, barely above a whisper. She looks at Aric. "It's eating her alive . . ."

Photo by Kate Gledhill of Kate Gledhill Photography

CECY ROBSON is a new adult and contemporary author of the Shattered Past series, the O'Brien Family novels and Carolina Beach novels, as well as the award-winning author of the Weird Girls urban fantasy romance series. A 2016 double nominated RITA® finalist for Once Pure and Once Kissed, Cecy is a recovering Jersey girl living in the South who enjoys carbs way too much, and exercise way too little. Gifted and cursed with an overactive imagination, you can typically find her on her laptop silencing the yappy characters in her head by telling their stories

www.cecyrobson.com

Facebook.com/Cecy.Robson.Author

instagram.com/cecyrobsonauthor

twitter.com/cecyrobson

www.goodreads.com/goodreadscomCecyRobsonAuthor